"They

"Get a forensic anthropologist up here," Brittles said to Pardee.

"Anthropologist?" Guzman started laughing wildly, her mouth wide open, revealing three missing teeth. "Them ain't human, you fools. What you all got here is dragonfly bones."

"We've got something else," Pardee said, holding out a baggie. He pulled on a clean pair of latex gloves and reached inside, removing several small colored objects.

"Nail polish?" Brittles asked, astonished.

"I've got a bad feeling about this, Nathan."

There were nine fingernails, the polish chipped on some and undisturbed on others. Five had color variations of brilliant red, another was black, another pale lavender, and two more had a French manicure.

All the nails were different sizes.

Nine different women, nine different bodies.

And they'd only begun to dig.

Other books by
David Cole

SCORPION RAIN
STALKING MOON
THE KILLING MAZE
BUTTERFLY LOST

DAVID COLE

DRAGONFLY BONES

AVON BOOKS
An Imprint of HarperCollinsPublishers

This is a work of fiction. Names, characters, places, and incidents are products of the author's imagination or are used fictitiously and are not to be construed as real. Any resemblance to actual events, locales, organizations, or persons, living or dead, is entirely coincidental.

AVON BOOKS
An Imprint of HarperCollins*Publishers*
10 East 53rd Street
New York, New York 10022-5299

First Avon Books paperback printing: September 2003

Avon Trademark Reg. U.S. Pat. Off. and in Other Countries, Marca Registrada, Hecho en U.S.A.
HarperCollins® is a registered trademark of HarperCollins Publishers Inc.

Printed in the U.S.A.

10 9 8 7 6 5 4 3 2 1

for Carol Jo Ellick
who reminded me why I write these books

Yesterday upon the stair
I saw a man who wasn't there
He wasn't there again today
Oh how I wish he'd go away

Old Nursery Rhyme

We who are alive and remain shall be caught up together with them in the clouds to meet the Lord in the
air and so shall we ever be with the Lord.

1 Thessalonians 4:16–17

Astronomers have gazed out at the universe for centuries, asking why it is the way it is. But lately a growing
number of them are dreaming of universes that never
were and asking, why not? Why, they ask, do we live in
3 dimensions of space and not 2, 10 or 25? Why is a
light ray so fast and a whisper so slow? Why are atoms
so tiny and stars so big? Why is the universe so old?
Does it have to be that way, or are there places, other
universes, where things are different?

Dennis Overbye
A New View of Our Universe: Only One of Many
The New York Times, October 29, 2002

DRAGONFLY
BONES

revelations

The landscapers arrived before sunrise.

Jack Klossberg drove the rented crane flatbed, loaded with three fifteen-foot palo verde trees, their root balls secure in heavy burlapping tied with twine. Emilia Guzman and Jesus Totexto followed in a brand new red three-quarter ton Chevy pickup, trailer-towing the backhoe. Both vehicles had bright spoked wheels, all the paint and chrome carefully polished that morning, and the Landmasters LLC logo freshly painted on both door panels.

Passing the access road to Casa Grande National Monument, Klossberg turned left onto State Route 287 and drove slowly, checking a hand drawn map as he turned right on Kenworthy Road. Reaching the end of the pavement, he stuck an arm out the window, motioning the Chevy to follow him up a rise onto a dirt access road into the staked area of a new housing development with three model homes. Two roofers sat on top of an unfinished fourth house, drinking coffee, while another man stacked half-moon shaped adobe roof tiles.

"Who's gonna buy these here houses?" Guzman said as she unloaded the ice chest and the twenty-gallon water cooler.

"People with money." Klossberg shrugged. "Except they don't have enough money to buy anything in Tucson."

All three of them walked behind the model homes, looking over the ten-acre tract rising gently to the east. Roughly half had been pretty much clearcut, except for some huge mesquite trees. Red stakes marked off the corners of different-sized lots, yellow stakes on both sides of rough graded streets. A bulldozer sat beyond the stakes, exhaust stack rattling as the engine warmed, the operator consulting a map where he'd begin clearing clumps of warm-season bunchgrass.

Klossberg liked upland bunchgrass, couldn't figure why the tract designer wanted to level all the mountain muhly, burrograss, sideoats and blue grama, and buffalo grass. Shaking his head, he crumpled dirt in his hand, feeling small lumps of decomposed granite and gritty limestone sand.

"Helluva place to plow off and landscape with city plantings," he said, kicking at an area of hardpan caliche. "They oughta just leave it natural."

"Then I'd earn no money for my kids," Guzman said. "Great view, anyway."

"If I had my scoped .30-30," Totexto said, pretending he was aiming west, "I could prolly hit some long haul trucker on I-10."

Klossberg shook his head.

"Come on, kids. Thirty holes to dig today."

They leaned against the flatbed, drinking some water, nobody talking anymore. Five in the morning, the July heat already near one hundred degrees. Birds calling their early warnings, a string of Gambel's quail chicks scurrying behind their indignant mother, red-tailed hawks already circling above the desert floor, and half a mile away he saw some mourning doves flying in and out of the tall, open shed that covered the Casa Grande ruins.

Klossberg finished his cup of water, consulted his map, pointed. Totexto shrugged off his sleeveless tee shirt and lowered the trailer ramp. Guzman stripped to her yellow tanktop and climbed into the seat of the backhoe. Its engine fired immediately, coughed some, settled into a purr. Guzman carefully backed it down the ramp and headed toward the bright pink stakes Klossberg was hammering into the hardpan desert floor, whacking the tops of the stakes with the flat of a shovel blade.

Half an hour later, Klossberg and Totexto had the first palo verde tree craned over the side of the flatbed, suspended above the first hole. A platinum-colored Ford Excursion came toward them, tinted windows closed and the aircon going.

Accelerating toward the unfinished home, the Excursion just barely slowed as the driver slalomed left past the flatbed. Rooster tails of dust and small stones blew back, cracking hard against the flatbed's front windshield, clanking off the paint.

"*Whoa,* dude!" Guzman shouted when a stone whacked her hardhat. "What's your hurry?"

Five minutes later, the first palo verde stood upright in the hole. Klossberg and Guzman started slashing the burlaping off the root ball. Another car came up the road. A Chevy Tahoe, stopping next to them. Painted whiter than white, so white that the reflections of green creosote bush and red-tipped ocotillos paled against the Tahoe's doors, the white bleaching out color, absorbing all other colors, even the brilliant red of the hand-painted sign on the door.

RAPTURE WARRIORS CAMP

"Yo," the driver said through the open passenger side window.

Klossberg nodded without speaking. Totexto stared at the beautiful black girl in the passenger seat.

"Where they at?" the driver said.

Klossberg pointed to the model homes and turned to the root ball. But the Excursion was already driving back toward them, braking abruptly but expertly so the front bumper was just inches from the Tahoe. Two men got out. Suits, ties, black Resistol hats, cowboy boots with roper heels, newly polished and shiny. One of the men came forward, already wiping road dust from his boots.

A deputy sheriff came out of the Tahoe, a Winchester twelve-gauge pump shotgun held upright, the barrel against his right shoulder.

"Howdy," he said. "Depitty Thumb. You them security people?"

"Brittles," the lead man said. "And Pardee."

Thumb extended a hand, but Brittles ignored it and quietly opened the Tahoe's passenger car. The girl came out, hesitantly, awkwardly. Anxious, eyes flicking from side to side, chewing gum hard. Leg chains, wrists cuffed with a two-foot chain. An orange jumpsuit, short sleeves. A teenager, barely sixteen, Brittles thought. Gorgeous face, model gorgeous, impossibly perfect and high cheekbones, skin completely unblemished. When she leaned forward to stretch some muscles, her jumpsuit gaped open at the top. Brittles saw her breasts and quickly cut his eyes away in the same moment he realized she'd leaned over on purpose.

"This here's Theresa Prejean," Thumb said.

"Please take off her cuffs and chains," Brittles asked quietly.

"Can't do that. She's pure bad dog."

Pardee, leaning against the Excursion, pulled away and walked a few steps in Thumb's direction.

"People aren't dogs," he said.

"Who the hell are *you*?" Thumb asked.

"Security," Brittles answered.

"Feebs? U.S. Marshals?"

"Not your concern. And who are you? I thought this girl was coming from a troubled teenagers boot camp."

"Rapture Warriors. But when they go bad, they be taken off property temporary-like to the Pinal County jail. Overnight, then on to Phoenix."

Thumb was a large man, flat-faced and barrel-chested like a Navajo, but his gut spread wider than his chest, his body soft and fleshy, and he moved awkwardly, leaning back slightly as though to counterbalance the weight of his gut and the twenty-pound police belt with radios, cuffs, ammo pouches, and a huge walnut-handled revolver in a worn red leather holster.

"You're a deputy sheriff," Brittles said. "But you're driving a private car?"

"So I moonlight. Well, I work graveyard as depitty, so guess I daylight. Rapture Warriors Camp pays me twice the hourly rate. For my expertise."

"Thumb," Pardee asked, not bothering to hide his smirk. "Is that really your name?"

"Early Thumb." Said defiantly, having seen the smirks all his life. "I'm Apache. That's my Apache name. Depitty sheriff, Pima County."

"But this is Pinal County. What are you doing all the way up from Tucson?"

"I live here. In Florence. Near the prison. You ready to get this on, or what?"

"Thumb," the other man said with a smile to himself.

"Don't you all make a mistake here," Thumb said. "I may look and talk desert, but I think city."

"It's her handcuffs and chains," Brittles said. "It's calling her a dog."

"Well. Y'all ain't never been prison correctional officers," Thumb said. "Some in prison worse than dogs 'n snakes. But it's not disrespect, calling her bad dog. That's how she's ranked, over at Rapture Warriors. If she didn't run her mouth all the time, she worked her tasks, she'd be upped to good dog and the chains come off. I come here like I was told, but I'm fixing to leave. Show me some ID."

"Miss Theresa Prejean?" Brittles said, taking out a leather badge holder, flashing a U.S. Marshal star for Thumb.

"Yessir," she mumbled.

"Where are you from?"

"Norleans."

He smiled, trying to calm her down. Frown lines deep between her narrowed eyes, she tried a smile, but only managed a flicker at the right corner of her lips. Brittles realized that she took him for Law, realized she was frightened out of her body about something, decided it would help if they just got on with it.

"You are the reason we're all out here, Theresa," Brittles said.

She fidgeted. Thumb pulled her wrist chain, trying to get her to step forward.

"No need to do that," Brittles said, and Thumb let go of the chain. "Does this man bother you, Miss Prejean?"

"Nossir."

"If he does, we can ask him to wait in his car."

"Nossir. Don't bother me none."

"All right. What did you have to tell us?"

"Umm . . ."

"A body. We heard something about a body buried here."

"Yes," she said. "A body."

"Buried here."

"Here."

"Exactly where," Brittles said carefully, "is 'here'?"

The sun flamed over the eastern horizon just then and she had to squint against the sudden brightness which sharply delineated trees and cars and bushes and people, drawing long, pencil-thin shadows stretching west.

"Way beyond that big mesquite tree," she said, pointing toward the far end of the red and yellow stakes.

Brittles offered his arm to her. Surprised, she shifted her cuffed wrists to place one palm on Brittles's arm. They walked through the razed ground to the mesquite, where she spent some time looking around.

"They told me—"

"*Who* told you, girl?" Thumb shouted.

Defiant, she looked to Brittles to see if she should answer.

"For now, we just want to see if there really is a body."

"Yessir," she said. " 'Bout fifteen paces directly that way."

"Here?" Brittles went to the spot outside the stakes.

"Yessir."

Brittles called Klossberg over.

"Can you get your backhoe in here?"

"Who's paying for the extra time?" Guzman asked, seeing money in this.

Brittles just nodded. Guzman hesitated, finally decided this was yes to more pay, and went back to bring the backhoe slowly across the desert floor.

"There could be relics in there," Totexto complained to Klossberg.

She looked to Klossberg for an okay, but he held up his hand.

"You can't just go ripping a trench or something," Totexto said. "You'll have the Park Service, all kinds of feds out here complaining you're disturbing an archeologically sensitive area."

"That could be," Brittles said, "but according to the GIS maps I've got of this area, the company that's building this housing development also owns all the land up to that ridge crest. And we've got the company's permission."

"You sure about this?" Klossberg said.

"What's your name?"

"Jack Klossberg."

"Nathan Brittles." He offered his hand. They shook once, a quick but firm up-and-down bob. "I've arrested pothunters. Up on Hopi. On Dinetah. All over Arizona. I appreciate you being so careful. But if there is a body . . . we have to dig."

"Don't let him do this, man!" Totexto complained.

"I'd need permission from the people who're putting in this development," Klossberg said finally.

"That's all arranged." Brittles took out a map of the development, marked into half-acre tracts. "We're only interested in this spot behind tract seventeen."

"Big spot, guy. Where do I dig?"

"Don't know, exactly."

"Okay," Klossberg said. "We'll do it one trench at a time. We look through the dirt and stuff, we don't find any pot-shards, we take another trench."

"Dude, you're making a *big* mistake," Totexto said. "This desert here, this ain't even gonna have no houses on it. This en*tire* area's gonna just be landscaped."

"Just get this over with," Klossberg said.

"*I'm* not working this."

"Suit yourself," Brittles said, motioning to Guzman to go start up the backhoe. "Bring it on. Right over here."

But the first three trenches, six feet deep, showed nothing. Eight-fifteen, the sun blazing, the temperature well over one hundred and ten. Even with the low humidity everyone was sweating. Brittles and Pardee took off their suit jackets. Both had guns, Brittles a Glock nine in a clip-on belt holster, and Pardee a Smith .40 in a shoulder rig.

"Hold it!" Klossberg shouted to Guzman, who'd just ripped out a fourth trench. "Lemme get a shovel."

Brittles knelt at the trench, now down about four feet.

Klossberg lay on the ground, reached in to pull out pieces of ornate potshards. Striped with wavy black lines. He started to look at them carefully, but Brittles pulled on latex gloves, stepped cautiously in the trench, and picked up a small fragment.

"We send all the pieces to the Anthro Department at UA." Klossberg held out his hand for the fragment. "They put everything together. Jigsaw puzzle."

"This looks like bone," Brittles said.

He motioned to Pardee, who went to his suit coat and brought back some plastic Baggies, using a marker pen to put #1 on the first bag, holding it open. Brittles started to drop the bone fragment, cut his head quickly to another spot in the trench, brushing dirt with both hands, picking out one bone fragment after another.

"*Jesus*," he said.

"Help me here," Brittles asked Guzman and Klossberg. "Pull the Baggies open, quickly, one at a time."

For half an hour Brittles handed up fragments until his quads cramped up and he had to stand up straight and finally step out of the trench. Everybody gathered around the piles of Baggies. Pardee had numbered one hundred and fifty-seven bags, each with a tiny bone fragment.

"What the hell are those?" Guzman asked.

"They ain't human," Thumb said. "That's for sure, that's for damn sure."

"Snake?" Klossberg asked. "Baby quail?"

"Hell," Thumb snorted. "Them must be from dragonflies."

"Get a forensic anthropologist up here," Brittles said to Pardee.

"Anthropologist?" Guzman started laughing wildly, her mouth wide open, revealing three missing teeth. "Them ain't human, you fools. What you all got here is dragonfly bones."

"Theresa," Brittles said. "Let's go talk somewhere."

Thumb started to accompany them, but Brittles waved him off. Back at the flatbed, Brittles poured out two cups of water, and Theresa drank hers so fast he gave her another and another until she poured the last one on her cornrow-braided hair and whipped her head side to side, shaking off drops like a dog coming out of a pond.

"You know what I've got to ask you," Brittles said.

"Yessir."

"So?"

"I was told," she said shortly.

"By who?"

"Sean."

"And Sean is . . . ?"

"Another Rapture Warrior."

"How did he know? How did Sean know, about the bodies?"

"You think those bones is from . . . is, like, body parts?"

Brittles nodded.

"Oh."

"How did Sean know the spot?"

"Work crew."

"What kind of work?" Brittles said patiently, wildly impatient inside but working hard not to show it and spook her.

"Clearing brush."

"Here? In the housing development?"

"Nah. Out in the desert. You know, we chop and pull weeds, uh, pick up plastic bags and bottles and trash."

"And is Sean still at this . . . what *is* the Rapture Warriors Camp anyway?"

"Enforced residence for troubled teenagers," she said by rote.

"Sean is still there?"

"Was at breakfast."

"Okay, Theresa. Thank you. I'll send you back to jail with the deputy."

"No!" Shouting in alarm, fear bugging out her eyes. "I can't go there. I told, you know, I told you, about the burial, if I go to that jail, I'll never leave."

Thumb heard her shouts and came over. Opened the rear door of the Tahoe. Brittles saw a D-ring welded to the floor, knew that Theresa would be chained to it.

"I'm not going back!"

"Why?" Brittles said.

"I'll never leave. They'll never ever let me leave."

Brittles went for his suit coat, pulled it on slowly, bent to brush off his boots, trying to find the right decision, but in the end shrugging his shoulders.

"Miss Prejean, sorry, but I have no authority to keep you here."

Thumb tried to pull her into the Tahoe's backseat. She raised her hands, clanked the wrist chain and cuffs on the roof again and again, digging through the white paint, sparks flying as she flailed to keep Thumb from pushing her inside.

"I'll have somebody at the jail to talk to you this after-noon," Brittles said.

Thumb dug a knee into her back, then kicked her legs out from underneath her. As Theresa lost her balance, he shoved her into the seat, in the same moment reaching for the open end of the handcuffs on the D-ring and snapping the cuff around her wrist chain. She spat into his face and spewed curses, but he slammed the door shut just in time, her face pressed against the window, distorted with rage.

"I apologize," Thumb said to Brittles. "We ain't never had to deal with somebody thisaway before. You say somebody will pick her up at the jail?"

"Sometime today."

"Piece of work," Pardee said from behind as Thumb drove away.

"She's afraid of something," Brittles said.

"Didn't mean her. What do we do now?"

They watched the Tahoe go around a bend, dust devils lin-gering in the air.

"You call the forensic anthropologist?"

"On his way. Sounded kinda excited, said we'd have to stop digging, lots of political problems involved with old In-dian bones."

"Keep that backhoe working. I've got to go to Perryville prison, that job's got priority. You handle these bones okay?"

"Just us dragonflies here, boss," Pardee said without smil-ing. "Just one thing." He held out two Baggies. "We've got something that sure doesn't come from an old Indian." He pulled on a clean pair of latex gloves, held up the first Baggie. "Some kind of bone. But there's still shreds of flesh on it."

"What's in the other Baggie?"

Pardee reached inside, took out several small colored ob-jects.

"Is that nail polish?" Brittles asked, astonished.

"Yup. Fingernails. I've got a bad feeling about this, Nathan."

"Stop digging until the anthro guy gets here. While you're waiting, get a federal warrant out for Theresa Prejean. Find out where that place is, Rapture Warriors Camp. Get her into protective custody, have them take her to that safe house we use in Tucson."

Pardee pushed the nails into a straight line on top of the Baggie. There were nine fingernails, the polish chipped on some and undisturbed on others. Five had color variations of brilliant red, another was black, another pale lavender, and two more had a French manicure.

"You figured out my bad feeling yet?" Pardee asked.

Brittles grimaced.

All the nails were different sizes.

Nine different women, nine different bodies.

And they'd only begun to dig.

laura

1

Badwater. Death Valley, California.

The three of us gathered at six in the morning around a small pool of saltwater, the lowest place in the United States.

"Ready?"

Rich held up a hand with fingers cocked like a starter's pistol.

Veronique Difiallos laughed.

I grinned.

"Bang!" Rich Thompson shouted.

Veronique coaxed her ancient VW camper van to life. She'd follow me, Rich driving his pickup ahead toward Furnace Creek Ranch. It was June twenty-third, the temperature already one hundred and seven degrees. Veronique's tape player started blasting an old Bink Dog rap.

I settled my lightweight headphones, turned on my iPod to get adrenaline ramped up with a Mad Squirrel rap, and started running.

> *Sunlight sometime, Moonlike Sunshine*
> *Moonlit nighttime, raccoon get in backroom fight time*
> *Mad Squirrel writes and recites rhymes*
> *Freestyle, written and, Laura Winslow high off the Ritalin*

You're in for dope rhyme spittin and
No I'm not kiddin

Mile three. These first few miles were fun miles. Long-before-dawn miles. Juiced-up, hydrated, pumped, before-you're-dry, ready-to-*fly* miles.

Veronique pulled alongside in the VW van.

"You okay?" she shouted.

I nodded without speaking.

"I can't *hear* you, lady."

She muted her CD player, leaned over to shout out the window at me.

Ring ring ring ring ring on my celly
Peeped the number was my homeboy Nelly
Askin, Girl, where you at?
I'm puffin on this twamp sack in the back of my man's
    Cadillac
Why you ask?
Cause them punk mothafuckas that we thought was
    gone
They back in the hood and once again it's on.

I shouted back.

Disrespectin women it's beginnin to get a little old
Like them tales that's ten times told
To your ten men friends on the same night
Your life's all fucked up and you're rappin like your
    game's tight.

"You're cooking," she shouted, dropping the van behind me.

Yeah, yeah, I'm fine.

I'm nuts to be running so far in this brain-frying heat, but I'm fine.

Left big toe blistering in the heat, my foot probably another twenty degrees hotter inside the running shoe. Right hamstring twingeing now and again, protesting and I'm wondering, *Why am I* doing *this? Like, remind me again, dear body?*

The Death Valley Badwater Run starts very early on a July morning. You run around the desert here and there, finally heading, uphill, a long way uphill, one hundred and thirty-five miles gradually uphill, climbing over eight thousand feet to the finish line, which was a third of the way up Mount Whitney.

It's the toughest extreme sports run in the U.S., and I loved it. The actual Badwater Run wasn't scheduled for another two weeks, but Rich and I had already made reservations that weekend down at Rocky Point on the Sea of Cortes.

So why exactly was I running?

I hadn't snorted Ritalin in months. I'd changed my addiction to long distance running. Extreme long distance. Plus hand weights. Rich had been my live-in partner for two months. We'd met one night at Nonie, downing Susie's dirty martinis and rubbing elbows until I decided it was time to end my long celibacy.

Rich made me conscious of my forty-six-year-old body to the point where I sought muscle definition, stamina, energy—oh, hell, let's be honest, I sought something more permanent than a methamphetamine addiction. When you're running, those fan*ta*stic endorphins kick in after a few miles. You get high. You don't get strung out, just really tired, and I had an ability to run farther and farther every week.

Veronique lived with a Tewa who'd given up his fiddle for a three-stringed cello to accompany her on homemade rap albums, which she sold on the Internet. She was somewhere in her fifties, he was ancient, their blissful lives a constant wonder. Veronique knew me at my down and out worst, when I'd first tried to kick Ritalin and wound up liking too many martinis. Veronique was half Venezuelan, half African-

American. Slim and beautiful, she tattooed her lips and eye-lids with impermanent ink that lasted two or three months. I'd thought it was a beauty thing, but she insisted that the tat-tooed lines made it easier to avoid daily makeup. She didn't drink, didn't do drugs, but brewed whole kettles of bancha tea every three days and infused my spirit with her energy, along the way teaching me hiphop and alternative rap. I loved rapping, and once I got past thug rap and the constant gangsta and ho routines, I gradually wrote my own raps, which the two of us would exchange in a weekly shoutdown.

She pulled alongside me again and motioned that we had a scheduled stop.

Mile six.

Gasping a bit, more from the heat than the physical exer-tion, hands on knees, greedy with the water bottle she handed me, greedier to sit in shade against the side of the van on the cardboard she laid out. We'd discovered early on that the pavement was hot enough to burn my thighs if I wasn't care-ful. But water loss was the death threat. Oceans of sweat poured down my face, my arms, under my running bra, into my shorts, down my thighs to soak my socks. We figured I had to drink a minimum of one gallon of water every hour, just to keep basically hydrated.

"What's my time?"

"Twenty-two minutes a mile. Not bad."

"I'm dying, Veronique. That works out to running the whole thing in about forty some hours. I'm gonna cut back."

"You can drive awhile. I'll run. Nobody will know the difference."

"Nobody but me."

I spritzed a whole water bottle on my ponytailed hair and shoulders, adjusted the loose fitting cotton blouse, and fas-tened my hat with sun-protection tenting at the back. The fresh water seemed to evaporate on contact.

"I'm not going much farther with these soggy socks, so get the next pair ready when I wave at you."

"Blisters?"

"Don't ask."

"You change your socks, we check for blisters. When we get to Furnace Creek Ranch, we decide how much longer you want to prove to yourself that you can do this crazy business."

She handed me a large paper cup full of some mineral-enhanced orange juice, then another eight ounces of water. I stretched, got out of the shade of the van, and started a slow jog after I got Mad Squirrel going again.

> *I keep it proper like the pop star*
> *Trying to act hard all chillin in the backyard*
> *Villain please,*
> *Conservative Individual Wannabes*
> *Get brushed back all up on my trees*
> *And heed the Weasel and the Dingo*
> *Sing your pop rap jingle at the "casingo"*
> *Bump the single, learn the lingo*
> *And then go back to grade school and try to play cool*
> *Gringo, or speaker of the Latin lingo*
> *African-American grow, Asian grow*
> *Where'd the half-breed Indian go?*

After stopping to rest for an hour at Furnace Creek Ranch, I decided I'd do the next major leg and quit there. I'd run seventeen point four miles, and I told Rich and Veronique I'd quit at Stove Pipe Wells, which would be about fifty miles total. We could eat something at the restaurant, maybe Rich and I could spend the night at the small motel. So we started off again, but it wasn't much fun anymore.

Until I saw the six-foot-long green caterpillar.

Somewhere along the route the actual physical effort of running becomes automatic, runners pulled along with a tractor beam right out of Star Trek, a magnetic force-field bubble that encases them with mystic energy. Some endurance runners take the stress and fatigue mainly so they'll

move way beyond endorphin rushes into hallucinations.
Runners from previous races reported seeing such things as a
Boeing 747 taxiing alongside, nude men and women
rollerblading with them for company.

I had no more hallucinations that day, but when my iPod
quit working I chanted some of my latest rap, modifying
some lines to fit this run.

> *I'm alone on my own*
> *On a road with no map to where I'm goin*
> *But my ambition's growin*
> *No knowin where I'll end up but welcoming adventure*
> *And free from dependence indenture*
> *Free from that affliction*
> *Ritalin addiction*
> *I center my mind on steps, not sure what I'm gonna*
>   *find next*
> *As I climb this hill I'm resigned to let*
> *Things unfold, unsure of some of the things I've been*
>   *told*
> *Or what the future might hold.*

I found myself repeating the last four lines again and
again, gradually reducing it to the phrase "resigned to let
things unfold," and that got so unsettling I slowed my pace.
Veronique pulled alongside and asked if I was okay, why was
I just walking, was I tired?

"Radio ahead to Rich," I said. "I've had enough of this.
Let's drive home."

2

Resigned to let things unfold.

That bothered me for several days after the Death Valley run, because I was weary of unfolding past events, weary of reading those events like tea leaves, like I Ching stalks. Enough unfolding, I finally said to myself, but what I mostly thought was that I wanted to fold up my life and move on somewhere.

Not just anywhere.

Somewhere permanent.

A home I could live in for years, for decades.

Most of all, a home where I could live beyond haunted memories.

After San Carlos, after Meg killed the man and I took her home, I had to clean up my entire life and it took me several weeks just to work out how to begin.

Months before, my best friend Meg Arizana arranged for me to accompany her on a drive from Perryville prison down to Nogales. At the border crossing, several people died in a monster shootout, Meg was kidnapped and held hostage in the Sonoran desert by the brother of a woman Meg had killed with a shotgun in my old Tucson house. I spent two weeks fulfilling my shouted promise that I'd come find her. The farther I got into Mexico, the more people died.

In the process, I wound up totally estranged from my second-best friend, Rey Villanueva, Meg's ex-husband, and thought I'd found my ideal man in Kyle Callaghan, a kidnap-rescue negotiator from New Zealand. Like Russell Crowe, in that movie *Proof of Life*. Except Kyle had a young daughter and still loved his dead wife.

Meg and Rey remarried, got divorced again after just a few months. Meg went to Alaska, the coldest place she could think of where she might forget being kidnapped and held for ransom in the desert. Rey moved on . . . somewhere. I'd not heard from him since.

I knew *I* also had to move somewhere.

But *where*?

I knew I had to leave my house, leave all those visual memories of life, but where should I go? What should I do?

With no goals in mind yet, I started by cleaning out the room I used for my office. This took several weeks; actually, the last week was when I did things, the first ten days I had to decide what to keep and what to throw away. I keep few mementos, souvenirs, reminders. But I don't discard things easily.

Most of my life I've been an outsider to my community, my few friends, myself. Be prepared, that's Laura's marching song. Prepared to move on when trouble happens. When Law gets too close, especially when Law gets in your face even if they don't know what they're staring at.

But like all people, I do have my souvenirs. My remembrances, memorabilia, mementos. So I had to sort through stuff carefully, had to form a willingness to throw it all out and just move on.

No. That's wrong.

Tired of moving on, I wanted to settle down, find a home. A real home. A *perm*anent home. A symbolic and physical place I could call Home. Most people have that all their lives, even when they move, they just pick up their sense of home and take it with them. When I've moved on, at the back of my head I already knew the move was temporary even before I made it.

So I sorted out my office things with a deliberate sense of importance, no matter how slight or peripheral to my past. Searching, I guess, for those things which had true importance. Oh, hell, let's face it, I tell you, I wasn't really searching for bits of the past, I was looking at all my stuff and wondering why I'd even bothered to save it.

I moved piles into my living room, other piles onto the kitchen table and counters, still more stuff into my office and bedroom. Piles of stuff right on the floor. On carpets, tiles, wood, bricks, even on top of clothing, because I was sorting all that, too. Gradually, I saw a pattern to the sorting according to which room I was in. Listen, you've all moved a few times in your life, some of you have moved on, a few of you know the sudden panic of not even being able to go home, you had to move on so fast you just left everything behind. Or you ran away from it.

Living room.

Books in a corner, CDs in another corner.

Office.

Paper trails of a few hacking solutions. A few photos, none of them showing people, just computer and networking hardware. Some hard copy of special hacks I'd done, software scripts I'd written, printouts of downloaded website articles.

Kitchen.

My DVDs. I had hundreds of them. I wanted to sort them into piles, wanted to classify them, you know, noir, classics, kung fu, romantic comedies, whatever. Maybe they were in the kitchen because I spent most of my time there, I wasn't sure about that, but I loved my DVDs, knew I'd be taking pretty much all of them. No way I'd even begun to figure out *where* I'd be taking them. But I knew they'd come for the ride.

Bedroom.

All kinds of storage devices. A few old floppies, a lot of data CDs, some zip drives that I couldn't even play back with my new iMac. At least a dozen hard drives. Firewire stuff, probably a few hundred gigabytes of important hacking scripts and locations and contacts. Everything of value I'd already backed up through the Web onto many servers, some at Don Ralph's new company in Phoenix, others parked on remote computers in Asia.

Rich. My housemate. My partner. I hadn't sorted him out yet.

So for the first week, all I'd done was sort these things without any real conscious effort to think about it. Somewhere in the second week I realized the arrangement of physical storage spaces, of what was getting piled where, and of Rich constantly neatening up the piles, stacking boxes in corners, aligning the edges of the boxes as I added haphazardly to the heaps.

At the beginning of the third week I laboriously went through all the stored files and documents and software programs. I read notations I'd made over the past ten years. Sometimes I'd hunt through the hard copy piles, wanting to correlate different versions of a document and surprising myself with my own handwriting. Often relaxed, usually when I had no contracts. But more usually cramped scribbles, cryptic, enigmatic, even eccentric comments that occasionally had no common sense at all, wildly inconsistent notes written in a riot of different-color inks and pencils and Magic Markers, scrawled with whatever writing instrument was nearest when I needed something. Although little of it was dated, I could make out comments from my years in Yakima, St. Louis, Phoenix, Tuba City, and, finally, Tucson.

So, in that random, nonlinear way, I haphazardly sorted and cataloged my past. At the end of the second month, my left brain began to assert itself against that indulgent right brain, an illogical way of dealing with my work and my life. I'd gone through this right to left progression many times, and only realized it when I turned up the sound of my TV set. Thinking was, for me, primarily visual. I know, I hear you saying how little sense that makes. But for me, I could watch one of my DVDs, any kind of movie, as long as the sound was off. It distracted my head, you see, until suddenly pieces of my mental puzzles snapped into place and I'd hit the Pause button and make notes of what to look for, write out computer hacking scripts in longhand, or put notations somewhere in the reams of data I was trying to organize for a client.

And through all this disjointed time, Rich came and went with his affable, ordered peace and quietness, his wonderful support and lack of questions. Except, somewhere in all my sorting out things, I realized I had to sort him out, too.

Like my notes, I cataloged the men from my past years. Jonathan Begay, my Navajo husband, who helped me run away from the Hopi reservation when I was only fifteen, and with whom I had a daughter, Spider, whom I'd not seen since she was two. *Another* Navajo, Ben Yazzie, a bounty hunter who'd bring in bail jumpers that I located through database searches. Kimo Biakeddy. *Another* Navajo. Rey Villanueva, a private detective.

Lost for a moment in these memories, I ended the reverie as always. Macho men, all of them. Men on the edge of understanding women, understanding me.

Once, avoiding yet again facing the concept of *moving on*, I went to a U-Haul yard and bought a dozen cardboard boxes and began throwing out things in that temporary way you always do, fill the carton but keep it handy in case you have to go through it again, you may have missed something.

Somewhere about the third month, I went to a personal trainer in Tucson and began, at last, dealing with the shreds of my Ritalin addiction. In time, all I did was displace one addiction with another. Wanting to make my body better, healthier, different, I began lifting free weights and three weeks later started running.

At first, I'd run a mile or two. Rich pedaling a mountain bike alongside. By the third week I was up to six miles, then seven, and one day eleven. Rich rode silently alongside, but as I began running in the desert, he'd stop to look over some promising fossil site, or to dig up a semiprecious stone.

In the fourth month I was running twelve miles or more every other day.

By this time, Rich had more or less moved into my house, and we settled for a domestic routine that included him cooking Thai and Mexican meals and me making sugar-free desserts, I mean no processed sugar or flours, none of that, but plenty of whole wheat and berries. I felt less and less consumed, frantic, and scattered about sorting things out, mostly because I'd long since sorted everything of value. Rich and I just stepped over or around the piles until he rearranged them. I really didn't notice the neatening up for two months, and Rich never commented one way or another.

One day he let slip that he'd been married.

"Divorced now?" I said.

"Lasted just five weeks," he said. "God, that woman talked like a faucet. Only thing she liked better than talking was buying women's magazines, which gave her most of her ideas of what to talk about. After two weeks, I got used to tossing out six or eight magazines a day, totally pissed her off. 'I *love* my magazines,' she told me, 'I can't live without those magazines giving me new ideas for cooking dinners and fixing my hair and pleasuring you.' Pleasuring herself, mainly. She only made frozen dinners, lots of frozen pizzas, and finally I realized that I couldn't see any sense in wasting all that time and energy on magazines, and that boiled up to my thinking that I couldn't much see wasting time with her."

One day I ran twenty miles, the last half by myself because Rich had stopped at what he said was a fantastic find of a dinosaur bone. That evening, he made enchiladas stuffed with crab meat and covered with suiza sauce, and I baked a raspberry pie. After two forkfuls of the pie, I looked at him contentedly eating a second piece and realized what a comfort he'd been over the past months. I felt a huge emotional debt for all he'd done to help me rid myself of anxieties and panic attacks and dependency on Ritalin to keep me going.

And watching him efficiently wash all the dishes and wipe down the counters and the table and all other surfaces, I also realized it was time to throw away all those cardboard cartons, gather the few things I wanted, and move on. Without him. That night, I tried many times to tell him this when we made love, but it took an enormous effort just to look at him, caress his shoulders, touch noses, and wordlessly make love again until he finally fell asleep.

I was going to tell him next morning, but Don Ralph made that unnecessary.

3

On the Fourth of July, three days after the Death Valley run, I slept in, late. Rich slipped out of bed sometime about five, I barely registered the time on our digital clock with the red numbers, and went back to sleep. He was going to Phoenix later that morning to set up and explain a large mock-up of a dinosaur to kids at an outdoor party.

I sat on the edge of the bed, fully awake. I've always been like that, not drowsy in between, one minute drooling on the pillow and the next my eyes popping open. Lay there for a minute or two, then sit on the edge of the water bed, start my morning stretches, then get into the first of my free weight routines.

After a hundred reps each of squats, military presses, dead lifts, and bicep curls, I showered, pulled on a pair of running shorts and nothing else, wandered toward the kitchen. Rich was outside, but had laid out all the makings for my breakfast, with the Gaggia espresso machine on and fresh triple-roast beans ready in the Braun grinder. I drank a whole twelve-ounce bottle of mineral water, enhanced with vitamins, turned to catch my upper body partially reflected in the glass fronts of our old handmade cabinets.

This was something new for me, probably a part of the hunger to move on, part of my addiction to my body. I turned my head sideways, shook my long hair like a TV model, flexed my biceps, knew my small breasts would never pass the pencil test. But that was okay. My body was okay. I liked my body. Another first in my forty-six years.

Behind me I heard Sunset snuffling in her food bowl, crunching the few remaining bits of dry dog food, scooting the bowl in front of her, never looking at me, but the wagging tail a strong hint that she wanted more. I opened a bottom cupboard and scooped out a full bowl from the forty-pound bag, something I'd never done before. Sunset was a five-year-old female purebred red Siberian husky. She weighed approximately forty-five pounds, stood eighteen inches high at the shoulder, and was four feet long from the tip of her nose to the tip of her tail. Sunset prowled the desert behind our house for hours at a time, no matter what the heat, so there was little fat on her rib cage. But if we let her eat a whole bag, she'd pig out, so we rationed her food. Today seemed different.

I looked at the half dozen or so cardboard boxes piled in the corner. *Today,* I thought, *I'll tape them shut and take them to St. Vinnies down in South Tucson.*

Eating some grapes, I stood at the open sliding glass door opening on the patio and leading down to the small grape-fruit and lemon grove. Sunset nudged me with his wet nose, wiping a few bits of dog food onto my thigh. Several mourning doves cooed at us, so familiar with our feeders and company that they barely moved aside if we came near. The resident mama Gambel's quail strutted by with her latest brood, this time seven chicks. There had been nine, but we'd heard a coyote near the house the last few nights and he'd probably eaten quail chicks for dessert.

Ten o'clock.

Already ninety-five degrees. I'd been to Houston on a whim just two weeks before and although it was also ninety-five degrees there, whenever I went outside the high humidity enveloped me like a sauna. One day I'd driven over to

Beaumont to get some financial data that a hacker refused to transmit on the Internet, no matter how much I assured him that I had nonpenetrable security for my network and satellite connections. The only safe computer, he reminded me in his Finnish accent, is one that's not connected to any other computer. Beaumont was incredibly more stifling than Houston. I couldn't even get the Cherokee's aircon to keep out the afternoon sauna. Another hacker connection of mine in New Orleans told me that Cajuns called southeast Texas the coonass Riviera.

But not Tucson. Higher elevation than Phoenix, somewhat cooler, and the summer humidity maybe just ten percent. Or lower.

I slid open the screen door. Sunset surged past me toward the orchard. At least he'd waited. I'd replaced the screen door seven times so far, because if Rich or I weren't around and Sunset saw anything else on four legs, he'd lunge through the screen door, making a wide hole, the mesh hardly slowing him at all.

Pouring some nonhoney muesli into a bowl, no soy milk today, I held it in one hand and ate with the other as I walked, half naked, after Sunset, figuring Rich was down there at the redwood picnic table he'd built from a kit.

Sunset disappeared quickly and came back in the next moment, frolicking, tail going *whoosh whoosh,* left to right to left, nonstop.

"Okay, girl," I said, putting down my empty bowl, getting into a race-start stance. "Let's go see him."

Off. Twenty feet later, I could see Rich's head and shoulders through the trees, half hidden behind a clump of creosote bushes. His long brown hair was loose, not being in his usual ponytail. Like a woman, Rich would twist the hair around to one side of his neck or the other, maybe roll it into a loose braid. A few steps closer, I could see he also was naked to the waist and I felt that conflict when you see somebody you like, somebody you really care about, but you don't love and you know that at some point the two of you will drift apart. Still, naked from the waist up, it was a good way to end breakfast.

But another ten feet of running and I heard voices. *Two* voices. Both men. The trail narrowed between two lemon trees and I couldn't stop in time, bursting into the picnic area to see Rich and Don Ralph drinking coffee and eating bagels. Don comfortable in his wheelchair and looking directly at my mostly naked body.

"Jesus," I said to Rich, stopping finally and crossing my arms over my breasts. "You could have told me."

"Hi, Laura," Don said, a slight smile crinkling his tanned face.

Rich laughed out loud and Sunset beat me with her tail as I started backtracking. If Don hadn't been in his wheelchair, Sunset would have warned me. She'd been trained to guard against any stranger standing on two legs. Anybody sitting down, though, usually meant friend or guest.

"Get some more clothes on," Don said. "Please. You look kinda, well, I think this is the first time I've ever seen you so . . . so em*bar*rassed."

4

Ten minutes later, when I came out of the bedroom with a tanktop and had brushed my teeth and hair, I heard the Gaggia wind up and groan several times. Rich had wheeled Don up to the house and they sat on the patio with small mugs of espresso, one set aside for me.

"Hey," Rich said.

He touched noses with me, somewhat apologetic that he'd not told me Don had come to the house.

"Hi, Laura," Don said. "Sorry to . . . well, intrude, I guess."

"Glad to see you, Don."

He poured some half-and-half into his espresso, drained the cup, held it out to Rich for some more. Rich's cell phone jingled and he started talking while he went for more espresso.

"Love that orchard," Don said. "Love the smell of lemon blossoms. What does a place like this cost? Down here in Tucson?"

"I'm leasing it. Twelve hundred a month."

"Good place for healing."

"Owner is in Italy," I said, ignoring his comment. "Don. Why exactly are you here?"

"Just driving through."

"From Phoenix?"

"Yeah."

"Just out for a drive? From Phoenix?"

"Mmmm."

Yeah, I thought. *Right.*

"And the business?"

"Heavy. Nine people now, about to hire another few. Contracts."

But he didn't make any effort to tell me about his new computer security company in Phoenix, his clients, his contracts, or his staff. He accepted another cup of espresso from Rich, slowly added some more half-and-half.

"Got to cancel Phoenix and go up to Casa Grande," Rich said. "Coolidge. Some housing development. They found some old bones, and I'm on call with NAGPRA."

"Good to meet you," Don said. "I might have some more small jobs for you, now and again. What's NAGPRA?"

"Native American Graves Protection and Repatriation Act." Rich bent to kiss me on the forehead and went in to get dressed. "Don, nice to meet you." He left.

"He's a keeper?" Don asked.

"Maybe." I ignored his question. "So?"

"So nothing."

"Nothing?"

"Just dropped in to say hello. He was a surprise."

"Out for drive."

"Nice surprise. Yeah. Driving over to Bisbee. See that big hole in the ground. That old Silver Queen mine. Or whatever they call it."

"Don't shit me, Don. You know ex*act*ly what it's called."

"That's a true fact."

"So," I said. "We're right back to this 'so what' routine."

"I've got this contract."

"No."

"Just hear me out."

"You gave me however long I wanted. After San Carlos, only small jobs. After all those . . . those people dead."

"Long as you want."

"Maybe even forever."

"If that's what you want. Yes. But it's been almost five months."

That's when I knew he really needed me for something he couldn't handle. I assumed the worst, which was that after I said no, he'd keep at me, and he saw that in my eyes and shook his head.

"Just hear me out," he said. "It's not what you think."

"I *think* you want me for a contract."

"Look. Laura. I know you've had some . . . some problems. With your friend Meg. Your friend Rey. With that whole messy business down in Mexico, down in San Carlos. I've never bothered you. Let you deal with it. Kept out of your way. Except for signing the partnership papers, for the Phoenix thing, I've just sent you your money, given you small jobs. Easy jobs. You don't ever have to come to the office. But I've got to push on you a bit. It's special, it's one-of-a-kind. Never quite had anything like this. So. Hear me out?"

"Sure," I said reluctantly. "Just this one time."

revelations

The gray Chevy Citation came north up Campbell Avenue, slowing as traffic bunched together in front of the movie theater just south of Grant Road. Windows tinted dark, a silvery mirror from the outside. Alongside, a plumber in a battered '55 Ford 150 pickup took out a pocket comb and used his reflection as a mirror, fiddling with his hair.

Theresa Prejean watched the plumber from the backseat of the Citation. Still wearing the orange jumpsuit, but no longer handcuffed, she shrank back and slid partway down the seatback.

"Can he see me?" she asked the driver.

"Don't worry. Just a plumber."

She worried at two fingernails on her left hand, frightened, anxious, with no idea where they were going. As he'd done for the past forty minutes, the driver paid close attention to his mirrors and her nervousness.

"Almost there." He turned to smile at her again.

"What's *there*?"

"A house we use. You'll be safe there."

"This red light is like going on for*ever*."

"Busy corner," the driver said.

"I don't like this. All I want is to get back to Norleans, and you're stuck here in the middle of goddam Tucson."

"For your own protection."

"Yeah. Well. I told my story. My best protection is back in my hood."

"Sorry. Maybe by tomorrow."

The driver's cell phone sounded a squeaky version of the Darth Vader music.

"Yeah," he said. "Yeah. No."

The plumber put his hand to a red sore on his neck, stretching his head to look at his profile. Theresa cringed, but the plumber switched to his rearview mirror, positioning it so he could rub his neck. Through traffic stopped on Grant as a long line of drivers snaked slowly into left turns onto Campbell, but the line cutting into northbound traffic got hung up in the intersection and when the lights turned green, traffic gridlocked in all directions.

"Come on, come *on*," Theresa said to herself.

"Five minutes," the driver said.

He caught Theresa's face in the middle of the center mirror.

"Please move away from the center," he said, and instead of moving she slid way down in the seat again. "Say what? Yeah. I'll keep the line open."

"Dealing drugs?" he said to Theresa. "In that camp?"

"Just a misunderstanding."

"Three grams of coke is not a misunderstanding."

"Momma was a turkey," Theresa sang to her herself, ignoring him. "But she thought she was a duck. Lookin for another bird to get herself a fuck."

"No no no," the driver said. "You got that wrong."

"Get out."

"Momma bought a chicken, but she thought she was a duck."

Behind them, breaking the monotonous, muted sound of vehicle engines in four lanes, a heavy rumble was working its way to the light.

"Put it in a pan and turned the oven up," the driver sang. "'Long came sister with a spoon and a glass, scooping out the gravy from the yass yass yass."

Looking out the back window, Theresa saw two motor-cycles weaving between the northbound traffic lanes. Her driver leaned toward the door, cocking his head until he picked up the motorcycles in his outside mirror.

"Whoa!" he said. "Those are Ducatis."

The first bike stopped just behind the Citation.

"A Multistrada 1000 Superbike. See the red wheels? Dark metallic gray body? I don't believe this, I've never seen one except on the Speed Channel. No, can't be a Superbike, not with that color, wow, it's got to be the Monster."

"Can you, like, get us going?" Theresa whined as the first bike came abreast of her window. "Like, please?"

For all his enthusiasm with the bikes, the driver kept checking his mirrors, checking out the other cars surrounding him, a slight frown at the blocked traffic.

"Helluva deal, you ask me." Theresa rubbed a hand over the door handle, testing it, but the driver had somehow set all the locks. "I shoulda just ran, once't I had the chance, shoulda ran."

"So why did you try for a deal? Telling about the bones?"

"Did Darth Vader tell you to ask me that?"

"Curious. Yes. We don't have much of a clue about you."

"Curious." She mimicked the comment in a singsong voice. "Well, it's my ass on the line. I'd be dead back there, you didn't pick me up."

"Dead? Why?"

Traffic cleared enough so all vehicles started moving, but the light switched yellow as the Citation came to the inter-section.

"For Christ's sake," Theresa said when the driver braked to a stop, "you could have run that yellow. We could be moving."

"Wanted to see the second bike," he said. "Yeah, oh, yeah. Another Monster. An 800. See? The wheels are metallic gray, and the tank and fairing are red, yellow, and black."

"I'm going to get out and walk, Jesus, I can walk across the street faster than you can drive there."

"Told you before, no rear door handles on these cruisers."

"Yeah, well, you got me locked up too tight in here."

"Almost there."

Both bikes sat directly between the Citation and a red Mercedes 500 convertible, whose driver paid more attention to the bikers than the bikes. Theresa tried to see the bikers; one of her New Orleans boyfriends owned a Harley. The bikers leaned forward on the seats, knees bent and angled ahead like their helmeted heads, a short rubber-banded ponytail emerging underneath the helmet of the biker in front. Neither wore leathers, both had identical faded denim jackets, stonewashed jeans, and black Nikes. Small, Theresa thought, they're both so small, they've got to be kids.

The light changed to green again. Reluctantly, the driver turned away from the bikes and started the Citation moving through the intersection. Both bikers let in their clutches at the same instant, Theresa expecting them to leap across the intersection, but the Mercedes kept pace with the bikes and the Citation, crossing Grant like a solid block, the Mercedes driver grinning at the bikers.

Ponytail waggled the lead bike slightly to the right, raising a hand to point ahead of the Citation, wanting to cut in. Theresa's driver already had his left turn signal on, trying to move over behind the Mercedes, so he slowed the Citation and motioned the lead biker to get in front.

"That asshole in the convertible," Theresa protested. "He's really pissing off these guys on the bikes."

Both bikers nodded their heads, maybe a slight thank you, maybe just relief that they could burst out of the jam, but the second bike sputtered, fell back, and turned sharply behind the Citation, the Mercedes driver now believing it was a game and keeping pace, slowing as the lead biker slowed. Cars honked from behind as suddenly the lead biker swiveled to a stop on an angle. The rear bike also stopped, the biker jumping off the seat and letting the bike fall to the pavement.

"It's a hit!" the driver said into the cell, trying to pull out his weapon from a clip holster that was snugged tight by the seatbelt. He dropped the cell, fought with both hands to get out the weapon.

"Get down, miss, get *down*."

"A hit? A *hit*?" Theresa screamed. "What the hell does that mean?"

The biker in front snapped open the carrier bag on the back of his seat and pulled out a chrome pistol, firing it deliberately at the Mercedes, the man frantically braking, throwing himself halfway over his door trying to get away until a shower of blood blossomed from his chest and right shoulder. The Mercedes jumped the divider strip, careened through southbound traffic until smashing into the tall neon sign of a Chinese takeout restaurant. The biker then turned the pistol toward the Citation. The driver cramped the steering wheel hard left, trying to run past the motorcycle but the biker taking careful aim, targeting the driver, hitting his shoulder, then his forehead. The Citation lurched sideways, the driver curled over the steering wheel, foot jamming the accelerator in the same moment so the Citation smashed *hard* against the biker, crushing one leg against the bike, knocking off his mirrored helmet.

The Citation's rear window disintegrated as the other biker, a pistol in each hand, fired one weapon after the other, thrusting each pistol slightly forward with the trigger pull, stalking after the Citation as it ground up over the curb into a strip mall, pushing the Ducati relentlessly ahead of it, the biker clawing up the hood of the Citation, but getting no purchase on the smooth metal. Theresa huddled on the floor, fingers stuck in both ears to shut out the noise of the bullets, the flying glass, her shrieks. The rear passenger window exploded, sunlight flooding into the Citation now that almost all the tinted glass had fragmented.

The Citation groaned relentlessly into the front of a music store, engine and tires screaming, but the storefront brick and steel construction held the Citation solid, unmoving. Theresa rolled on her back, hands crossed in front of her face, palms outward, pleading as the biker thrust both hands inside the car and hit her chest *thumpthump* with a double tap and then one last bullet in her head.

The biker turned around, firing several shots randomly toward all the cars and people on the streets. Releasing the clips of both pistols, calmly inserting new clips, he fired again at the cars, drivers abandoning them or ducking on the floor. The biker ran around the Citation, looked down at the second biker, trapped between the Citation and the storefront, one leg bent almost perpendicular out from his hip, raw stumps of bone sticking out of the jeans, a bloodied young face nodding at the biker, who shot the injured boy in the head.

Firing again and again at nothing in particular, the biker ran to his machine, cranked the engine into life, and roared down Campbell, swiveling the bike at high speed around parked cars, the biker low on the seat, and abruptly disappearing in a right-hand turn onto a side street.

laura

5

"What do you know about 800 number call centers?" Don asked.

"Computer help lines?"

"Ordering merchandise."

"Like . . . Land's End? Call an 800 number, order a pair of pants?"

I noticed that Don had his Moroccan leather briefcase stuffed into a pocket of his wheelchair.

"Sure. Whatever. Say, a pair of pants," he said, ignoring the question. Typical Don Ralph. He'd tell you only what he wanted you to know. "You dial the number. Order the pants. What happens?"

"I give them my credit card info."

"And your shipping address."

"And my billing address."

"Plus a phone number. All of that for some pants or tee shirts or pajamas. You call that number and you trust that somebody, somewhere, takes down all that personal info and the company keeps it private. Keeps it secure."

"Somebody you don't know," I emphasized.

"Exactly right. Somebody you don't know, you'll never meet."

38

"So you're here about credit card theft. Identity theft. Same old, same old."

"Not exactly."

"What? Exactly?"

I shifted my chair out of the sun. He didn't even touch his wheels, didn't unlock the brakes to move into some shade. Once Don was on scent, he rarely noticed what happened to his body.

"In time. In time."

"I've got months," I reminded him. "Maybe forever. But we're not talking about pajamas. So where are these calling centers?"

"Exactly right. Do you know how they work?"

"I've ordered. A few times. From some fake ID. Like, say, a credit card that's untraceable."

"But you've seen the catalog. You've seen the pajamas."

"At the bottom of the catalog page, there's an 800 number. I call it."

"Unless you ask the operator, you have no idea where they are."

"North Dakota," I said, thinking about it. "Some state that's mostly in the boonies. Not in a big city. Wages are good. Cubicles. Headsets."

"Private enterprise. Capitalism at its best."

"What makes our country great. We're not talking North Dakota, are we?"

He smiled. Gotcha, I thought. One of Don's very few tells. When you had that ace in the hole, when you knew he only had a ten or a three, and you called him on it, he smiled. He knew it was a tell, he couldn't help smiling anyway.

"In the U.S.," he said.

"In the continental U.S."

"Of course. The 800 numbers are cheapest to rent in the mainland."

"So . . . where?"

"You've hacked into a few call centers, I know that."

"Kansas city, one time. That's all I remember."

"Ever heard of them being in a prison?" he asked.

I had to think about that one.

"Upstate New York, maybe. Or . . . guess I don't really know."

"How about closer to home. In Florence?"

"North of here? That Florence?"

"Arizona Department of Corrections," he said. "Florence facility."

"But that's a maximum complex. Hard timers there. And the death house."

"Yes, it's a big complex, with several different facilities. Much of it is for level five inmates. The nasties. Thugs, rapists, murderers, they can be level five or, if they're on good behavior, they can be lower. Level three, say."

"Don, wait, wait. So I call Land's End."

"They don't handle that company. But yeah. Somebody reputable."

"I really want those pajamas. Nobody else has the style I want."

"From the looks of you half an hour ago, you don't even wear them."

I blushed. That's really hard to do, make me blush.

"Okay, Don. So you've seen my boobs."

"I've seen them before," he said. "Remember that contract in Houston?"

"Oh. Yeah."

"I saw it all," he said. "So have we got your boobs out of the way now?"

"Pick up the phone, call the 800 order number. No idea, really, who I'm talking to. But I assume . . . I assume, 'cause it's the American way, that they're company people. That I'm talking to a company rep. Paid with a company check."

"Wages are going up. So. Some companies, some very *big* companies, contract out the call center."

"To prisons like Florence."

"It's a test contract. A new contract. But far from the first in a prison."

"How long have they been up and running?" I had no idea where he was going, but so far I couldn't see what he needed me for.

"Half a year. Eight months, outside."

"Don, that's . . . this is . . . you run one of the top legit security-penetration companies around. We are talking some kind of hacking, right?"

"Right."

"This doesn't compute," I said. A stupid cliché. "This doesn't make sense. If a credit card call center is running inside a prison, no legit company is going to allow convicts to take down personal information. Credit card numbers."

"When the operator enters data—"

"The inmate."

"When the *con*vict, I mean, when the *in*mate enters the data, first of all, he sees just asterisks."

"Like a log on password."

"Just like a password. You log into MSN, AOL, whatever, type your password and all you see is a series of asterisks. Because you can't read it, you have to enter it twice. In the Florence call center, there's a small script running on the main data servers that verifies the credit card number and the inmate never really sees it."

"Networked computers?" I asked.

"Closed network. Each inmate has his workstation. Networked with several data servers. But entirely combined within that operation."

"But you just said the data server verifies the credit card number. How does it do that without dialing outside? Without some Internet connection?"

"It doesn't. It just verifies that the inmate has entered the right number of digits from a credit card."

"Who sees the real numbers?"

"Prison officials, Correction Officers with special computer training, they burn encrypted CDs with the data. They take the CDs to a completely separate computer network. Orders go to the company."

"What am I missing, Don?"

"Missing?"

"Oh, don't get cute. You're stringing me along here. You're trying to sell me on something and I don't have a clue what. But in ten minutes I'm going to get my running clothes on and go out for ten miles or so."

"Two more things, then."

"Let *me* ask two more things. Number one," I said. "Somehow, all these pajamas getting ordered are winding up in credit card theft."

"And identity theft."

"How much damage are we talking about?"

"Don't you mean, how is the data getting out of the prison?"

"I figure that's why you're here, Don. You can't figure it out, you decided to come down and titillate me with something different."

"Something unusual. That's for sure."

"Working for a prison. That's not just unusual, that's weird."

"Not why I'm here. Laura, I realize I'm giving you pretty thin stuff."

"Thin? It's so goddam thin it's invisible."

He grinned, wide, showed his teeth.

"Gotcha," he said. I usually didn't start swearing until I was aggravated about not getting the right details.

"Fucking goddam A," I said, but we both laughed.

"Come on, Don," I said finally. "You've got all those people in your new building up there in Scottsdale. You've got somebody else that can handle this."

"We."

"You. We. Whatever."

"Laura, you're a partner. You and I go a long way back. *We* did the work that made enough money to set up this company. So we're partners. You get a third of the profit. Whether you ever go back to work full-time or not."

"What's the hook, Don?"

"Hook?" he said innocently.

"However you figured you'd get me back to computer hacking."

"Ah," he said. "*That* hook. You feel it?"

"Jesus Christ, Don! It's hanging right in front of me, I guess. So put your goddam bait on it, I'm sure not going to swallow bare metal."

"Nobody else can fill this contract," he insisted.

I snorted.

"No. Really."

"Really. Come on. Identity theft is minor league stuff these days for people like you. Right?"

"Right, yes. We mostly do security penetrations, offer contracts to guarantee high level computer and database security. But this time . . . a client asked for you."

"That's hardly a first. People have been asking for me a long time."

"You, Laura. It has to be you."

"Who's the client?"

"Don't know."

Sunset came out of the shrubs, finally hot enough to quit chasing birds and rodents. She sprawled at my feet, moved to get into the shade under the table. Put both paws over her eyes, her invitation for play, but I ignored her. Finally, Sunset scratched her left ear, slowly, languidly, gave a big yawn showing her yellowed teeth, and settled into rest mode.

"See a vet," Don said. "Get your dog's teeth scraped."

A tail whacked at his leg. He reached down to rub Sunset's muzzle. She let him, but I wasn't giving off the right vibes, so she didn't give her affection yet.

"Here's the deal," Don said.

"I haven't accepted any deal."

"If you do, no coming to the office."

"Get this over, Don. What's the hook? What's the *real* hook?"

He scratched Sunset's nose, rubbed the back of his hand gently back and forth across her nose, and scratched under her jaw until Sunset dropped her head next to the metal platforms holding Don's feet.

"You *know* who the client is," I said. "Don't you."

"Can't tell you that."

"It's somebody I've worked with before?"

"In a way."

"What if I don't want the contract?"

"You just don't."

"But I'm going to lose out on something, right?" He shrugged. "What?"

Don folded his hands in his lap. Looked me in the eye. Said nothing more. Knew that was the only way to really bait the hook, to get me back. I had no reason at all to *want* to go back to hacking, other than occasional, small-time jobs where I had absolutely *no* contact with the client.

I had bank accounts totaling in the high six figures. All cash. I got steady, monthly, large payments from the company, wired electronically and randomly to one of those bank accounts. I didn't need money. I didn't even think I needed to be juiced by the game. A good part of me never wanted to be juiced again. In four years, four contracts had ended with at least one person dead. Several of them right in front of my eyes. I'd shot people. Although I now owned several handguns, I never wanted to shoot anybody again unless my life depended on it.

"She asked for you, Laura."

"Oh, you bastard," I said.

But he'd set the hook. I thought about all those packed cardboard boxes, stacked haphazardly, waiting to be taped up or flung into a dumpster. I went inside the house, got a plate of green grapes, brought them out. Don shook his head.

I ate fifteen grapes. I got up again, went inside again, went from room to room, looking at all I possessed, all I wanted to throw away, all I wanted to change.

"I'd be working only with you?"

"No."

"Pass."

"Not working in the office," he said. "That's what I meant. I'm in the office. I'm too tired to get out, you know that."

"So. By myself, then."

"Didn't say that, either."

"You know I don't like working with strangers."

"I vouch for him."

"Oh, gee, Don."

"He's been working with me for three months. He's part of the package."

"Why?"

"Used to work for the Arizona Prison CIU. Investigator. He knows the different complexes. He knows Florence. Use to work up there."

"Pass."

"He's also a U.S. Marshal. Nathan Brittles."

"You gotta be kidding me," I said.

"You know him?"

"John Wayne. Played somebody named Brittles. Cavalry officer. I can't remember which film."

"Well, this guy's legit. I checked him out."

"Brittles," I said to myself.

"Good man. He just doesn't know computers."

"Why does he work for you?"

"He knows security."

Rich came through the front door just at that moment, stopped dead still when he saw me. I'd never talked about Don, never talked about computers or the Internet or hacking or my friend Meg's kidnapping or all those people I'd watched die. He smiled his gentle smile, came over to rub my nose, but I turned away from him and went back outside, standing in front of Don. He already had his hands on the wheelchair brakes, unlocking them. Wanting to leave, he only waited for me to swallow the hook or swim away. Bye bye.

"Okay," I said. "What's next?"

6

I watched Don lower the wheelchair ramp of his van and roll onto it. The ramp rose, the panel doors slid shut. Through the passenger-side door I could see him levering himself into the driver's seat. When he saw me watching, he waved me over.

"One more thing. I should have said how soon it's gotta go down."

"You want me to drive up to Phoenix tomorrow?"

"Tomorrow?" He shifted into Drive. "Somebody will get you in an hour."

The van moved slowly around the twin palo verdes near the front door, dust rising from the crushed shell and rock driveway, and the van quickly accelerated and turned onto the paved street.

"You going to do it?"

Rich stood several feet behind me, startling me. I moved to him, but he stepped aside, careful not to touch any part of my body. Sadness, frustration, anger, I couldn't tell what he was feeling. I went to the fridge and got out some Gatorade.

"Maybe."

"Like, maybe you'll dump those cartons of junk?"

"Or not."

He went outside, stood underneath the thatched ramada, his back to me.

"Rich. I don't know. Okay?"

"Is it something ordinary?"

"He wouldn't say."

"He said enough."

"You were listening?"

"Some."

He gathered his long hair, rolling it around and around, finally pulling out a thick rubber band and fastening the ponytail so it hung down to his shoulder blades. "You want to talk about it?"

I really *didn't* want to talk about it.

"I'm not sure what you mean."

"It. Them. The things you do. Not that I really know the things you do."

"Did."

"Okay, the things you did. The things that got you wound so tight you were snorting Ritalin when I met you. You want to go back to that? Back to . . . *it*?"

"I never thought about it until today."

"What about your life here?"

"With you?" I said, touching his arm, holding it with both hands.

"It's not about me. You're relaxed, Laura. I've never asked what you used to do, I never *cared* what you used to do. I've never read your papers, I've never snooped on your computer, I've never even asked why you don't touch your computer for days. I don't care about that stuff."

"Going back," I said. "It wouldn't be anything I haven't done before. Are you worried that somehow I'll go back to a job and go away from you?"

"Are you healthy enough?"

"Excuse me?"

"Capable."

"Say what?"

"You were on the ragged edge when I met you, Laura. Like that song. Alanis Morrisette. You were on a bunch of jagged little pills, you ground them up, you snorted them, you snorted a *lot* of them. Are you going back to that?"

"You want me to stay? Here?"

"With me, you mean."

"Stay with you," I said, a little too slow and deliberate. "Yes. Stay. Not take this . . . job, whatever. Just continue like we're doing? Is that what you want?"

"Laura. I just want you to stay healthy."

"You mean, emotionally healthy," I said bitterly.

"Dammit, I mean stay the way you are now. For your sake. I don't care about us as much as I care that you don't go back to whatever work you used to do. I've seen you come away from that work."

"It's only one job."

"Right." I'd never seen him so angry. Rarely angry, that's my Rich. "Whatever."

"Rich. I think I need to do just one more small job. I need to make sure I can leave it after one more job. Leave it. Junk it, can it, walk away from the life."

"The life?" He was appalled. "You mean, like, The Life? You were in The Life?"

"Jesus Christ!" Now I *was* angry. "If you're saying I was a working girl, if you're saying I was a whore, that's ridiculous."

"What*ever* it was, Laura, you could walk away from it now. Other people move on."

"Rich," I said. "What's your bottom line here?"

"When I told you I never checked your computers, your private stuff, I mostly meant that. Except. The first two months after I met you, I'd check out your bathroom, your bedside, wherever I thought you might be hiding that Ritalin. I can't go back to doing that, Laura."

"That'll never happen again."

"My sister," he said. "She drank. A lot. When I was a teenager, mom and I would search the entire house, looking for my sister's booze. No matter how much we poured down the toilet, she'd always find more. No matter how many times she'd promise the boozing was over, it never ended. Never. I can't go through that again. I shouldn't even talk about it. I forgot about it for some years now."

"Just this one more job, Rich. I promise."

"Yeah. You promise. I've got to get going."

Buzzing, somewhere, a drone, getting louder.

"What the *hell* is that?" Rich said, angry we'd been interrupted.

I knew that *whopwhopwhop* sound and a minute later a small Bell helicopter flew twenty feet over the house and settled into the desert lot across the street. The pilot kept the blades rotating as somebody jumped out of the left seat and came toward us.

"Fuck this," Rich said, picking up his forensic tool kit. "We'll talk later."

"I could be up in Coolidge for days. Maybe I'll get a motel room there."

The man from the chopper loped up the driveway, saw me at the door. "Mrs. Burdick?"

How like Don to keep names and titles secret from people he'd hired for a job but whom he didn't trust.

"Yes."

"When you're quite ready."

"I'll need some clothes," I said to the pilot. "Five minutes."

When he left, Rich set his forensic tool kit in the middle of the floor and walked around and around it. Not a good sign, since he only traveled in circles when he was so angry he didn't trust himself to head straight out anywhere.

"I've *got* to do this," I said, getting angrier with each of his circles.

"No, you *don't*!" he shouted.

"What?"

"You just stay here. You just chill, I'll come back tonight."

"Not this girl," I said. "You must be talking about one of

those horny little undergraduates you said always want to see your bones."

I put on some Mad Squirrel, amped the stereo to max.

"Turn that crap off!" he shouted.

Why'd you have to go and say that?
Now all these people gonna think I'm a bitch
But now I'm pissed off and don't give a shit
You can fuck a freshman if that's your go
But don't think you gettin' in this ass no mo.

Rich picked up the stereo, ripped off the speaker cables, and smashed the hard metal case against the floor. He stood back suddenly, afraid of what he'd done so unconsciously, awed by his anger. Palms up, arms out, pleading for my forgiveness in the total silence of the room, even the birds and insects frightened away by the noise.

Rich strode angrily to his pickup, ground the starter.

When I came back out, after locking the door and getting into the chopper, we rose above the road, and before the chopper headed north I could see Rich's pickup, swerving around and around on the desert floor, driving in ever widening circles, and long after his pickup lurched off to the west I could see a tall, thin cloud of dust motes lingering in that spiral of uncertainty.

revelations

The black Lincoln Town Car arrived promptly at four-fifteen.

Exactly as promised.

Yayo saw the dust trail when it came through the Rapture Warriors main gate. She stopped pacing, wrapped both hands around the woven silk handles of her Takashimaya shopping bag, stood absolutely straight up, pushing her shoulders back to relieve neck tension due to anticipation. Finally squaring the shoulders, she wondered, if she held them back, whether her small breasts would show better. But because she was wearing a XXL tee shirt on her small-boned body, nobody would be able to tell about the breasts, so she just waited until the Lincoln pulled up beside her and an immaculately tailored and groomed chauffeur came briskly around from the driver's side to open the rear door for her.

"Miss Yayo," he said, unsmiling, precise.

"*Arrigato,*" she said, making a slight bow, wondering how Japanese she should be with him, wondering if he reported on her behavior. She spoke perfect Japanese. Tokyo born and Kyoto raised by a geisha mother, now in the U.S. for just two months of her sixteen years. Knew how to please men, knew which men *not* to please, knew the chauffeur wasn't important, swung her legs easily into the backseat, knees and ankles pressed together as though she were wearing a geisha's kimono instead of the jeans.

"I'll take that, Miss Yayo."

He held out a gloved hand, pointing at her bag.

"These are my things. From the camp."

"Yes, Miss Yayo."

She hooked the twined handles around his glove. He shut her door with a solid clunk, walked briskly to a large trash receptacle, and dumped the bag into it.

"Those are my things," she protested.

"Tamár has all new things for you."

"Are you taking me to meet her?"

"Of course. Fasten your seatbelt, please."

He drove in through Oro Valley, swinging along Sunrise Highway to the canyoned foothill area of rich Tucson. She sat without moving, content to look, head moving slowly, elegantly from side to side as different homes caught her eye. The limo turned into a gated community, the security box barrier raised so quickly the limo barely slowed.

The Lincoln wound easily along the curved street, heavily and expensively landscaped. Thirty-foot high mesquites, carefully planted palo verde trees, and many different shrubs, mingling with an occasional saguaro left where it had grown for decades, protected by state law against removal.

"Here we are," the driver said.

Yayo had expected a mansion, a palace in this summer land, but the Lincoln turned onto a driveway of crushed coral and up a long, winding hill to an ordinary one-story house. She unclipped her seatbelt, expecting to be let off at the front door, but the driver pressed a garage-door opener in the sun visor, waited for the door to rise, and drove the Lincoln inside.

Eager, excited, more than a little bit anxious, Yayo started to get out of the Lincoln, but the driver was already coming around to help her. When the garage door closed, banks of indirect lighting came on. He held a gloved hand to assist her out of the Lincoln. She expected to see a small door from garage to house, was startled to find one entire side of the garage had been decorated as though *it* were the front of the house. Elaborate golden carriage lamps on either side of a huge double door, knobs of fourteen-carat gold in the absolute dead centers of both doors. There were no visible locks. The driver motioned her toward the door. Standing in front of it, looking for a bell, she gasped as the doors swung inward.

A tall, beautiful woman stood there. Wearing a short-sleeved blouse in a blue paisley print, with a sheer bodice, fluttery collar and sleeves, and lace inserts at the Empire waist above a slim inch or two of bare skin. Stonewashed indigo blue denim skirt, slit up the front, and indigo Manolo Blahniks.

"Welcome," she said in a modulated English accent. "Do come in."

"Are you Tamár?"

"Tamár, yes."

"I wanted to have better clothes. I look awful."

"We've got plenty of nice clothes for you in a few moments. But business first. Let's have some tea. I've oodles of different teas. What is your favorite?"

She adjusted a perfect faded green celadon teapot, opening a large box with packets of tea leaves. Yayo chose a green tea and Tamár put it in a silver tea strainer, pouring hot water into the teapot from a silvered pitcher, and offering Yayo her choice from a delicate china platter carefully arranged with ginger cookies.

"Digestives," Tamár said. "I much prefer the chocolate ones. Do you?"

"*Arrigato gozaimus,*" Yayo said, teacup in hand, unable to bow, so she cast her eyes down, head forward and back in one gracious movement.

"I don't doubt your ability to speak Japanese," Tamár said. "It's your English that the men desire. And I also. How *is* your English?"

She handed Yayo a *Newsweek* magazine, folded to a page.

" 'Top of the Week.' " Yayo read carefully, not too fast, not too loud. " 'Cover Story. With a blunt tough-love message that says we have to stop complaining and take responsibility for our lives, Dr. Phil McGraw has become America's hottest self-help guru.' "

"Good, except . . . the men will want that quality you Japanese women have, the voice pitched up, a bit of singsong, that clear indication that Men Rule. Now. Read it again. Your natural voice. A bit of insistence. A certain quality, let's call it Women Rule."

Yayo faltered with the first words. Eyes lowered, she stopped, but didn't look up, began again, and gained enough confidence halfway through to raise her head and eyes to deliver the last words directly at Tamár, who smiled and clapped her satisfaction.

"I'm told you are sixteen," she said.

"And two months."

"Are you a virgin?"

"No."

"Good. You're too old for that market. Now. Come over here."

She crossed the room to an antique desk, took out a book. Yayo tried to comprehend the shape of the house, where the bedrooms were, confused that no kitchen seemed evident, even more confused that the expansive living room, on three levels, seemed to have no doors except the ones through which she'd entered. Tamár sat on a long sofa, watching Yayo for a moment.

"In good time, my dear. Look at the pictures."

Yayo opened a large photo album, the chrysanthemum-color covers of heavy leather, with a dozen soft leather tabs.

"I thought I would be working here," Yayo said.

"You'll start here. Let me explain how the Circuit works. This book shows thirteen other houses, just like this one. Like mine. You'll see pictures of all the other houses in that book. Each house has its own manager. Like me."

"I thought . . ." Yayo hesitated.

"You thought?"

"That you were in charge. That this was the only house."

"Women need to protect themselves from those men who usually manage working girls. Women need to organize. As women. Cut out those men, those pimps who take your money. The Circuit started at least sixty years ago. Now we have so many houses that we've regionalized. You're looking at the Southwest Circuit. Arizona, Nevada, Colorado, California. For the first year or so, you'll be moving between houses in the Southwest."

She paused to pour Yayo more tea.

"You do understand why you'll move around?"

"Louis Vuitton. Prada. Fendi."

Tamár smiled, clapped her hands together with soft enthusiasm.

"Exactly. Our customers want to see new faces. Our customers *pay* to see new faces. They pay very well. And most important, they keep paying *us* instead of going elsewhere. You're very good. Who designed my clothes?"

"The blouse, Cynthia Steffe. I believe the skirt is . . . is Michael Kors?"

"Very, *very* good. You are special. What is he wearing?"

Tamár tinkled a silver bell and a tall, handsome Latino man came into the room. He wore a black silk turtleneck underneath the jacket of an off-white linen suit. The top edge of the turtleneck almost, but not quite covered heavy pockmarks on the left side of his neck.

"Not European," Yayo said hesitantly. "Not American. Not U.S., anyway. Are you from Mexico, sir?"

He moved his head sideways, neither a no nor a yes.

"Yayo, I want you to meet Mr. Galliano."

Galliano bent to take Yayo's hand and brush it against his lips. Not a kiss, really, just a constant motion of picking up her hand as he bowed his head, moving the hand smoothly past his lips and letting it go slowly, delicately.

"Mr. Galliano is in charge of all security," Tamár said. "He takes very good care of my problems. And even better care of any problems you girls have."

"I don't solve problems," Galliano said. "I just make them go away."

"And now, dear. If you'll go down that hallway, to the last room on the left, you'll find many clothes laid out. That will be your bedroom, while you're at this house. Pick the clothes you most like and come back to model them for us."

Galliano watched her bow and leave the room.

"What do you think?" Tamár asked.

"We've got problems."

"You told me that the black girl wouldn't be a problem anymore."

"She's not. But she's unlocked a big surprise. Somehow, she found out about the burial site. She met some U.S. Marshals there. And all kinds of bones are getting dug up. How many girls do you have left to bring into the Circuit?"

"A dozen. Maybe more. How did that black girl find out?"

"Don't know yet. She tried to sell some coke inside the camp. Other infractions, the camp usually calls the sponsor, dismisses the client. But drugs, that's an arrest offense."

"Did our man pick her up?" Tamár asked

"Yes."

"Does he know about your special young friends? The bikers?"

"Nobody knows about them," he said. "They're all from Colombia, they're all vicious, they've all made their bones over and over, and it's time to send them back to Colombia for a long visit."

" 'Made their bones.' " Tamár grimaced. "Not a great metaphor. Do you really want to send them back?"

"You mean, should I whack them, too? Too early to tell."

"All right. You know best. I'll call Micah and arrange to get the rest of the girls. Let's meet here, I'll tell you when. Here's my list."

She removed a folded piece of paper from a beige clutch purse, ticked off one name with a gold Cross pen.

"She's taken care. See to the rest. Start with him."

"You want to shut down the whole food chain?"

"All that computer information trail, yes. We've mined it enough. I've taken what we needed, sold off the rest. Can you get to this man?" Pointing at one of the names. "The one inside?"

"Difficult," Galliano said, but he nodded, working out some details.

"Those bones. We shouldn't have trusted that . . . that laborer."

Galliano took her pen and wrote numbers beside the remaining names.

"We're *all* laborers," he said. "And Micah?"

"We have to be the only two left. And then . . . we'll leave. Will you go back to Colombia?"

Galliano shrugged, barely raising his right shoulder an inch and cocking his head slightly the other way.

"First I'll make all our problems go away," he said. "One at a time."

He folded the list, handed her the Cross pen.

Before he could put the list in a jacket pocket, she grasped his closed fist with both her hands. "It would be foolish to add my name to the bottom of your list."

"We've done too well, Tamár. And once we've both moved on, we'll do something else even better. For now . . . one problem at a time."

laura

7

The chopper circled the Perryville prison complex, but landed at a nearby hospital emergency helipad. Reaching across me, the pilot opened my door, his right hand, palm facing inward, making scooting-out motions. I stepped onto the skid, bent low and duckwaddled beyond the whirling blades, knelt with hands over my ears as the chopper rose with a sudden roar, and darted off into the morning haze.

Nobody else on the helipad. I waited a few minutes before I got angry enough to head toward the exit stairway, saw an elevator, and jammed my thumb repeatedly on the Down button. The door opened with loud chimes and a tall man strode out, bumping my shoulder before realizing I was there.

"Sorry," he said, stepping sideways, a little bow to acknowledge the bump. "Sorry. Didn't see you."

He tugged his red beret tighter on short black hair. The only people I knew who wore red berets were either military or air marshals. Just what I needed. A U.S. Marshal. I'd had a very bad experience with the last one.

"I'm Nathan Brittles," he said. "Will you come with me, please?"

"Why?"

"Why am I Nathan Brittles?" he said with a smile. A charmer. But then, I've met a lot of charmers, including the

ones who tried to kill me. "I know, I know. That's not what
you meant. Look. Spend five minutes with me. You'll understand. Here. This is for you. From Don."

He handed me a photo ID badge.

WINSLOW, LAURA NMI
AQUITEK

"That sounds like a toothpaste," I said. "You're kidding
me, right? Don Ralph's business is named after a brand of
Mexican toothpaste?"

Chin tucked to his chest, he studied the ID badge.

"Thought it was scuba gear, first time he told me about it."

"You got ID?"

"Why?"

I fingered the laminated tag hanging from his neck.

BRITTLES, NATHAN C.T.
US MARSHAL

"Cuz I could get one of these with my own picture and any
name I wanted. Twenty-four hours, maximum wait. It's not
that I don't trust you. I don't. I just want to know if you
rigged an identity in a hurry and forgot to put something extra in your wallet, like, I might see you're really somebody
else."

Without hesitation he reached inside his coat and handed
me a battered, stuffed leather billfold. Waited, charm in his
smile, but not in his eyes. I quickly rifled through a Texas driver's license and several credit cards, all for Nathan Brittles.
The finger-worn AARP membership card convinced me.

"What do those middle initials stand for?"

"Cutting Tongue."

I took in his barrel chest, slightly flat and elongated nose,
his black hair.

"Keep talking," he said. A smile crinkled his upper lip.

"Why are you staring at me like that?" I said.

"Don't know that I'm staring."

"Don't want to work with me," I said. "Worries you, working with a woman. That's the kind of stare I'm seeing."

"You're the one who seems worried."

I was either disgusted with him or angry at myself, I didn't know which.

"Sorry," I said. "You probably think I'm one of those strong women that are just waiting for you to take me to your home."

"Actually, I don't think I've ever brought a woman to bed in my home."

"What are you?" I said, his humor thawing me out some. "A priest?"

"I play Indian flutes," he said. "Sometimes, playing one on a spring evening, I feel like a priest. But that's another time."

"Don't think you'll play me into bed."

We both nodded, the banter having gone on just long enough to make each of us uncomfortable.

"You're Navajo."

"And you're part Hopi. Can we talk about that later?"

"Don't want to talk about it at all," I said shortly. "Okay. Where do you want to spend your five minutes?"

Hospital cafeteria food rarely looks any different. I passed up the Jell-O and flan, desperately wanting some caffeine, but took nothing. Brittles loaded a plate with scrambled eggs, bacon, link sausages, and a soupy pile of grits.

He picked a table against the wall, nobody nearby, and dug into his food.

"Haven't eaten in a long time," he said without apology, shoveling eggs into his mouth with one hand while fumbling with the other in his briefcase. Laid a manila envelope on the table, but didn't unseal it.

I waited, silent.

"You're a hacker."

It wasn't a question. He pulled out a thick dossier, laid it in front of me, flecks of sausage meat dropping on the top sheet.

"Very good hacker, Don tells me. Computer forensic specialist. I had to look that one up. Okay, we've got a proposition for you."

"I'm booked up this month."

He laid another sheet of paper in front of me.

"This says you do very little for Don. Small jobs only. No jobs involving personal contact?"

"So?"

"Way I hear it, you're taking time off. Running and such. Free weights."

"I work out," I said finally, part of me angry at the surveillance of my personal life, but mostly resigned to technology's intrusion on privacy. I'd done it myself, many times, too many times to think that others wouldn't hesitate to use the same snooper stuff I did.

"We know that," he said, using a piece of wheat toast to sop up the last bits of egg and grits. "I'm not here to threaten you in any way. To threaten your privacy. I know you've been threatened before. I know all about that mess down in Mexico. Your friend being kidnapped. So that's why you don't want any more jobs involving personal contact?"

I got out my cell phone and the set of numbers Don had given to me. Still our old code, I noticed, deciphering what he'd written so I'd call the right number at the exact right time.

"Laura." Don answered immediately. "You're looking for bona fides?"

"Who is this handsome guy?" I asked.

"Nathan Brittles. Two tours of duty in Nam. One of the original members of the Shadow Wolves. Ask him what that is."

"You were a shadow wolf?" I said to Brittles.

"Indian trackers. U.S. Customs. Mostly involving drug smuggling across the border and through the Tohono O'Odham reservation. I think the current bunch is working on terrorist stuff."

"What else?" I asked Don.

"Spent some time as an investigator for the Arizona Department of Prisons. I think he quit in disgust at the politics. Been a U.S. Marshal for a while. I've been trying to hire him that last five months. That enough?"

I pushed PWR, shut down the cell phone, snapped it shut.

"So you're who you say you are."

"Look. Can we, like, get beyond this adversarial posture for a while?"

He swiped the papers back into the briefcase, except the sealed envelope.

Now, here's the crazy part, I mean, I tell you, this is *really* crazy. I'd described him as handsome to Don, one of those words that comes out from your gut before your head can stop them and once they're out, they're in the air. Maybe it was him being Navajo, I don't know, there was something about him. I'd seen his smile at the word, a sardonic smile, though, not narcissistic or self-involved, just a recognition of something about him that he never really acknowledged to himself. But he *was* handsome, he was incredibly trim, he looked like . . . *Stupid stupid don't go there,* I thought. Enough Navajo men in my life.

"Do you lift free weights?" I found myself saying.

"Every other day. I also believe there are many universes. Like science fiction. Like, there's another version of you and me operating in another universe."

"Now, that really freaks me out," I said.

"Okay. Here's why Don had you meet me here. Three days ago, a federal prisoner at Leavenworth asked to see the deputy warden. Told the warden that she had information on a monster identity-theft ring being operated from inside a prison. You've heard, I'm sure? Some of the 800 number call centers have contracts with prisons? Help lines, customer service, catalog ordering?"

"Heard about it, yes. Never came across it personally."

"Everybody orders from catalogs. Don't you?"

I nodded.

"And you called some toll-free number, right?" I nodded. "You ever really know, even care, where that person was? *Who* that person was?"

"Don already went through that dance with me. This federal prisoner, what's he got to do with me?"

"Not he. She."

I waited. He tapped the manila envelope, pushed his plate and silverware aside, cleaned the plastic tabletop, started spinning the envelope by flicking a corner with his fingernails.

"I'm not sure."

The spinning envelope started to annoy me, I knew it was a tell, a giveaway sign that he was nervous, possibly because he didn't know what was inside the envelope, possibly because, in spite of his promise, it was some threat to me, some government document, a warrant, I'd violated security somewhere, hard to know, I violated computer security regularly. I slapped my hands down on the envelope and startled him for a few seconds. He stretched out his fingers.

"I'm not supposed to look in this envelope unless you agree to help us."

Picking it up, I looked at the flap, glued shut, threw it down again.

I'm getting good at social exchanges. I'm not anywhere near as intimidated as I used to be.

"This prisoner—"

"Who is it?"

"A young woman. Abbe Consuelo Dominguez. Abbe pronounced like 'Abbie,' but spelled *A-b-b-e*. Early twenties, doing eighteen months on federal mail fraud. Actually a hacker. Like you. But got nailed when she sent a list of a thousand credit card numbers through the mail."

"So?"

"Ms. Dominguez says she'll identify the prison which functioned as a source for identity theft."

"So?" I said again.

"But *only*," he stressed, "only if *you* would get involved."

"Me? Involved?"

"You. Asked for you by name. Told us where to find you."

Mind-boggling.

I quickly ran through some of the names of people I'd been responsible for prison terms. No young women. Quickly ran through the revenge thing, wanted nothing to do with revenge seekers, not after Meg Arizana being kidnapped, that crazy son of a woman we'd once exposed.

"Where's this woman now?"

"At Perryville prison. I brought her down two days ago, from Leavenworth. But I've been tied up with another . . . another case, on federal land. Couldn't get to you until just now."

"And you want me to talk to this woman?"

"She wants to talk to you."

"But you have no real idea what she wants to tell me."

"Nope."

He started spinning the envelope again, stared at what he was doing, stopped abruptly, and smiled.

"You're on to that one, aren't you? I don't have many tells. I play high-stakes poker, I'm very good at keeping signals from other players. Now you've got me wondering if I play with cards in front of me like this when I'm a little nervous."

"If I meet this woman," I said. "If she talks to me, I'm out of it then? This envelope thing is kinda dumb, anyway. Like a Hollywood spy movie without any logic. So what's really inside?"

"Yeah. We peeked. Sealed it back up again. It's just a long, detailed list of financial transactions using stolen credit cards. But we don't know how they were stolen except through some prison 800 number call center. Lots of prisons in this country, even private prisons that have a bottom line to earn money. You talk to Ms. Dominguez, she gives up the specific prison."

"Don said it was Florence."

"Just a guess. She teased us with a list of fifty prisons."

"But why me?"

"Don't you want to find out?"

Sure I did. But not that I cared about the identity thefts. I always wanted to know about people who knew my name, knew what I did. It's supposed to be a private thing, hacking into computers, supposed to be done through cutouts, although I'd been doing it long enough to have an international reputation.

"Can we go there right now?"

"In my car, I've got something you have to wear. They're expecting two people. U.S. Marshal, somebody from Aquitek. Don's cleared the way. But you'll have to put on a uniform."

"Do I get a red beret?"

At the time, I thought all of this was getting to be a lark. Wheeeee! Some fun in the Phoenix sun. Of course, a handsome Navajo man will blind me to the truth all the time. *Not this time,* I thought.

"So you're Navajo," I said, mouth way ahead of my brain.

"Mother was from the Biihtsoh Dine'é clan. Big Deer People. Father was Deeshchii'nii clan. Start-of-the-Red-Streaked People."

"From where on the rez?"

"Medicine Water. You? Which Hopi mesa?"

"Hotevilla. Look, uh, I *so* don't want to talk about this."

"No problem. Ready to go?"

And how strange, to feel so . . . conflicted about the difference between this man and Rich Thompson.

No. I won't go there.

8

He didn't have my size quite right.

The black khaki uniform trousers fit tight in the crotch, the shirt molded around my shoulders and biceps, layered on like paint, like a second skin. I refused the holstered Smith & Wesson nine, but snugged the red beret against my shoulder-length dirty-brown hair. It would take more than a beret to give me helmet hair. I liked the cool black band around the bottom, hated what the beret signified, marveled at how far I'd come to working *with* Law instead of against it.

"What's your color?" he said when I swiveled his rearview mirror around so I could see myself with the beret, adjust its fit. I liked that. Most men would have a cow if you even touched their mirrors while they were driving, but his only physical reaction was to snuggle against the left door, steer with his left hand while he looked me over at seventy miles an hour.

"Color?"

"Your hair. What coloring, what brand of coloring do you use?"

"That's not flattering, you know. That I'm old enough to cover the gray."

"I do. So, what do you use?"

"L'Oréal."

"Hey. Use it myself."

He stretched a fist to me, we knocked fists. And again, I had to check him out, I'd been doing this ever since we'd met, but not obvious, keeping up my part-angry, part-frustrated, part-I-don't-care image. Unlike most older men who fixate on total black coloring, Brittle's hair was somewhere between black and brown, not even noticeably colored.

He slid over to the I-10 right lane, turned on his blinker for the Cotton Lane exit. We headed north on Cotton Lane, my heart thumping. I'd been here before, been here just last year, the start of one of the worst days in my life, the day Meg Arizana was kidnapped down at Nogales. Tried not to show my anxiety at being here as he turned left at McDowell Road and then right on Citrus Road for approximately half a mile.

"What's wrong?" he asked, pulling into a parking lot instead of the main prison complex entrance.

"I've been here once."

"A friend in there?"

"No." Licking my lips, tugging at the beret. "I've never been inside."

"Want to talk about it?"

"Let's just get this over with."

This time, I paid more attention, saw a bunch of gray buildings, looking like blockhouses, spread out within the confines of the entire Perryville grounds. I knew that "complex" actually meant specific buildings in a prison.

"Explain to me what I'm going to see," I said, alerted by the remembered anxiety of my last visit.

"Arizona Department of Corrections. Each complex is run by a warden and each unit within the complex is run by a deputy warden. Each complex warden is assisted by a complex deputy warden, each unit DW is assisted by an associate deputy warden, an ADW."

"Forget the alphabet soup."

"I don't know many details about Perryville regarding units. I never worked here. All I know, it's a woman's prison, there's a Criminal Investigation Unit here. My impression is of a fairly large complex of single-story gray buildings with this large parking lot out front, facing the flat, one-storied admin building. Here."

He got out, moved to the front of the car before realizing I was still inside. He laid his briefcase on the hood and waited. His cell phone rang, he flipped it out and open. A Samsung a310—I notice these things, it helps when I'm anxious or frustrated, I focus in on technology, my safety valve, my emotional throttle-down escape.

One Mississippi, two Mississippi . . . ten deep breaths, and I got out of the car, eyes on the pavement and then up, defiant, ready to deal with it.

"She's supposed to be at the camp," I heard him say. "*Shit!* I authorized one of my men to pick her up. To hold her as a material witness."

An Anna's hummingbird buzzed past my ear, flirting with the red ocotillo flowers. A male, its gorget and crown a brilliant iridescent red, the helmet absolutely glowing when you saw it head-on, but turning dark as it flew the other way.

"See if you can find that guy, that . . . Sean, the guy who supposedly told her about the bones. Okay, bodies. Whatever. Call me when you leave the camp."

"Problems?" I said.

"No."

If I'd have known right then that Theresa Prejean had been assassinated on a Tucson street, on a corner only *six blocks* from where I used to live, if I'd have known, I'd have . . . what? I thought, *What the hell would I have done anyway?*

He folded the cell, tucked it away, and gestured toward the entrance. He followed me inside to the front desk, showed his ID, and we were escorted through a barred-door sally port into a long hallway and then a windowless visitors' room. Twenty feet wide, over fifty feet long, chairs set on either side of tables, aligned perfectly in a row stretching the length of the room.

"You can leave us," he told the correctional officer.

"Can't do that, sir."

Brittles slapped his coat pockets, found another ID card

with a green border around a bright yellow background. Shielding it from me, maybe just an accident, but I couldn't make out what it said. The CO's eyes widened, he was young and seemed a bit awed.

"Yes, sir!"

He snapped a salute and left.

"Who are you?" I asked.

"Just who I said I am. Okay. I'm going to leave you here. You'll talk to the prisoner alone."

"No way."

"That was part of her condition. I'll be right outside. Slap the door or holler, I'll come in."

Alone in the antiseptic room. Orange plastic chairs, tables bolted to the floor, the chairs burned with cigarettes and full of dings where they must have been hurled at the wall. The chairs looked as heavy as the tables, I wondered why everything wasn't bolted down.

A CO escorted a black woman in an orange jumpsuit into the room. She wiped down all the tabletops, mopped half the floor, never once looking at me once she caught me staring. She started on the second half of the floor, but the CO checked his wristwatch and told her it was time for her lunch break. They left.

I fiddled, I breathed, I unbuttoned and rebuttoned the top of the tight shirt, and started as a door banged open at the opposite end of the room. Another CO ushered a woman in, took off her handcuffs, exited, shutting the door behind him.

The woman didn't move. Staring at me. Dark, curly hair, shoulder-length but not stylish at all, looked like she'd cut it hurriedly, not anything important, just had to be cut, keep it out of her eyes, probably. She wore institutional blue jeans, no belt, an orange tee shirt, sneakers without laces. She didn't move.

I got up, but she still didn't move, so I started walking the length of the room. She looked somehow familiar, but I knew I'd never seen her before. As I got within ten feet I saw deep frown lines burrow into her forehead, just for a moment; she was steeling herself, getting ready for me. Five feet away, I stopped abruptly in shock. She smiled, a cynical hook at the right corner of her lips which flattened against perfectly white teeth.

I dug into my purse, found the old picture my ex-husband Jonathan had given me two years before. A twenty-one-year-old woman, laughing, happy.

"Yeah," she said, voice brittle with tension.

"Is it . . . are you . . . ?"

I hadn't seen her in twenty years. Shock waves. I had to reach for a tabletop, steady myself, my legs weak, felt like one of my old panic anxiety attacks, it was *brutal*, I tell you.

I couldn't stand and wobbled into a chair, mouth wide open, stunned.

"Hello, *Mom*," she said sarcastically, all the tension released in those words as though she'd been waiting to say that for years and years.

It was my daughter from my brief marriage to Jonathan Begay.

Spider.

9

"Spider," I said, lips dry, tongue in knots, my whole *head* in knots.

"Dominguez."

She cut me off, her lips barely a pencil line, they were clenched so tight, the word emerging like a hiss, lingering on the last *ahhh* syllable, teeth apart, for a moment I thought her tongue would dart out. Like a stinger. Like a snake.

"Help me here, Spider," I said.

She fingered the ID badge clipped to her orange tee. Waited for me to read it.

DOMINGUEZ, ABBE CONSUELO
ADC 49-353424-F

Finally, not knowing what else to do, I took out the photo that Jonathan gave me two years before. I traced my finger over the smiling woman, trying to discover some link, some blood, some connection between my memories of her at two years old, when Jonathan took her from me and disappeared.

Trying to make a connection between the smiling photo and the enraged face in front of me. I just kept staring at her, a tiny smile flickering on my lips, fading, more a twitch than a smile. I had so much invested in discovering this moment, meeting her for the first time in twenty years, I'd built this mythic meeting scene, I don't know what I'd built, but the daughter I'd imagined was nothing like the woman across the table.

Her concentration broke. Blinking, suddenly looking down, nothing else changing in her body, still sitting like she had a pole up her ass, years of anger at me, at somebody, and here I was as a release for the anger. And then she took a deep breath, hunched her shoulders, let the breath out with a slow sigh, and rolled her head side to side, muscle tension probably cramping her neck.

It was something to build on.

"Dominguez. Where did you get that name?"

"Run one of your hacker searches. You'd find out."

Rude.

A whole different attitude. For the first time, I wondered if she really knew what to do with me, with her mother, facing her mother, two adults, two strangers.

"I've searched for your real name for years."

"I have no *real* name," she snorted. "Like you, I have lots of identities."

"Spider Begay." She shrugged. "I filed the birth certificate. In Flagstaff."

She shrugged again.

"So Spider Begay disappeared two years after that birth certificate?"

"*You* disappeared. That's what he said. What Daddy said. When I met him in Mexico. Do you know where he is now?"

"No."

She nodded toward the steel door at the far end of the room.

"Where is he?" she asked.

"Who?"

"Mister Law."

"Nathan Brittles?"

"Oh, c'mon, mom. You don't believe that's his real name, do you?"

"He has a lot of ID. But I really don't care about him right now."

She saw I was curious.

"Check out John Wayne," she said cryptically.

"I saw the movie. What do we do here? *Why* are we here?"

"He coming in? Or what?

"Tell me, Spider."

"Dominguez!"

"Abbie, then."

"It's not *aaaaa-beeee*." Flat A sound, long E sound, said derisively. "*Ah. Bay*. Ahbay. Don't you, like, know any Mexican?"

I swore. A border phrase, a slang phrase, the rudest I could think of. That shocked her. No telling if it was because of the insult, or because it was said by her mother. Another attitude. Negotiation with anger.

"Let's get to it," she said flatly. "Call him in."

"This is between us," I said, standing up. "You want him in here, you deal with him and I'll just go home."

After a minute of standoff defiance, I headed toward the door. I'd only gone a few steps when she surged out of her chair, slamming it against chairs behind her, grabbed a plastic ashtray from another table, and hurled it like a Frisbee, like a discus, like a deer slug out of a twelve-gauge, sailing it three inches from my head. I ducked, but she wasn't aiming it at me. Flew all the way down the room in a flat trajectory, cracking against the door and dissolving in shards. The bolt shot back with a loud click, a CO appeared with her hand on a baton.

"Get John Wayne," Spider yelled.

The CO cocked her head at me.

"Brittles," I said.

"Wait one."

She closed the door, the bolt shot home. Neither Spider nor I moved. Two minutes later the CO came in again.

"On the phone."

"Get him *off* the fucking phone, get him in here!" Spider screamed.

"Your call," the CO said to me, arms out wide, palms up, a shrug.

"We'll wait."

Spider immediately went to the other door and pounded on it with her hands. The CO quickly shut and locked her door, the second door opened, a second CO appeared. Spider held out her wrists to be hooked up. Once the handcuffs were on, she left without a word.

Brittles arrived fifteen minutes later. There wasn't anything I could do, alone in the visiting room. No other inmate received a visitor, whether by accident or planning to keep the room empty for me.

"Sorry." Panting, slightly out of breath. "I was out in the parking lot. Cell phones don't work so good in here. Listen. I've got other problems. Bad problems."

He had the envelope, still sealed.

"I thought I was more important to you."

"You're important right now. How did it go?"

"Ever had kids?" I asked.

"Three. But I see them once in a while. Seeing your daughter in here, in a prison. Bad?"

"Horrible."

I started to cry. Began sobbing. He offered me a clean purple handkerchief. After a few minutes, he put a hand on my shoulder, not a grip, not a pat, he just laid it there until I got things together enough to wipe my face dry, mascara streaking across the purple hankie.

"What did she say?" he asked, his voice gentle, with an underlying urgency.

I tried a smile, managed a laugh, more a wet giggle.

"She said . . . something like, ask you if you're John Wayne."

"Interesting."

He actually began *spinning the envelope*. I slapped his hand. He looked down, unaware of what he'd been doing.

"You're good," he said. "You find a tell, you use it. Except the secret in poker is to never reveal that you know a tell."

"What did she mean?" I said with emphasis.

"Who knows? Let's get her in here."

I watched him stride to the nearest door. Noticed his cowboy boots. Hand-tooled kangaroo uppers, intricate stitching, uppers dyed black, tops lined with an inch-wide strip dyed a soft orange. He pressed a button on the wall, and the door opened quickly. Spider held out her wrists again for the CO to unhook her, never looking at her wrists or the CO, staring at me. Unhooked, she came directly to our table, snagged another chair, sat down.

"Here's the deal—" she said.

"Not quite yet," Brittles said. "Take her back inside for five minutes."

"What!"

She resisted, but the CO took orders only from Law.

Brittles began twirling the envelope, became conscious he was doing it, nodded to himself, slapped the envelope himself this time.

"So. You found one of my tells. She has a tell of her own. She left you waiting in the room, left you alone to stew. If she'd been really good at any of her attitudes, if she'd really played out any of those roles, she'd have demanded to be returned to her cell. Then, when we wanted her, they'd have to call up, release her, all those prison rituals with doors and keys, she'd have been at least ten or fifteen minutes. But she was waiting right on the other side of the door. This woman has an agenda. For now, her emotional need to press the agenda overrides her head."

"What's the agenda?"

"I have no idea. But. We've got an edge. Let's push it. Usually these visitation rooms are filled with all kinds of vending machines. We need some food in here."

Calling the CO, Brittles talked a moment and turned to me.

"Sandwiches. Tuna salad, chicken salad, or egg salad?"

"Tuna."

"Coming up. Look. I've got to make another phone call." He left.

Alone in the room again. Nothing to do. So anxious I could hear the linoleum floor expanding as I pressed on it. Heard the walls breathing, my senses so acute for *something* to happen, if there was a lawn nearby I'd be able to hear individual blades of grass grow.

The envelope.

I ripped it open, pulled out a single sheet of paper. A spreadsheet printout dated three days before. Names, Social Security numbers, addresses, gender, age, credit card numbers, all checking and savings account numbers and balances. Old-hat stuff to me, I could get anything like this, I could use it, transfer money, whatever I wanted. But I had ethics about it. Something told me that this list had nothing to do with ethics or morality, it was nothing more than a cookie jar waiting to be emptied.

Flannel-lined jeans, 34 waist, 33 long, 2 pairs. Orbit hiking boots, black, Gore-Tex in uppers, women's European size 36. Every spreadsheet entry involved ordering either clothing or towels and sheets.

There was no 800 number listed, nothing to indicate the company.

Brittles came back with a green plastic tray, two shrink-wrapped sandwiches, two diet Cokes, heavy worry lines in his face, cell phone open on the tray.

"Can we get my daughter back in here now?"

"Eat first."

"I don't want to eat. I want to see my daughter."

"Then wait while I eat. Let's see if this time she figured out the game and went back to her cell. If not, we've got a bigger edge."

"This is no game for me."

"Law and not-Law is always a game. They're always out to screw us, we're always out to con them. Everybody looks for a tell, an edge, an advantage, leverage. When you're inside here, or when you're the person who's gonna put somebody in here, you bank any leverages you get, whether you use them now or in five years."

"I can't wait."

Moving to the door, I pressed the button. When the CO opened the door, I saw Spider sitting on a bench. She came back to the visitors' room, went through the ritual with the handcuffs. She came to the table as though it hadn't mattered, but I saw her smile to herself. She *knew* she'd made a mistake. Brittles caught my eye, shrugged. Edge. Leverage. I could care less.

10

"Okay," Brittles said to Spider. "Your mother will find out how the information is being sent."

"Now I want my part of the deal."

"That's what I'm trying to tell you. The deal is to find *every*thing. What's being stolen. Who's doing the dirty work. Where's it going. We don't know where the information is going. Until we know all that, there is no deal."

Spider's face muscles constricted as though she were either going to spit or shout. I could see her clenching her teeth in an effort to do neither.

"It's not like finding the clues in a video game," Brittles said. "The first clues are the easiest. Like having a bunch of keys and finding the one that opens a door. But these cases are always more complicated than that. Not like a TV show. Not like a movie or a book. Where everything gets solved in one hour or two or four hundred pages. So we've learned what one of those keys unlocks. There are still lots of keys left, we know nothing about what they open."

"It's just . . . just so goddam *frus*trating," she said.

"Yeah, well, now you know how crime pays. With a prison sentence. For you, eighteen months. This is only month three, and you want out already. Be realistic. It doesn't happen like a movie."

"Yeah. And you're no Dirty Harry Clint Eastwood, solving the case."

Brittles turned his face in profile to me.

"Oh, I don't know about that," he said. "Don't I kinda remind you of Clint? The older Clint? *Unforgiven? Blood Work? True Crime?*"

"Here's the deal," Spider finally said.

"Here's *our* deal," Brittles said, removing papers from his briefcase but never breaking eye contact with her.

"No," she insisted. "You did your part, getting her here. Here's *my* deal. I'll give up this identity-theft ring on two conditions. One. Plea bargain. I give you the ring, you get me released. No. Not just released. Pardoned."

"Not possible."

"Two. She helps."

"Help you?" I said.

"I can give you the place," Spider said to Brittles. "I can't give you the people. With her, we can find them."

"No deal."

"Wait," I said, "wait, wait. Spider—"

"Abbe."

"You'll always be Spider to me."

"That's your problem."

"Why did you ask for me?" I pleaded.

"I don't like being in prison."

"Why are you in prison?"

She sighed, disgusted, the question not worth answering.

"Federal mail fraud," Brittles said. "She was sending confidential credit card information to Mexico. Sentenced to two years."

"Eighteen months," Spider said, "with good behavior. I've been there only three months. The longer I stay, my behavior is only going to get worse. Then I'll have to serve the full deuce. I don't want to."

"Can I help her?" I asked Brittles.

"No no no," Spider said. "The right question, the only question that matters to me, is whether he can cut me loose. If I come through."

"Can you?" I asked Brittles.

"It's possible."

"Then it's a deal."

"Laura. First things first. You don't make deals unless you know details."

"Laura." Spider mimicked his voice. "How sweet."

"No," I said to Brittles. "It's a deal."

"You don't even know what you want us to do," he answered.

"Sure she does, Mister Law. She's a hacker, she's a cracker, she's a down south smacker, and she's better than I am. So far."

"Which prison?" Brittles asked her.

"Hey. Deal with Laura here means nothing to me. Deal has to be with you. I give you what you want, you give me unconditional release. A pardon."

"You're assuming this is a major thing," he said. "It's just stealing another few hundred credit cards. It's minor, it's almost meaningless. Tell me what prison, how many people involved. Then I'll decide what kind of deal to offer."

"It's not the crime," Spider said to me. "He's pretending this is just about identity theft. Check it out with him. Whisper in his ear."

"What is she talking about?" I asked Brittles.

I could visualize him playing poker. Holding cards, holding *good* cards, a winning hand, but Spider still in the pot, maybe an even better hand. He sat even straighter, smiled with a very slight nod, and I knew she'd won the pot.

"Deal," he said.

"Florence," she answered immediately.

"How?"

"Don't know."

"But it's coming from there?"

"The 800 number call center. Some inmate in the center. All I know."

"Whoa," he said. "I've been to that call center. All the computers are on a closed network. No access to the Internet.

Credit card and Social Security numbers are hidden from the inmate operators. Show up as asterisks."

"Five seven two Gates Pass Road," she said.

"What's that?"

"Where I lived in Tucson."

"You live in Tucson?"

I was incredulous. I'd searched all over the U.S., I'd tracked her from Pasadena to New York City, and she once lived in Tucson?

"Eleven years ago."

"And your point is that you remember the address?" Brittles asked.

"No. Memory training."

"Explain that."

"When Don Ralph was shot down in Viet Nam, he got rescued. But he knew a guy who spent five years in the Hanoi Hilton. With Senator McCain. This guy, bored out of his mind, cramped in a tiger cage and slowly going crazy with nothing to do, he hung a string across the bamboo bars one day. Went back to his math training, recreated his whole memory of calculus and differential equations, worked out the equation for that hanging string. From there, he trained his memory, sharpened his ability to retain details."

"And inmates . . . smart inmates . . ." I could almost see Brittles's head buzzing as he worked out the implications. "They could remember credit card numbers. I've thought of that. But how does that information get out of prison within twelve hours? Rarely more than twenty-four hours. That's how long it takes for somebody to run up massive debts using those cards."

"I don't know."

"And just how were you . . . how were we going to find that out?" I asked.

"Easy," Brittles said. "You go inside."

"You can't ask me to do that," I said to Spider. "No way."

"Way," she said with a smirk.

"They'd never trust me. An outsider. A woman."

"It's good," Brittles said. "That's good."

"Ooooeee. You're so smart, Mr. Law," Spider said.

"Well, I'm not that smart," I shouted. "I'm not taking any chance of going inside a prison."

"As a computer expert," Brittles said. "From the company that installed the call-center computer network. You come in to fix a problem. I like it."

"So, mom."

The word still hung in her throat, came out coated with sarcasm, cynicism, and solid anger, as though it were a pill she'd been waiting to fling at me for years.

"You really in?"

"If I say no?"

"You'll never see me again."

Not a pill. A fishing line, not even baited, just thrown out there with a naked metal hook that she was ready to reel in, she was that confident I'd say yes. I knew she had much more anger.

"When?" I asked.

Brittles pulled two thick envelopes from his briefcase, dropped them on the table. Spider ripped one of them open, shoved it to me after a quick scan, ripped open the other. I sorted through a mass of identity papers, most of them arrest and sentencing papers, including two prison photo cards of my face with the name Susan Elliott McBride.

"You bastard," I said, flinging all the papers at him. "You planned this all along. You weaseling bastard."

"What happens now?" Spider asked.

"You go back to your cell and wait. No, no, I'll keep those papers. Tomorrow morning we should be ready. Laura, you come with me."

"I want to talk with my daughter."

"Too late, mom." She stood up, went to ring the bell. "You should have thought of that earlier, to stall me." The CO came out, hooked her up for the third time, and she left without another word.

11

His cell phone jingled again, his face grimmer as he listened.

"What am I supposed to do now?" I demanded, fuming while he made three more calls and then waved at an unmarked Ford Excursion.

"I can have the chopper take you back to Tucson."

"We need to talk about the deal. About my daughter's pardon."

He started to get into the Excursion. I piled into the backseat.

"Whoa, whoa," the driver said. "Get out, lady."

"We have to talk!" I insisted to Brittles.

"You haven't seen her for twenty years," he said curtly. "Why are you so dead set on helping her now?"

"She's my *daughter*. Tell me if this deal is possible. A complete pardon, if I go along with what you want."

"Come with me, we'll talk on the way."

"Where are we going?"

"Near the Casa Grande ruins. But I don't think I can arrange for the chopper to meet us there. You'll have to find a ride back to Tucson."

He refused all conversation during the fifty minute trip.

We flew at nearly one hundred miles an hour, the Excursion rocking on its springs. Once on the freeway, Brittles took a portable flashing lamp, fed the cord out his window, and clamped the magnet to the roof. Every time I tried to say something to him, I could barely hear myself, wind whistling into his window, and I wondered if he'd put the lamp outside just as an excuse to shut me off. Somewhere past the Chandler exit an Arizona DPS cruiser picked us up, tried to pull us over until Brittles got patched through on his radio and the cruiser pulled in front of us, bubblegum lights rotating, clearing traffic all the way to Casa Grande.

Another DPS cruiser sat slantwise across the entrance road to what looked like the beginnings of a housing development. The officer checked Brittles's ID and pulled the bright yellow barrier back so we could pass. Fifty feet or so down the road I could see a backhoe, yards of yellow crime scene tape wrapped around bushes and trees, several men and women sifting dirt through large screened boxes. Somebody in a double-banded Tilley Stampede hat directed them, several of the park's picnic tables pulled up outside the crime scene tape, objects sorted onto each of the tables. Another man saw us coming, waved us over.

Brittles got out to talk to him quickly, talked directly into his ear before I could join them.

"Laura Wilson," Brittles said. "Zeke Pardee. Another U.S. Marshal."

"Just spend five minutes with me," I pleaded. "I don't have a clue why we're here, I don't even *want* to be here, just tell me what you'll do for my daughter."

"That's in transition."

"Excuse me?"

"I had something worked out. It won't work now."

"Why?"

The man in the Tilley hat climbed out of one of the trenches and walked up to us, casually brushing dirt from his encrusted jeans as though he really didn't care if dirt was there or not. It was Rich.

Both of us were astonished to see the other. I started to smile, but he turned quickly to face Brittles. As though I was nobody, which shocked me.

"You the paleontologist?" Brittles asked.

"Rich Thompson. NAGPRA. Remains Repatriation Coordinator. Arizona State Museum, on the AU campus."

Brittles hesitated only for a moment, shook the offered hand. He didn't bother to introduce Pardee, but Rich grinned at each of us in turn, extending a hand to Brittles and Pardee, repeating his name. Brittles ignored him and strode to the three tables.

"Anything?" he asked Rich.

"Some great stuff. This whole Casa Grande area is built mostly on alluvium ground, not too old, a few hundred thousand years."

"What's on this table?" Brittles ignored the archeological lesson.

"Pleistocene fossils, maybe mammoth, camel, bison, horse, llama, dire lion, very big tortoise, glyptodont, that's a very cool-looking thing, I've got some pictures in my office."

"Fossils. This next table?"

"Haven't identified them yet. Probably came down from nearby hills and mountains, probably volcanic or metamorphic."

"Fossils. Lava. Why have you even bothered collecting them?"

"This is a prime archeological area."

"This is a crime scene."

"True, true. But . . . it's also just outside a famous national monument. There are rules about how to dig through these grounds. They're holy grounds. Sacred grounds."

"Bones. I just want to hear about the bones," Brittles insisted.

"Especially bones. Bones are sacred. Bones are assumed to be Indian bones. Under NAGPRA, we have to take special care to retrieve the bones and return them to the proper Indian nation."

"This is a crime scene. This is evidence."

Rich pressed his lips together. He started his lecture.

"In 1990, the Arizona legislature passed laws that protect human burials and associated objects on state, county, and municipal lands and private lands. These laws provide Arizona's Indian tribes and descendants of Hispanic and Anglo settlers an opportunity to ensure that the remains of their ancestors are treated with respect and dignity. Both laws require that the discovery of burials more than fifty years old must be reported to the Arizona State Museum if the burials are in danger of disturbance. The museum identifies groups that might be related to the dead and coordinates discussions about how the burials should be treated."

"Whoa, whoa," Brittles said. "I appreciate your concerns for history, but I don't want history. I need to know about these bones. The housing development can deal with your museum."

I smiled at that and Rich saw my smile, shot me an amazed look before he pushed a finger into Brittles's chest.

"These laws are often misunderstood," Rich said emphatically. "The museum is prepared to respond promptly to reports of isolated discoveries and to remove remains and associated objects at its own expense. This housing developer is free to continue construction within a statutory maximum of ten days after discovery. They'll have to begin consultation through the museum before continuing construction and they'll have to make plans either to identify and remove burials before construction begins or to have appropriate personnel available to identify and remove burials as they are found."

"Is the lecture over?" Pardee asked.

"Just tell us what you've found," Brittles said. "Will you do that? Please?"

We all gathered around at least four hundred bone fragments scattered on the third table. Rich had made some effort to sort the bones according to size and shape, but it seemed a hopeless task.

"It's a lot of bones," Rich said.

"Are any of them old bones?" Brittles asked. "Animals?"

"No." Rich took off his hat, clutched it with both hands

over his chest. "No. They're all human. The oldest haven't been here more than a few years."

"Why are they all broken up?" I asked.

"*Fargo,*" Rich said.

"The wood chipper?" I said.

"Yes."

"What the hell are you talking about?" Pardee said.

"In the movie. *Fargo.* One of the bad guys stuffs the other bad guy's body into a wood chipper." Rich shuffled his feet, apologetic but firm. "I've heard through the Internet it's something the Mexican drug cartels do to dispose of bodies. When they can't just dump the bodies in the desert, I mean."

"So, these bones," Brittles said, poking his finger at a three-inch fragment.

"Don't touch them. Please."

"Okay. I'll call in a forensic anthropologist, see what he thinks."

"That's a rip, man. I've spent fifteen years looking at bones of pretty much anything, dead or alive, that's ever walked or crawled."

Rich pulled on a fresh pair of latex gloves, carefully separated half of the tabletop of bones from the other. I could see a pattern in what was left. Not immediately noticeable, but piles, more like groupings of similar bone fragments.

"Totally raw guess," Rich said. "We're looking at a dozen people."

"A dozen?"

"Give or take. It's my gut talking here, but . . . these just feel like different people. These twelve piles . . . these fragments."

"Gut." Brittles snorted at Pardee. "Zeke. Call Tucson. Get a forensic pathologist up here."

"All women," Rich said with a grimace. "I mean, probably. You can tell. This fragment, from a pelvis, it's not full-grown, it's female."

"How many women?" I said.

"Women. Girls. Who knows? You wanted my take. That's it."

"Altogether," Brittles said, licking his lips, trying to avoid the obvious question, "how many people are we talking about?"

"Best guess?" Rich said to himself. "I'd say you've got a real nightmare here. At the *least,* a dozen bodies. At the most . . . I can't even say."

revelations

William Little Bill Marriott stripped down for a full body cavity search. Bending over, he watched, not protesting, not making any facial expressions or sounds, while the Correctional Officers tossed his lockdown cell. Some COs didn't hassle the inmates while doing this. A few COs were kickstarters, out to make trouble, not at all happy when humiliated by an inmate using the CO as a target for urine or feces. *All* COs got things hurled at them. Most survived the indignities by publicly ignoring them. A few couldn't restrain their anger and humiliation, occasionally taking it out on the inmates, often griping to other COs. Kickstarters. Usually male COs, macho alpha-dog males, sniffing for trouble, baring their teeth. In some backward state prisons and jails, nearly all the COs were kickstarters. A way of life, but not one tolerated in the Arizona prison system.

Odd, that they'd spend so much time searching him, when he was the person who feared attack from somebody else.

Little Bill had been shanked before. Once in the right thigh, once a glancing strike across his rib cage, the last time a serious attempt to disembowel him.

Shanks are prison knives.

Totally improvised, hand-manufactured from silverware, metal scraps, including bits of motors from razors and tape recorders, from bits of wood, plastic, Plexiglas shards, sharpened toothbrushes or toothbrushes with the heads broken off, cafeteria cutlery, or just about anything that could be turned into a stabbing weapon.

For most inmates, some degree of intelligent information comes from the physical characteristics of the shank: what it was made from; who made it; how it got passed from one inmate to another; even the gift of design balanced against the quality of the shank and how long it took to be made.

Simple shanks come from a piece of found material. A sliver of wood or glass, for instance, a metal shaving from a machine shop, a discarded toothbrush melted enough so the con can jam a razor blade in a carefully filed slot at the end. Most shanks aren't even sharpened by design. A sliver of Plexiglas or a razor blade needs no sharpening. A random piece of metal *must* be honed to an edge, usually by days of continually rubbing the metal against something as simple as a concrete floor, although COs look on cell floors and walls for signs of rubbing.

Inmates never ever have the opportunity to get a sliver of glass because they just don't exist in prison. Toothbrush handles are available, even though inmates only get special super-short-handle toothbrushes, about one and a half inches long, and razor blades always are available from their single-use-type razors, which are supposedly counted when given out and then collected every time they shave.

Supposedly collected. Not always.

So shanks can be as found, like the occasional Plexiglas shard or sliver of hard wood, or manufactured. Either way, a shank is a deadly weapon if used correctly on the first strike. Even a good shank has to be used just right or it will slip so the victim won't be stabbed, just scraped. COs wear stab vests, but most inmates know the vulnerable spots around the vest and occasionally succeed in wounding a CO. Inmates don't have stab vests, so stabbing is easier. If an inmate goes after his cellmate, stabbing can mean death. One inmate, sentenced to life for three murders, had actually stabbed his roommate forty-seven times, and when the COs came to subdue him, he said he'd make no fuss if they'd give him some over-easy eggs and an extra link of sausage.

Unlike the movies, Little Bill never worried that somebody would use a shank on him while demanding sex. Or even for murder. Inmates shank other inmates for any reason, usually a gangbanger thing that happens fast, with everybody disappearing even faster. The COs just find a patch of blood on the concrete floor. Most shanked inmates don't even go to the hospital for treatment, insisting that it was an "accident" and refusing to rat out another inmate, which would only lead to being shanked again.

Little Bill knew that shanks rarely survive a shakedown search, but that they are made in such numbers that all searches turned up a fairly large quantity. But a lot more shanks are kept in a neutral place. Hidden in the yard, in the machine shops, in the laundry, the cafeteria, in every common area of the prison, usually hidden by somebody to be used either by a gang or by another individual con.

Anybody in Florence could be shanked.

Inmates, COs, administrative staff, visiting teachers or preachers, even the warden himself. Nobody was exempt, if the conditions were right.

Little Bill heard it whispered down the lane that somebody had a contract on him. Little Bill wouldn't say why he was a target, but he was believed by the warden, who put him in PS, professional segregation, which was essentially being put in the hole. Total lockdown in an individual cell, no contact with anybody except the COs who brought his meals and who supervised his one hour a day out of PS to walk around a walled yard, with nobody else present. Little Bill knew that PS offered him additional protection against being shanked, but there was no absolute protection, no guarantee at all.

The old name was protective custody. PC or PS, when an inmate believed he was in danger from other inmates, he PC's up. In prison jargon that means the inmate demands protective segregation. Many times this is done by the inmate approaching an officer and quietly saying, 'I need PC,' or something like that. Or the inmate may make a small sign and sit in the back of his cell until the count officer goes by. Then the inmate gives him the sign without saying anything. The point is that if the other inmates find out he's asked for PC, his ass is grass and he becomes a very serious target; his life is immediately in danger.

Despite his loneliness in PS, Little Bill sometimes refused his one-hour walk in the yard. He knew that most attacks were like a blitzkrieg. Somebody rushed at you, maybe that somebody got passed the shank at the very last moment, he came past you and stabbed, sometimes stabbed many times if no CO was nearby, then the shank got passed off to yet another person and the only real evidence was somebody like Little Bill bleeding to death on some dirty concrete floor.

He felt truly vulnerable. Little Bill had applied to be transferred out of Florence, but even urgent paperwork took its time working through the red-tape cycle. So he finally refused even the hour's freedom from his cell, refused all contact with any other inmates in Florence, even inmates he knew to be friends.

The only people in Florence called convicts were the real old-timers, the professionals. A few old-time white brothers from the South called the black brothers coonmates, but all other people were inmates.

Segregated in PS, even Little Bill had no control over the COs.

One morning CO III Beethoven came to Little Bill's PS cell and said the warden wanted to see him. Little Bill said there was nothing to discuss with the warden and he wasn't leaving his cell anyway, even if Jesus Christ himself wanted a visit. CO III Beethoven had a Taser and shot it twice into Little Bill, the second time a freak where one hook and wire of the Taser stuck into his shirt pocket and the other hook went into his right pants leg, so the heavy voltage went clear down his body and pretty much drove Little Bill out of his mind.

Unfortunately, Little Bill thought that CO III Beethoven was just another kickstarter, going out of his way to cause trouble. This was a bad mistake.

Fifteen minutes later, he was walking from Unit Three to Unit Six when CO III Beethoven stepped into the hallway, turned toward Little Bill, walked on past him, and that was it. A five-inch-long nail went neatly between two ribs and directly into Little Bill's heart, killing him almost instantly.

The criminal investigators' attention was turned away from CO III Beethoven, who left work early that day, pleading stress and fatigue, drove to the Tucson airport, and paid cash for a one-way ticket to Nome, Alaska.

laura

12

I hadn't done this for over ten years. In one day, leave my lover in a helicopter to meet another guy, have that *new* guy *and* my lover together with me, and wind up that same night invited to the new guy's house.

Brittles lived near Casa Grande National Monument. Somewhat north, out in the desert, but we drove through Coolidge, past the entrance to the monument, on our way from the place where Rich was examining all the bones.

"You ever been in there?" Brittles asked.

"Never."

He turned around and onto the entrance road, then up to the main building.

"I know a lot of the park rangers. I come here often, I have a season pass. I come here just to get some peace from the day."

Parking, he led me through the door, said hello to the ranger on duty, and we went through an exhibit to the back glass doors that opened up on the monument itself about fifty feet away. It was an old, simple place. An ancient building from many centuries before. A tour of high school kids chattered past us to the exit, and when we got near the monument we were all alone.

"Want to go inside?" Brittles asked.

"No."

"Me neither. I just like to look at it against the sunset."

Probably four stories high, the wind-and-rain-worn reddish building sat underneath an elaborate metal roof set on four huge corner posts. We sat on a wooden Park Service bench amid the low-lying smooth ruins of the original complex, but the monument was the only real building left.

"Grand, isn't it?" Brittles said. "Built by the Old People."

"Anasazi?"

"Hohokam. Maybe the same thing. Who knows, six centuries later?"

"Hey, Nathan."

A park ranger stopped to shake his hand.

"Laura, this is Dave Winchester. Dave, Laura Winslow. Her first visit here."

"Visiting the state?" Winchester said.

I really didn't want to talk at all.

"Yeah," Brittles said, "you could say that."

"Well, park's closing in five minutes. You know the way out."

"How do I get back to Tucson?" I said as Winchester moved away.

"I'll drive you down."

"I'm so tired. Too much today."

"How long since you've seen your daughter?" he asked.

"Don't want to talk about her," I said, leaning back on the bench and falling asleep in an instant, groggy and defensive when Brittles palmed my shoulder.

"My house is only five minutes away," he said. "I've got lots of extra rooms. Why don't you just come, spend the night, take care of yourself?"

"I can't do that. *You* can't do that. You've got to start the process, get me to this call center, to these computers, so I can find out whatever you want to know and my daughter can get out of prison."

"It's not that simple," he said. "Some other things have happened."

"I don't care about other things. Fix the deal. Get me to work, then get my daughter pardoned."

"We have to talk about this."

Next thing I knew, he was shaking me again.

"Look. I've really got lots of space. Five minutes away. I'll fix you something to eat. You sleep. When you're ready, I'll have worked out exactly what we're going to do with this whole mess."

"Were you really named after John Wayne?"

"Yup. Nathan Cutting Brittles. That's the character he played, and my father was one of the extras for John Ford. Made a lot of movies with Wayne and Ford at Monument Valley. My Navajo name is actually Cutting Tongue. When I was five or six and kinda wild, my mother said I ran right through some wooden fence slats, broke two of them apart with my nose."

Ran his tongue around his lips, remembering.

"Just a scratch on my nose, but I bit through my tongue, blood everywhere. They thought I'd broken the fence with my tongue. Before I could convince them they were wrong, it was all over the village. Cutting Tongue."

"What's the Navajo name?"

"I don't remember. Getting too far away from my roots, I guess. You got a Hopi name?"

I hesitated. Many Indians don't like to say their special name. Maybe Brittles *hadn't* forgotten, he just didn't want to say it.

"Kauwanyama," I said. "Butterfly With Wings of Beauty."

"You're one good-looking butterfly, Laura."

"Just drive," I said with a smile. "Just take me away, wherever."

Set a hundred feet from the nearest road, Brittles's house spread out in modules around an atrium center. His dirt driveway led to a six-car garage separate from the house.

Parking in front of a roll-up door, he opened it for me, turned on some overhead lights and showed me three motorcycles.

"Some people paint, sculpt, throw pots, whatever. I restore old motorcycles, and these are my babies. Over there is a 1952 Vincent Black Lightning. Guy set a world speed record on it. Made several runs, couldn't break the old record, finally took all his clothes off, laid on his belly flat-out horizontal. Set the record. I paid sixty-two thousand for that one. Not many around. Jay Leno has one.

"Over there is a 1931 Henderson KL inline four-cylinder. Back at that time, it was clocked at almost one-twenty miles an hour. I got it from a guy named Dennis Henderson. Henderson, selling one of his Henderson bikes. Couldn't resist. This one's my prize. A 1928 Cleveland inline four-cylinder."

I briefly thought of Rey Villanueva, my onetime partner. Meg Arizana's husband, who rebuilt old cars and took me on the only bike ride I ever had, in Sonora, Mexico, when we were looking for my ex-husband Jonathan Begay.

Inside the house, he took me straight down a hallway to a room filled with photographs. Picking up an ornate silver frame, he showed me an old picture of a woman in typical Navajo dress, a velveteen blouse and long skirt, sitting at a weaving loom. I couldn't see it well, so he turned on a strong light, revealing two walls of the room that were covered from floor to ceiling with photographs. Many of them were of Indians, but some were also of smiling young soldiers around helicopters.

"Nam," he said when I looked closely on one picture. "That's me, on the right, with my crew chief for that bird. I had a lot of crew chiefs. I was kinda crazy back then. A young, wild guy from the rez, never been farther than Phoenix until I enlisted at sixteen, my mother signing a paper that I was two years older. I flew the old Huey gunships, I flew slicks, carried Marines in and out of LZs that were so hot nobody else would take the chance. I was drunk or coked

up all the time. Guys would say, over there, the greater the in-
coming fire, the tighter your ass puckered. The pucker factor.
I never had it. I was crazy."

I studied his young face, an insane grin, arms around two
buddies.

"Doesn't even look like you," I said.

"Ever think about being something else?" Brittles asked
abruptly.

"Like . . . who? What?"

"Anybody. Anything."

"No."

"Not ever?" he said.

"Well. Yeah. Sure."

"Sure, what?" he asked.

"I think about it," I said.

"Doing something else? Or *being* somebody else?"

"Done that. I've had so many fake identities, I've lost track
of the real ones."

"Lost track of the real you?" he asked.

"Yeah. God, why am I telling you this?"

"Because you know I've got the same problem."

"You've been thinking about this lately?" I said, more than
a bit incredulous.

"For years."

"Huh."

"Yeah. How about that?"

"Do you ever really let your head just relax?"

"You mean, relax from thinking about it?"

"Yes."

"Never," he said. "Not since that first group of North Vietnamese regulars I lit up with three rockets in 1974. My crew
chief raked them with the .50 cal. Made sure they were KIA.
Come on. Let me show you your bedroom, get you settled."

But I never made it to the bedroom that night. We had more
wine, I watched him light some incense stalks, watched him

play with his two German shepherds, listened to several of his Indian flute CDs while I looked over his monster collection of DVDs.

"You watch a lot of movies," I said. "Why?"

He finished playing something on the CD, set it back in the rack.

"Nobody's ever asked me that."

"I watch them with the sound off."

"So do I," he said. "Sometimes I do. Like, I watch continuity. You know, from scene to scene, where the continuity checker is supposed to take Polaroids and make sure both costume and makeup fit the matching scene before. Like, my favorite example is *Run Lola Run.* Most all the edits show her bra straps in different places."

"And you watch bra straps because . . . ?"

"When I'm trying to piece together bits of a case I'm working on. Like this thing with the bones and all. None of it fits. So I look at the jump cuts, try to imagine what happened between."

"When do you turn the sound on?" I asked.

"Say, Robert Altman. Say, *McCabe and Mrs. Miller.* Altman had all these different sound mikes set up on the set. He'd take all the voices, throw them in the pot, do a master mix, totally confuse the obsessive in the audience who had to hear every word. With Altman, you *never* really heard every word. He layered them on top of each other in crowd scenes. So I close my eyes and listen. Same kind of thing as the jump cuts. Try to eliminate the crap. Sort out what's important."

"Look," I said, setting my wine glass on the floor, standing up. "I can't do this stuff right now. "I . . . this is confusing . . . I really need to go home."

"Let me drive you."

"No! Just loan me a car."

"You're in no shape to drive all the way to Tucson," Brittles said.

"A car. Just . . . anything."

"Okay."

He wrote a cell phone number on my palm.

"Call me. Here. If there are any problems."

"Sure," I said, not wanting to call him at all.

He saw that in my eyes and wrote the number on my other palm.

"It's nothing personal. Just don't forget your daughter."

"You bastard," I said. "You're playing me."

"So go home. Get a good night's sleep. We'll talk again tomorrow. Just don't go washing your hands before you write this number down on a piece of paper. Promise?"

"Sure," I lied. "You've got this all figured. You've got *me* all figured."

"No!" he said, folding both my hands into fists, holding the fists. "I have absolutely no idea what this is all about. I have absolutely no idea why your daughter just happens to be the one person who connects to the prison, and connects me to you. Like it or not, you're in this now. Up to your neck."

"That's from a movie." I giggled. "Gregory Peck says it to David Niven. *Guns of Navarone*. But Gregory threatened David with a pistol. All you've got are words."

He folded a set of car keys into one of my hands.

"Ford Taurus. Government car. Don't ding the fenders."

13

Brittles had tried to stop me from returning to my house, but I needed too much gear. My Mac titanium laptop, some special software and data backed up on CDs, and my running shoes and some clean underwear. But when I got there, Rich was waiting.

"Can we talk about things?" Rich asked.

"Not tonight."

"When?"

I hoped he'd go out for a walk or clean the fridge or wash the dishes again.

"Why?" he asked.

"Rich, I don't know what to say."

"Maybe . . . we could just talk. We could find out what you don't know. Talking's good, you know."

"What would we talk about, if I don't know what to say?"

"Things."

"Things," I said to myself.

"Yeah. What you're feeling. What's happening."

"Between us, you mean."

"Well, yeah," he said. "What's happening between us."

"Nothing's happening, Rich."

"It's that guy, isn't it?"

"What guy?"

"The fed, the whatever he is. Who brought you to the excavations."

"He's nothing," I said

"Yeah. I saw you looking at him."

"Rich. Please. Nothing's happening between us."

"I know," he said reluctantly. "That's how I feel, too."

"This has nothing to do with you, Rich."

"Bullshit! It has *every*thing to do with me."

Angry, he started to straighten up the bookshelf, caught himself doing that, swiveled his head in wide circles, trying to loosen up his neck muscles, trying to loosen up his attitude so he'd gain control of his emotions enough to start talking to me again. But I didn't give him the chance. I went out on the patio, went down through the lemon trees to the place where Don had seen me half naked, just a short time ago.

Years ago, I thought. In another life.

An open bottle of cabernet sauvignon sat on the wooden table. I drank from the bottle, scarcely breathing the first time I held it to my lips. Cradling the bottle between my thighs, I sat there for a long, long time. Sunset, sundown, twilight, evening, dark.

There are few cities in the world with such dark nights. Decades before, Tucson adopted special zoning ordinances that prohibited street lighting because of all the astronomy telescopes in the surrounding area. My rented house sat in a newer developed area, but even with zoning variances the builders and developers informally agreed to not install streetlights.

I could see the night stars, the evening and morning planets.

I sat there all night, emptying the wine bottle, moving only to go up to the house to the bathroom and get more wine. At some point I fell asleep and awoke with moonlight on my face.

I showered, ate some Total and blueberries without soy milk, trying to decide how I was going to handle my life. Mostly, I didn't know what to think, let alone what to do, about dealing with my daughter.

Five in the morning.

Finally, I decided to run and run, to avoid thinking and just listen to hiphop. I laced up one of my favorite pairs of New Balance 990s, stretched for ten minutes, and started out on one of my familiar routes among the quiet streets. I loved running in the Tucson foothills because of the constant up-and-down pacing, which gave me the chance to work all kinds of muscle groups. Your ankle, if you think at all about how it moves, lets your foot be perpendicular to your leg if you're on the flat. Start uphill, the angle changes to less than ninety degrees. Go downhill, the angle is more than ninety degrees. A small thing to most people, probably a nothing thing. To an extreme runner, it's important to keep all the muscles, tendons, ligaments, and joints well aligned and working right.

I ran for two hours, probably seven or eight miles, my

MP3 player moving from alternate hiphop to my own tracks. I mouthed the words to all of them, tinkered with my rhyming schemes and the words in combination and alone.

Turning finally into the street that led to my house, I gradually became aware that I'd seen the same red and metallic gray motorcycle at least three or four times, the rider crouched low on the seat, leaning forward, knees tucked in and pointing ahead. I watched the rider take a corner at a fairly high speed, saw the bike lean over, a booted foot extended to just above the pavement in case the bike leaned too far.

Inside my house, I stripped off my running gear and took a shower. My water pressure was low, so I could hear Sunset's paws as he ran back and forth from the front door to the patio door. Toweling dry, I couldn't remember if I'd left either of them open. I put on clean panties and a running bra, pulled up some green workout shorts to go out on the patio and begin some free weight workouts. I checked that the front door was shut and locked, went into the kitchen, and saw the helmeted biker looking at me ten feet beyond the patio sliding screen. Sunlight glinted off the face mask of the biker's helmet. I thought he was distracted, so I jumped toward the heavy glass door to slide it shut and lock it, but the biker quickly ripped off the helmet with one hand and raised a .40 chromed Llama with the other.

Hispanic, young, male, hardly more than a boy, these things registered in the same instant he pointed the gun at me and triggered off half a clip as I dived toward the left wall, thinking it would give me some protection, but the heavy slugs ripped easily through the annulated stucco exterior and the Sheetrock. Sunset put his nose against the screen, growling, and the boy must have moved the Llama toward Sunset, who scrabbled backward and out of the kitchen as the boy emptied his clip. I heard the *snick* of the clip release, realized that sliding the heavy glass door shut would give me no protection at all, and wondered if I could get my shotgun out of the bedroom closet in time, wondered if it was even loaded, knew I'd left four double-ought slugs in the storage slots of the stock. Bunching my body like a runner about to explode into a one-hundred-yard dash, I launched myself past the window to see the boy smile when I appeared, another clip just sliding home in the gun. But Sunset charged into the kitchen, barely slowing as he crashed effortlessly through the screen door and in just two bounds started working the boy's throat in his jaws. I skittered down the hallway, found the Mossberg shotgun, loaded the four slugs into the tube, and came back to the kitchen to watch the boy wrestle Sunset, twisting backward so both of them fell to the ground, and in the same fluid motion, as they were falling, the Llama wrenched across the boy's body to fire two bullets across Sunset's back. He howled with pain, letting go of the boy's throat, trying to lick at his back. I stood at the screen, pumping the shotgun to load a shell, unable to shoot because Sunset moved back and forth in front of the boy, who saw me pointing the shotgun at him, his Llama out of position to shoot me but he fired it anyway, smashing bits and pieces off the ramada poles and thatched roofing, the noise startling me so that I pulled the shotgun trigger without aiming, blowing a hole in a potted agave. The boy leapt to his feet and ran around the house. I lunged through the shredded screen door, saw that Sunset's wounds were only minor, pumped another shell home thinking, *Three, I've got three left,* and started around the corner of the house, but before I got to the front yard I heard the motorcycle start up fifty feet away. I stood in the middle of the street, aiming at the back of the bike, letting off two shells, but he wove the bike from side to side, moving quickly up through the gears and going so fast that his bike started a wheelie before he leaned forward and brought the bike down to the pavement and cut a sharp left onto a cross street and out of sight.

I could hear the bike another street over, and thinking he might come back I ran into the house for more shells. But the roar slowly faded as the biker went out of the neighborhood in the direction of Tanque Verde Road.

I wasted no time. Gathering up my laptop, I shoved it into a backpack, tore my dresser drawers open, onto the floor, grabbing whatever clothes were on top, cramming the clothes down on the laptop, slinging the backpack over one shoulder before I went out back to find Sunset. She'd already decided her wounds weren't severe, although I could see two shallow trenches cut right through the hair and skin, each wound at least two inches long and deep enough to continue bleeding. I clucked my tongue with the *Come* sound, led Sunset to my pickup, where she jumped immediately into the bed. I headed out the driveway, turning in the opposite direction from where the bike had gone, and finally worked my way to I-10 north, heading to Phoenix.

At Picacho Peak I pulled off the road to make a call to a vet I knew in Casa Grande, and after dropping off Sunset, I sat in the parking lot for an hour, deep breathing, waiting for a panic anxiety attack, always happened to me before in a crisis, I'd be cruising at the speed limit, confident, secure, knowing exactly where I was going and all of a sudden my heart's pushing down the accelerator of a Shelby Cobra Mustang and I'm running in the red here, I'm *way* beyond safe RPMs, my anxiety swinging toward the peg and ready to blow.

I could blow any second.

But the attack never happened.

Gradually, my pulse rate slowed back to normal. I fiddled with the car radio, looking for a hiphop station, wanting the familiar and wonderful energy as a backbeat so I could work out a plan. It seemed ages since I'd listened to hiphop.

Finding no stations I wanted, I went through some of my own raps, ending with a few more lines to my latest.

So I'm taking small steps with my eyes on
The western horizon

Even when the sun's rising I'm trying
To envision a sunset that hasn't come yet
And a truth that I've been denying
On a path that I've been defying
As I pass another butterfly flying

I called Brittles and told him I'd be at his house in twenty minutes, told him all about the biker with the chrome Llama.

Ten minutes after I got there, we tumbled into his bed.

14

"I have to tell you," he said. "Any relationship that begins under extreme emotional duress is doomed to failure."

"Keanu Reeves to Sandra Bullock. *Speed.*"

I thought of Rey Villanueva's inability to discuss anything emotional unless he related it to something in a movie.

"Seemed like a good line to use," he said. "But it was just a movie. I think when he says that, after they've escaped from the bus, the airplane blows up, she says something like, 'Okay, I guess we'll have to base things on sex.'"

"I like your house," I said. "I like you."

"You're a little drunk."

"I'm a lot drunk. I'm a lot tired."

"At least you're relaxed."

"I work at that. I know how to deal with stress without taking drugs."

"Just a bottle of chardonnay."

"I like your house."

"So do I. When I settle in here, it gives me a root vegetable feeling."

"Root vegetables," I said. "I like that. Kind of a root cellar mode, except I hate root cellars, they get me to thinking of how those old pioneers got truly depressed when all they had was life in a root cellar. Especially the women."

"Aah, no." Brittles frowned. "I don't think of it as the root cellar. More like . . . like actual growing root vegetables. Carrots. Beets. Turnips."

"Rutabagas."

"Potatoes."

"Potatoes?" I asked.

"Yeah. Potatoes."

"Isn't a potato a starch?"

"Whatever. We're not talking actual things here, we're talking a concept."

"Roots in the ground," I said. "But not in a sterile cellar."

"Roots underground, storing up energy and sweetness for eventual harvest and creative combination. I get that way, sometimes. When I get weary of being manic, when my head is ready to explode, I hibernate."

"Yeah," I said. "Me, too."

"It's a very active, if quiet, stage for me. It's actually just as manic as the other stage, but the action is all below the surface. I'm not sure why I hibernate."

"I turn off my phones. Turn off the lights. Turn on the TV, mostly. But no sound. Just the visual."

"The visual." He worked at the thought, agreed. "Yeah, I guess. Like when I watch movies to study the continuity."

It's like, left brain, right brain. Left brain logic, language, listen to the sound. Right brain, not logic at all, but symbols, patterns. Really different. If I have the sound one, sometimes I don't even look at the picture. Sound off, I get sucked into the visuals. I don't want to be distracted in any way.

"No. I mean entirely visual. I watch in the dark, sometimes. But we're both seeing things without the sound on. So why do we do that?"

"There's clearly some research or information-gathering agenda here, or maybe just a rabid curiosity, but it's totally typical for me. I can neither really explain nor justify it. I know a lot about physics. The big bang, creation myths, other universes."

"For me, it just is." I sat up. "It's the way I learn things."

"Like a sponge, right?"

"A sponge?"

"Yeah. Like a sponge."

"You soak things up. I see that, like a sponge."

"Maybe thinking is more like devouring good food. I have a quick mind, so stringing the learning experience out over a long period of time feels torturous and frustrating. I do better with total immersion."

"And when you come out on the other side, you're new in some way and ready to tackle things again. Right?"

"Right. You go underground, you come out refreshed."

"Underground. Maybe underwater?"

"Water?"

"Yeah. You used the word . . . 'immersion.' "

"Oh, I see it. Sounds like baptism, doesn't it? Odd, because there is a kind of religious fervor to it."

"In a small way," I said, "it's also why I occasionally look at tarot cards or I Ching readings. I don't want answers from them because that's for the psychic hot lines. But by studying what's revealed and using it as a backboard for my own explorations, I can often work out solutions or else find new directions."

"So if you had some tarot cards right now—"

He pronounced it to rhyme with *carrot*.

"Tear-oh."

"So if you had them. If you were reading them."

"Right now?"

"Now."

"I don't have any with me."

"But if you *did* have them, *if* you were reading them."

"Uhhh," I said. "Where are you going with this?"

"Here," he said, kissing me.

"Oh."

"And here."

"This is, like, so clichéd," I said, "like, so Hollywood. You've seen too many fake love scenes to believe those clichés really work."

I touched the back of his hand, touched the side of his neck, right on the main artery, felt his pulse thumping, his neck warm, just inside his blood running wild up and down his head, around his arteries and veins and capillaries, the wonder of the human body.

"It's so complicated," I said, thinking of how the body worked.

"Not so complicated," he whispered, misunderstanding me and touching my breasts. "How about here? Let me tell you some more about the big bang theory."

Oh. Drop out the bottom of the frame. Fade to the next morning.

I caught Brittles's face, lying sideways on the pillow, eyes shut, lips open and relaxed as he breathed. It was the first time I'd seen him so relaxed. No vertical furrows on his forehead between the eyes, sleep even softening the lines which runneled down from the sides of his nose to the corners of his lips. I realized he was the kind of person who had to compose a business face, probably a Law face, tighten things down, form a skin barrier against showing emotions, eyes narrowed with a private, encoded life force and lips that would never reveal it.

A face so guarded it reminded me of mine.

15

But in the morning, after a dozen phone calls, he was all business.

"Here's the deal," he said. "I'm not even going to explain most of this. I've got two major caseloads. One of them involves you and your daughter and the credit card scam. The other has something to do with all those bones you saw yesterday. And with a dead girl, down in Tucson. I think they're connected. But I've got to work both cases. So here's what we're going to do with your daughter, and don't argue with me because I've been calling in favors and making payoff promises all morning. Tomorrow, you and I will go to the Florence prison complex. To that call center, where you'll try to figure out how information is getting out."

"And my daughter?"

"She's got to help me in another way. I've arranged to transfer her from the Perryville prison to a troubled teenager boot camp that's only a few miles north of the Florence complex."

"That's ridiculous. That's not even close to what I'll allow."

"Yes, you will," he said. "You work the prison, your daughter will work inside this boot camp for me."

"Why? What will she be doing?"

"I don't know."

"You *do* know!" I shouted. "No deal."

"We discovered all those bones because of a young girl who was in the camp. That girl was murdered yesterday in Tucson."

"Whoa," I shrieked, "just goddam whoa right there. If somebody from the camp was just murdered, you're not sending my daughter in there."

"Only way," he said. "You can come to it now or later. But until you get your head around accepting this agreement, your daughter stays in federal prison."

"I'm going back to my house. In Tucson."

"Think carefully about what I've said."

"You're using me, Nathan."

"Yes. I am. But just think about getting your daughter out of prison."

Brittles told me of the bikers who killed Theresa Prejean and a U.S. Marshal, and connected the bikers somehow with the Rapture Warriors Camp. With the biker at my home.

"You can't put my daughter there now," I said.

"*Got* to do it."

"No way."

"The only way."

"Nathan, you're not putting my daughter in jeopardy."

But he'd already made plans for the transfer and explained the details.

"A female U.S. Marshal is flying in from Denver. She'll take your daughter to the camp and sign her in."

"No! I'll do it."

"Laura, you're not thinking. Two different assaults by young bikers. Two different targets, who'd never met. I don't know the connection, but you've been identified. You go to the camp, they'll automatically tie you to your daughter. That puts her in even more danger."

"You take her, then."

"Think, think. The only place you've been, outside of the Perryville prison, is that housing development. Where the bones were found. The bodies. Women's bodies. I don't know the connection, but it has to involve somebody who knows I'm working the case and saw you there with me."

"When will Spider be taken over there?"

"It's already being arranged."

"Damn you!" I shouted. "You didn't even ask me first?"

"No time. You and I have to go to Florence."

"The call center? That's not even on my radar anymore."

"It's a contract," he said. "With Aquitek. We can deal with it in one day, if you're half as good as Don says you are. By the time we've finished, your daughter will have been enrolled in the camp, and you'll get a full report."

"I don't like it. I don't like it at all."

"One more thing," he said. "I want you to move into this house. For now. I'm somehow responsible for getting you involved with these bikers. I want to make sure you're protected."

"I'll find a place of my own."

"No, Laura. *This* is going to be your place. You can just call it home until I'm satisfied you're no longer in danger."

Home. What a concept. And it wasn't even my choice.

"There's something else," he said hesitantly.

Hesitation always drives me really nuts. Somebody's usually got bad news, doesn't really want to give you this news, but knows he has to be the messenger. But he hesitated, fiddled, walked in circles like Rich.

"What?" I said. "What else?"

"Don ran a trace on Abbe Consuelo Dominguez."

"My daughter."

"On the woman who *calls* herself your daughter."

I fumbled out the only picture I had of her, the one Jonathan had given me two years before.

"It *is* her!"

"Don couldn't find any database records out there that link Abbe Dominguez with anybody named Spider Begay."

"I've used a dozen different names over the last ten years."

"Anything's possible," he said slowly. "But . . ."

"But *what*?"

"Abbe Dominguez was sentenced to two years in Leavenworth for federal mail fraud. Dominguez was also suspected of involvement in a huge identity theft ring working out of New York City."

"I want to see her. She called me Mom. I want her to tell me, to my face, that she's really my daughter. When I was fifteen, I ran away from the Hopi rez with this guy, Jonathan Begay. We had a baby. We drank a lot. We smoked a lot of pot, we did a lot of radical Indian stuff. AIM stuff. I was at Pine Ridge when the FBI men and Joe Stuntz were killed. When my daughter was two, Jonathan just . . . disappeared with her one day. We were in some motel, I don't remember where just now. I woke up, they were both gone. Now, twenty years later, I'm not letting her out of my sight again."

"You can't go near her," Brittles said. "Somebody knows who you are. Knows who *I* am."

I turned on my cell phone, but he put his hand around it, folding it shut.

"If you're going to call Don, he's with me on this. For now, Laura, we've got to consider the possibility that the Dominguez woman is not your daughter. That she's a convicted felon and is working a scam on us, on you, to get out of jail free."

"Whatever makes you even say a thing like that?"

He hesitated. "Don checked her records, found nothing in her background before she wound up in the courtroom for sentencing. Don thinks . . . and I agree . . . Don thinks you have to look at the initials of her name. Abbe Consuelo Dominguez. A. B. C. D."

"Ridiculous!"

But I trusted Don's intuition on things like this. And I'd *al*ways trusted his ability for data mining. If Don couldn't turn up any traces of that name before the prison sentence, it probably didn't exist. *She* didn't exist. It was phony ID.

"Okay," I said finally. "But how about a close friend of mine taking her to the camp?"

"Who?"

"Veronique Difiallos."

"When was the last time you saw her?"

"At least a week ago," I said.

"Still . . . how about, for a few extra inches of protection for your daughter, or whoever she is, how about we disguise her somehow?"

"I've already thought of how to do that. Listen. Nathan. Let's be clear about something. What happened here, it's a one time thing."

"If that's what you want."

"I hardly know *what* I want these days. Except to get my daughter out of prison. Find a home for the two of us."

16

"This will take most of the day," Michael Craven said. "Right, Shelly?"

Michalle Sasha looked closely at Spider's hair, at the roots and ends. Michalle had cut my hair for years, although she lost interest in trying to persuade me to do something creative beyond L'Oréal coloring. A loud techno track came from the giant sound system and Michalle wiggled her hips slightly to the beat.

Spider slouched in the green leather chrome-armed chair in front of Michael's station. She fiddled with his tool case, slipping different kinds of scissors and combs out of it until he finally took the entire kit away from her.

"I'd give it four hours, tops," Michalle told me.

"Bring it on," Spider said. "Just do me. Get me outa here."

"Great mood you got, missy," Michael said.

"Yeah. Tickle me so I can die laughing."

Brittles grabbed the back of her chair and swung her around to face him.

"Look, girl," he said in a low, stern voice. "We've got a deal, right?"

Spider didn't answer.

"Right?" he said louder. She nodded. "Okay. Part of this deal is that you go into that camp, you try to find out anything that might help us. Right?"

"Yeah, okay, okay. Right, okay?"

"If anybody connects you with your mother, I mean very *bad* anybodies, you could be in serious trouble. So get this hair thing over with, then we'll buy you some different kinds of clothes. Right?"

He released the chair.

"I'll be back in three hours," he said to me, and left the salon.

Spider jerked her body, like a child trying to get a swing started, and got the chair swiveled around so she looked at herself in the mirror. Michael arranged some Goldwell products on a side table.

" 'Oxycure Platin,' " she read. "Is this, like, bleach?"

"We call it stripping out color."

"Bleaching my goddam hair," she said. "B.F.D., dudes. Like I *really* always wanted to be a platinum blond."

"Do mine, too," I said to Michalle.

"Oh pu*leeze!*" Spider said.

But I settled into the chair at Michalle's station. Both Michael and Michalle mixed a scoop of the Oxycure with a careful measure of Topchic solution, twelve percent alcohol, it said on the container. They brushed the solution onto just the ends of our hair.

"I thought you'd cut it first," I said.

"No way," Michael answered, grabbing Spider's head at the top so she'd stop squirming. "We've got to let this stuff stay on until we've stripped all the color out, till there's no color on the ends."

"Great," Spider said. "How many times are you going to put this crap on?"

Michael yanked a plastic cap over her head.

"Just sit there for a while," he said. "What kind of music you like?"

"Who cares?"

"Got any hiphop?" I said, as Michalle put a similar cap on my head.

Michael sorted through a few hundred CDs.

"Got some Scarface. Mystikal. Snoop Dogg. Boo Yaa Tribe."

"Anything," I said, and he sorted the CDs like a deck of cards, fanning them in front of me until I picked one at random. He slotted it into the player.

I gotta a tattoo on my lower back
Sayin no dirty dicks allowed and if it's fishy I'ma throw
    it back
And it's startin to smell like the coastline
When you startin to tell me
Which of these young hoes you think is most fine
And I don't play that
I don't stay that way at home
Don't play with your bone
So doncha never say that
Just get your hat, I'm leaving you flat
You really fucked up when you thought that it was okay
    to say that

"Jesus Christ," Spider complained. "Lemme hear some thug gangsta tracks if I gotta sit here all day."

Michael picked out another CD.

Fifteenth of the month just got my county check
Rollin down the block watchin hoes break their necks
I'm the pimp nigga that they wanna be on topa
Ridin my dick as I serve that ass propa
When up come these fools wearing blue
This is a blood town so I told em that they better duck
    down
Shot a couple rounds in their direction
Maybe I could hit em or at least I would scare em
One mothafucka rollin strapped shot back
Punks shoulda known that my block got my back
Once again it's on, Tucson Vietnam
Like rat-tat-tat-tat and the bitch niggas gone
Like that.

A timer dinged. Michalle hit the Stop button on the CD player. She and Michael mixed a fresh batch of their goo, but this time applied it to the roots, snapped fresh plastic caps on.

We repeated the process one more time until both of them were satisfied.

"This is it?" Spider groaned. "This is *shit,* man."

"Over here, kid," Michael said, motioning for both of us to sit at the shampoo basins and lean our heads backward.

"Who you calling kid?" Spider said to Michael with some humor. "You can't be more than five years older than me. Six, tops."

"All potty mouth brats are kids to me," he said, spraying cold water on her head and rubbing in shampoo.

"Whoa," she said, "that tickles."

"You complain any more and I'll tickle you to death."

Back in the chairs again. Delighted that Spider's mood had improved, I tried to get her to talk to me, but she focused entirely on Michael, with an occasional comment to Michalle that whatever happened to my hair it wouldn't improve my personality.

"So now, like, you gonna cut it finally?" Spider said.

"Nope. We're gonna give you some Ellumen."

Michael showed her a platinum bottle with a red cap, spraying it on her head as Michalle did the same to me.

"Take out all your color, Laura?" Michalle said. "You going full platinum, like the girl?" I nodded. "Short cut?"

"Not too short," I said. "I've always wanted to look like Annie Lennox."

Once our hair was a brilliant platinum blond, the haircuts took very little time. Michael used both thinning and texturing shears and a clipper on top. Michalle used only a clipper. As Michael spun Spider's chair around, Spider caught my eyes in the mirror and she nodded to the techno beat as she checked out my hair. She grinned, gave me a thumbs up, then shut down the grin and cut her eyes away.

I savored that grin, that thumbs-up gesture. *A small thing,* I thought, *but even more than I'd hoped for. If it takes a simple haircut,* I thought, *to get me closer to my daughter, great.* I'd do more, I'd do anything.

"Good sweet Jesus," Brittles said from the door.

Spider and I whipped off the protective sheets, turned to face him, standing side by side. Impulsively, I stuck my arm around Spider's shoulders, and she let it stay for at least a minute.

"Get a good look at this," she finally said to me. "Once I go into that camp, once the deal is complete, you'll never see me again. You thought it was funky, getting your hair done like mine. It *was* funky. You made me laugh, for a little while."

She gestured at all the hair clippings on the floor that Michael was sweeping into a dustpan.

"But nothing more than a moment. Like that hair."

"Spider. Please."

"You're pathetic, mom," she said sarcastically. "You're fixated on a two-year-old baby. I'm no diaper brat anymore. And you're . . . you're history. Like the hair."

"It'll be all right," Brittles said halfheartedly.

That I *didn't* want to hear. If *he* was wary, I was downright scared.

"It's a risk," Brittles said to Spider as she snorted. "One of those times when you've got to trust somebody. You're headed into risky business and not knowing what to expect. Don't be so young. Long ago, in another part of the world, I had absolutely no fear. I'd push into the jungle without knowing what was on the other side of the next clump of bamboo. I *wel*comed what might be waiting there for me."

"How old were you then?" she asked.

"Eighteen."

"I'm five years beyond that. Don't go lecturing me with your past."

"She's a pistol," Brittles said after Spider went out the door. He stared at my haircut. "I'm revising my outlook on you every day."

"So you going to play your flute again for me?"

"I moved it into my bedroom. With all my other good stuff."

"So I guess I'm not going to see it again?"

"Sometime. When we've got time."

"Maybe," I said, "you're just the kind of man who's not really available."

"Think I'll just wait until you take me out to dinner. Been ages since a woman bought me a great meal."

"Hey," I said. "Let's give this thing some time to breathe. Maybe a few dinners, a picnic would be nice, some sightseeing or hiking in the canyons. Something not quite so . . . so, spur-of-the-moment-hop-into-the-sack kind of things."

"It's that hair bleach," he said, opening the door for me. "Can't know yet if it leached all your good sense out or refreshed your mind with curiosity."

revelations

"Abbe Dominguez," Father Micah said, looking over the completed application form. "Age twenty-three. We don't usually accept people that old. And you are the mother or the guardian?"

"I'm her stepmother," Veronique Difiallos said. "Divorced from her actual father. But I'm the one who decided to take responsibility for young Abbe."

"And why did you come to our place? There are many different facilities that offer programs for young people who struggle in their homes, their schools, or their social environment in the community. Why did you choose Rapture Warriors Camp?"

"I heard about your successes."

"From whom, if I may ask?"

"I called around," Veronique said. "Called friends in similar situations. Friends who had financial resources to get only the very best. Three places were recommended. One in California, one in Utah. And Rapture Warriors. I lived in Phoenix for some years. I liked the idea of Abbe being in a remote area, like the desert, where there are no large cities too close."

"Minimize distractions," Father Micah said. "Maximize healing."

"Exactly right."

"And you, Miss Dominguez. What do you think about this?"

"Whatever."

"Whatever." Father Micah sighed. "Maybe you're younger than your years. You certainly exhibit teenage indifference."

"How do you handle security?" Veronique asked.

"Rapture Warriors Camp is run by very strict disciplines. We have no bars, no real locks, no resident restraints. However, we do classify each resident according to certain risk factors. New residents are considered flight risks. We assign them to special dormitories under constant supervision. In extreme cases, we may classify a resident as a 'bad dog.' Part of the discipline at this level involves wearing handcuffs and leg chains for a twenty-four-hour period. This is all voluntary. If the resident refuses that discipline, the resident is dismissed on the spot."

"Do you have many runaways?" Veronique asked.

"Not as often as you'd suspect. Instead, we put residents into groups. Most of the residents here need schooling. We offer an accelerated program toward a high school GED. Plus therapy groups, crafts, arts. If a resident needs medical assistance that our staff nurse practitioners cannot provide, the resident is escorted to Tucson. Stop that, Miss Dominguez."

Abbe was walking around the room, humming to herself.

"Sit down."

They all waited until she sat, shrugging.

"We have zero tolerance for negative behavior. We specialize in really troubled young people. From those dealing with the bad effects of peer pressure on up the scale. Depression, using drugs or alcohol, people with behavioral disorders, like ADD, and young people who are sexually promiscuous."

"Cut to the chase," Abbe said to Veronique. "You going to dump me here or what?"

"We have an agreement," Veronique said to Father Micah. "If Abbe stays here for a full month, I will pay her ten thousand dollars. Another month, another ten thousand. Until you think she's ready to go outside."

"She's gonna dump me," Abbe said to the ceiling. "So get on with it."

"The fee," Veronique said, taking out a checkbook.

"Seventy-five hundred for the first month. Twenty thousand total for three months, if you pay all of it up front."

"That's excessively expensive," Veronique said.

"Half our residents have severe addition behaviors. Drugs, alcohol, sex, self-mutilations, and serious depression. We charge a lot, we guarantee a lot."

She wrote out a check, tore it carefully from her book, and placed it squarely on the desk, neatening up everything else on the desk at the same time. Father Micah watched this neatening, cutting his eyes back and forth between Veronique and Abbe.

"There's one other thing," he said as Veronique stood up to leave. "Rapture Warriors Camp is founded on the biblical plan for humans."

"Oh, for Christ's sake!" Abbe said.

"Exactly right. We don't teach it, we don't preach it, unless you want to hear it. Otherwise, you're only influenced by the Raptures as a metaphor for improving your own life in this world."

"So that you become worthy," Veronique said.

"Are you a believer?"

"I'm a Catholic. I've heard of the Raptures, but I've never understood what it meant for Catholics."

"The Lord comes below the clouds, but above the earth. He takes the saints and the dead in Christ back up to Heaven. Then the Antichrist begins a seven-year reign. After His first three and a half years, many Jews are taken up to Heaven. At the end of the seven years, Christ returns to earth. The Second Coming, which will last one thousand years. The devil is imprisoned in the bottomless pit, and the earth is ravaged by fire."

"Do I have to listen to this crap?" Abbe said. "Or can you just put those golden handcuffs on me?"

"You don't have to listen at all," Father Micah said. "But let me show you two of your new friends."

He escorted them from his office into a windowless room, carpeted, expensive chairs and tables scattered randomly in groups. A young girl sat at one of the tables, a young black boy at another.

"Chloe. This is Abbe. She'll be in your dormitory."

One look at Chloe would tell anybody that she wasn't going to make it in the camp or in life anywhere. Her unwashed red hair looked like dreads and it just lay clumped and matted. Freckles strewn like the milky way across her face, chest, and arms. Beautiful face, that peaches and cream look with the freckles, but her hands were pale and big-boned, the knuckles red and cracked like she'd washed dishes and clothes for a living. The rest of her body was slender, a Barbie figure, improbably big boobs and wasp-thin waist, but the hands gave her that alien look, so nobody really knew how to react to her.

"Hello," she said, her voice, pitched low, hesitant, and so weak it sounded as though it had no spine in it, no bones, no skeleton. The voice of a loser, Abbe thought. No, of somebody who'd just plain given up on life.

"And this is Rafterman," Father Micah said, pointing at the black boy, who immediately went into a singsong rap.

These mothafuckas always fuckin wit me
Like them police mothafuckas always fuckin wit me
An in the yard mothafuckas still fuckin wit me
Unless you're hard mothafucka don't fuck wit me
Cause I'm the kinda nigga that'll beat your son
And go fuck your baby's mama to increase the fun

"Rafterman stutters," Father Micah said. "Unless he's singing."

"Ah . . . ah-rapping," Rafterman said.

"Rap. Hiphop. I'm still learning to appreciate it. Tell Abbe and her mother where you're from, Rafterman."

"Ah I'm, ah . . . from, ah I'm from ah . . . ah—South LA."

"We encourage his rapping because he gets out his feelings."

Forty ounce freezin my balls, St. Ides my brand
I'm the mothafuckin man
With a forty ounce can
With a gun in my lap, always gotta roll strapped
Cause it's hot in these streets gotta watch for the jack
Caps get peeled when I'm packin steel
These fuckin streets is real and wit the rappin' skill
As my meal ticket
I'm not Ice Cube but I can still get wicked
Surrounded by bitches in like a Hollywood flick
Only five foot six but I gotta big dick

"That's pretty disgusting," Veronique said. "Perhaps I'll just leave now."

"Hey, man," Abbe said. "That's one motherfucking cool rap."

"Ah . . . ah, thanks."

"I'll just show you one more thing," Father Micah said, leading them both outside where an adult was counseling a young girl with fiery red hair. "Miss Cameron. Please speak up so Abbe, our newest resident, can learn about discipline."

Miss Cameron raised her voice, never taking her eyes off of the redhead.

"You earned the demotion. So you work your way out of it in the way you walk for the next two days. You count your steps. You make it a ritual, a habit, you'll get demerits if you look down, sideways, at somebody else, or if you smile or didn't pay attention to me or you lose track of the cadence. From here, it's one hundred and fifty-one steps to the parade ground, left turn, another sixty-three steps, halt. So you learn to count the steps without looking down, if the steps are exact from one exercise to another, it's a good thing, and a good way to concentrate and avoid demerits. Am I clear?"

"Clear, yes, ma'am, clear."

Abbe looked at the unfenced yard, the entrance road leading out to the world.

"Do I ever get out there?" she asked.

"Absolutely. Part of our discipline is fulfilling a contract with Pinal County to clean brush and litter. You'll be taken on your first work crew later this week."

"Well, Abbe," Veronique said. "Good-bye. This could be just the right place."

"Whatever."

Veronique bent to kiss her, but Abbe ducked her head away. Veronique walked to her Mercedes without a backward look and drove away.

"You don't have to like her to succeed here," Father Micah said.

"Do I need to like you?"

"No. Respect is what we work for."

"I can't respect somebody I don't like," Abbe snorted.

"A word in your ear, dear girl. Whether you do or do not like me, or the staff, you'll learn to respect us. Without respect, your hill will get mighty steep to climb."

"You got that right out of an old western movie," Abbe said. "Richard Boone says it to Randolph Scott in *The Tall T*."

"Well. We are in the West. Just remember. Respect."

"Or my elevator won't go all the way to the top. I'll be less than a six-pack in the fridge, up the creek without a paddle, rowing with one oar."

"Miss Cameron," Father Micah said. "Why don't you instruct Abbe in the proper way to walk to her dormitory?"

laura

17

"We've got to walk from here."

He strode off several paces, stopped when he realized I was standing with my door open, my hands on top of the doorframe.

"What's wrong?" he asked.

Wordless, frowning, I gestured at the prison complex.

"It's a waste of time," I said. "This is nothing."

"Oranges," he said after a moment. "Remember the oranges."

"I don't . . . what . . . I don't . . . *oranges*?"

"Oranges," Brittles said. "In all the *Godfather* movies. When you see an orange, something bad's gonna happen. Vito Corleone is buying oranges when he's shot in the street. There's an orange atop a bowl of fruit right in front of Don Barzini in that scene where the heads of all the families agree to stop the war. Don Fanucci, that thug in the early parts of *Godfather II*. He's juggling an orange just before he goes upstairs, when Robert De Niro shoots him through the towel and the towel catches fire."

"Sure," I said sarcastically. "Brando sticks a piece of orange peel over his teeth just before he dies. That's what *I* remember."

"Coppola wants to tip off the audience, something's gonna

happen, something not so nice. Whenever I'm about to go into a place that makes my scalp tingle, I stop and think of the oranges. Just a ritual, just . . . I guess, a way to ramp up my alertness."

"Now you're really scaring me."

"Can you do this?" He walked back, put his hands on top of mine. "You'll never be safer than inside there."

"It's just . . . it makes me think of my daughter being in prison."

"You're going in there," he said gently, wiping my eyes with a clean handkerchief. "You're going into one prison so you can get your daughter out of another. That's the only way to think of it."

"To get her out," I sniffled, nodding.

"It's not you going in. It's her coming out."

He took my hands off the door, nudged it shut with his hips.

"Ready?" Holding my hands, turning me sideways, facing the prison, holding hands with me like we were teenagers.

"Yeah," I said. "Let's do this."

We bypassed the roadway and climbed an old stairway to the admin building. A screened-in gallery surrounded the entire third floor.

"Warden used to walk around there," Brittles said. "Make sure things were locked down tight."

"Are we going inside? To meet the warden?"

"No."

"Where's the call center?"

"Not even here," he said after a moment.

"So explain to me. We're to work with computers, but they're somewhere else in this prison?"

"Another complex."

"There's more than this?"

"Half a dozen or so. Florence is a big place."

"So . . . if this *isn't* where the computers are, why are we here?"

"I want you to see who you're dealing with."

"I can see that at the call center."

Hesitating, unsure of what to tell me.

"Laura. The worst of the inmates are in here. This is level five, maximum security. You see how carefully inmates are treated here, you'll understand how dangerous they can be. You get to the call center, I don't want you forgetting for a moment who you're working with. So get over whatever hesitation you've got. Let's just go inside."

He led me to heavy iron gates underneath an arched entrance to the main prison yard. A man in a brown Correctional Officer's uniform waited for us, jangling a huge ring of keys as he studied a clipboard.

"Aquitek Security?" he said, looking at his clipboard again. "Mister Nathan Brittles? Missus Laura Winslow?"

"Miss," I said.

"Sorry about that, ma'am. I'm CO Champlain, I'll be your guide."

Selecting a huge old brass key, he fitted it into a massive lock on the gate and swung the door open.

"Folger Adam key, ma'am," he said. "From Joliet, Illinoise."

Ignoring his mispronunciation, I read the sign over the gate, listing all restrictions. No children allowed. No animals allowed. Nobody in a uniform, law enforcement officers an exception if notified in advance.

We walk into an area closed on all four sides, but open to the sky. Above me, straight ahead in a guard tower, another uniformed man with sunglasses and an AR-15 studied us closely, the gun held at port arms.

"I'll need a photo ID. No more than twenty dollars allowed inside. Nothing metal in your pockets?"

We'd already been briefed on what not to carry with us, so Brittles had locked all our money, our watches, keys, and my bracelet in his car. We passed single-file through a metal detector, showed our IDs to a woman CO, and received visitor badges to clip on our shirt pockets.

"This is worse than airline check-in," I said, trying to make a joke, "except it's so claustrophobic. What do you call this . . . this . . ." I waved my arms.

"Sally port, ma'am. Double-gated security. You'll see sally ports all through the prisons. Unlock one door, go inside, lock the first door before you unlock the second. You ready?"

He opened the second gateway and we walked into bright sunlight. I thought I'd see a lot of inmates, playing basketball, lifting weights, doing all those things you see inmates doing in movies showing the yard. But all I could see were buildings, green grass, some flowers, and khaki uniforms. No inmates.

"Nobody's home today?" I joked.

"Everybody's home," Champlain answered. "They're just all locked up."

He turned back to the gate we'd just gone through, gesturing at the walls.

"Them walls. Those gates. All this stuff came from the old Yuma Territorial Prison. Hundred years ago, the state decided to build a new prison here. So everybody at Yuma, I mean the guards, the staff, the prisoners, everybody dismantled parts of the Yuma prison and trekked it over here. Took more than a year to walk that far. Look at that wall. See the lines that look like the walls were built against wood? All this stuff came from Yuma. Wagons, lots of wagons. But the prisoners walked."

The guard in the tower faced us again, but he'd swapped his AR-15 for a strange shotgun. Champlain saw me looking up.

"Thirty-seven-millimeter tear gas gun, ma'am. Except loaded up with knee knockers. Wooden slugs. Fire them suckers at an inmate, kneecap him right quick. This way."

An old building, a sign outside saying it had been constructed in 1912. Champlain led us up the stairway and I could hear the buzz of many voices. Another CO came out of the gates, stood at the top of the steps waiting for us. He didn't introduce himself, just checked our badges. He wore a black flak jacket over his uniform shirt, a holstered Taser hung from his belt, and his face was covered by a plastic visor that looked like a welder's mask.

"Stab vest," Champlain said. "Heavy duty Taser for inmate control. Plus a face shield. Substance guard. When they spit at you. Or worse."

"Looks like my dentist," I said, "when he wants to avoid getting pieces of my teeth in his face while he's drilling."

Champlain and Brittles exchanged a cynical smile, but said nothing. The CO in the stab vest unlocked the gateway and we went into a much smaller sally port. The buzzing swelled to a loud, continuous roar of many voices as soon as we stopped at metal bars surrounding all three interior sides of the sally port. Three tiers of cells stretched all around the walls, each cell holding one inmate. In the middle of the open area, an elevated glass-walled control booth rose above stairways. Several COs inside the booth moved about constantly, checking the cells, watching everything and everybody. None of the voices was understandable. I could see many inmates with arms hanging on bars of the cell door. Some moved their hands and fingers in sign language, but no signs that I'd ever seen before.

"They're talking to each other," Champlain said. "See that one holding a mirror? Second floor, left side, right about in the middle? He's reading notes from the guy next to him. In a bit, you'll see them switch off from who talks, who listens."

"Why am I in here?" I said to Brittles.

"Explain the face shield to her," he said to Champlain.

"They spit on you?" I said.

"Spitting ain't nothing. They throw urine. Feces. They store it up, hoping to catch a CO without a face shield. They'll take anything peppery the kitchen sends up on their meal trays. Hot sauce. Chiles. Whatever. They'll hide it in their cells with their urine and feces, load it into their plastic water or soda bottles. When a CO without a face shield walks by, *BAM,* they let him have it. Man, I've been stung by pepper spray, by Mace. That's nothing compared to the shit these guys try to squirt in your eye."

I turned sideways to shut out most of the cells.

"See the TV?" Brittles asked.

In the closest cell I saw a TV picture flickering without sound. The working electronics of the TV set were encased in clear plastic, with the speaker removed. The inmate pulled out ear buds when he saw I was looking at him.

"That's the real reason I brought you in here," Brittles said. "The TVs, their radios, these guys can remove parts of the electronics to make things. Clear cases, making it harder for them to hide contraband and weapons from the CO who checks out the cell. Seen enough?"

Another CO came through the open area, escorting an inmate with handcuffs attached to a two-foot-long chain which was looped through a padlocked security belt at his waist. Led to a pay phone, the inmate awkwardly picked up the handset.

"This is grim," I said, head down.

"We're outa here," Brittles said to Champlain.

Back on the yard, Champlain started to talk about the rest of the buildings surrounding the grassy yard. A door opened somewhere, an armed CO came down a sidewalk and crossed to the door of another building, waited until the door there was unlocked, then waved a fisted hand in a circle. An inmate appeared at the first doorway in leg irons, hands cuffed behind, shuffling along the sidewalk. When he reached the second door, a second inmate shuffled ahead, then another and another, but only one at a time. I tried to separate the men I saw, tried to understand their individuality beyond the handcuffs and chains and blue clothing. Many had ponytails, many more had jailhouse tattoos. The seventh man, a heavyset Mexican, was a full-sleever, with tats running down and around the entire skin area of both arms.

"Doesn't anybody ever come out to play?" I asked.

"No, ma'am," Champlain said. "Work crews are allowed. If some inmate shows up out here and he's not legit, he's not supposed to be here, he'll be shot."

"Wounded? Actually shot and wounded?"

"Or shot dead. This is a no man's zone, ma'am. We've got lots of rules. And we've got a lot of scumbags in here who don't want to play by our rules."

"Take me to the computers," I said to Brittles.

"Y'all want a tour of the death house?" Champlain said. "Most tours, that's the highlight. That's the place people most want to see."

"Not today," Brittles answered.

"Not ever," I said to myself as we went out the main sally port to the parking lot and the hot sun and green trees and freedom. Then I turned to Brittles. "Where now?"

18

Back in the parking lot, Brittles opened the doors to let out some of the heat.

"You're getting kinda pink," he said.

I picked up the Aquitek baseball hat, wiped my forehead. The hat fit so easily on my short hair I had to take it off, rub the hair for the umpteenth time.

"Annie Lennox," he said. "I'm old enough to remember."

"Just turn on the aircon."

"We're just going across the street."

"The call center is over there?" I asked, eying what looked like trailers or temporary buildings behind a fence.

"Nope. Come on."

"We're walking?"

"Put the hat back on."

Across the road, Brittles went up to a solid chain-link

doorway and pressed a call button. As though waiting for us, a man in khaki dress slacks and a green Polo shirt came up to check our ID.

"Friedlander," he said, satisfied. "CIU. Car's over here."

"He doesn't say much," I said quietly to Brittles as Friedlander went quickly ahead of us to an old white Taurus with almost two hundred thousand miles on the odometer.

"He's a detective."

"Working with us?"

"Nope. He's my contact here to escort us into the call center."

We drove slowly past the main complex, headed east.

"Why do you have horses?" I asked Friedlander as we drove by a stable.

"Pursuit," he said shortly. "Chase horses. Haven't been used in years. State would save a lot of money by disbanding the unit. But I guess some idiot in the director's office must like horses."

"You mean, they chase whoever escapes?" I asked.

"*No*body escapes from this place. Not on my watch, anyway."

We drove another few miles past several other complex buildings and a maintenance garage, dipped around a sharp S-curve over a narrow bridge, finally arriving at a guard post. Friedlander stopped, showed the guard his ID. The guard flicked his eyes over me, asked for ID from Brittles, then waved us through.

"This is Eyman Complex," Friedlander said.

More gates. More COs. More prison units. More sally ports. And, finally, a large one-story building with galvanized siding and a shiny new microwave dish atop a tarpaper roof. I recognized the dish immediately as an Internet uplink. Friedlander escorted us into the building, waiting while IDs were checked again, and left us in a makeshift sally port area looking out on a sea of waist-high cubicles with clear plastic walls. Although each cubicle had a computer, only a third were occupied.

"That Friedlander doesn't talk much," Brittles said.

I paid no attention, recognizing the computers.

"Let's get to these machines," I said. "I've had enough of people."

"Wait. There's a protocol everywhere in this prison."

"And I'm yours," a voice said behind us. "Miss Winslow, I've admired your work for years. I'm Shane Caraveo."

Now, that I don't like. People knowing who I am. No, that's not quite right. A lot of people in the hacker world know my name, but almost nobody would be able to recognize my face. My face flushed with anger, but before I could say anything he held up a large folder, the cover turned back to show a picture of me in my Aquitek uniform. Puzzling, since the picture was obviously of me, but I'd never posed for it.

"Let me show you around."

The three of us went up to a narrow catwalk around the work center, and Brittles stayed in a corner to talk with an armed CO. I could hear the muted whispers of voices, none of them distinct.

"Here's the setup," Caraveo explained. "It's a closed, secure network. Three dozen workstations cabled by ethernet to a server farm over in that locked cage."

"Workstations?"

"Yes. Like the old terminal and server setups. No hard drives, no floppy or CD drives. Motherboards very simple, designed to connect the workstation to the server, run the dedicated software. Workstation box also houses the monitor. Only things outside the box are keyboards and mice."

"Network cards?"

"Nope. All the hardware is on the motherboards. Actually, an inmate designed them. Have you seen inmate TV sets?"

"Clear plastic cases."

"Same here," Caraveo said. I inched along the catwalk, wanting a closer look at how the operators worked. "Uh, Miss Winslow, don't move by yourself."

"Excuse me?"

"Look across the room."

The armed CO held his AR-15 loosely at his side, the barrel pointing at me.

"I'll take you down on the floor. I'll even let you talk with a few inmates. But at all times, I have to be with you. You can't move independently. All the time, remember where you are."

"But these people must be serving minor sentences," I protested.

"Two counts of murder." Caraveo pointed at one man. "Murder, arson." Pointing at another. "Armed robbery, assault. It's not the crime. It's the behavior. Every inmate at Florence is rated according to risk factors, to make it simple. In the main complex you visited earlier, almost every unit there holds level fives. Maximum security. These men here are all level threes. Lower risk."

"Who built the system?"

"Our company. We're based in Miami. Call centers, help centers, catalog centers, that's all we do. Hardware assembled in China to our specifications. I wrote the database programs. I lived in Finland for a while, worked with anonymous email resenders over there, before the religious nuts shut us down. That's how I know your name. We handled some of your accounts. Years ago. Five years ago, I think."

Well. A lot has changed in five years, I thought. Including my reputation, since I didn't remember routing anything through Finland because Japanese networks were notoriously insecure.

"So. What do you want to see first? What's in the cage?"

"This whole place is a cage," I said.

"Yeah. Well. The small server farm is down in that cage. I meant, do you want to see the servers, or the operators?"

"Downstairs."

"I won't introduce you to anybody. Don't make eye contact. You are, after all, a woman. These guys don't see many women, except a CO with a gun or a taser."

He reached to my shirt lapels and I slapped his hands away.
"Don't," I said.

"Fasten your top button. Pull your cap tight. Look official.
Look like you know what you're doing and do it quickly."

He led me down the metal staircase and across metal
flooring into the maze of cubicles, stopping at one that
wasn't occupied. I sat in a surprisingly comfortable chair, adjusted myself to the keyboard, flexing my fingers.

"Good ergonomics," I said.

"They are people," Caraveo answered. "Whatever other
punishment they get in here, my company won't give them
carpal tunnel problems or bad backs."

Inside its case, the workstation hardware consisted of just
the motherboard and the monitor tube.

"No fan?"

"These guys. They take motors apart, they make things
from them. Keys, shanks. They use the wire from motors for
lots of things."

Three cables ran out the back of the case, all of them anchored inside, all running down and underneath the metal
flooring. I knelt on the floor, saw how the cables went
through a tight rubber grommet. I tugged on the white power
cable. It didn't move. Nor did the blue ethernet cable. Some
small slack in what looked like standard telephone wire.

"Anchored underneath," Caraveo said. "No inmate can get
to the cabling. If we have problems, we just unbolt some of
the cubicle partitions, then there's a special key that unlocks
the metal flooring plates."

"And everything runs to your servers?"

"Not the power cables, no. They're connected in nodes under the cubicles. All the ethernet cabling goes through a couple of routers, an electronic switch, then to the servers."

"And how do people input the information?" I couldn't see
any telephones. "How do they even get the calls?"

"Headsets. Plug in here."

He showed me a plug on the side of the workstation.

"All in one box," he said. "Like everybody in here. All packaged in a box."

"Show me how it works."

Caraveo took me past the empty cubicles toward the other end of the room. We stopped outside and slightly behind a cubicle. A thickset black man slouched comfortably in his chair, his voice barely louder than a murmur, his fingers flying across the keyboard. He moved his eyes to the side, knowing somebody was behind him, but not looking around.

"Yes, Miss Sampson. That item is currently in stock at twenty-four dollars and ninety-five cents. What is your next item?"

Hardly a big-ticket sale, I thought.

"Thank you, Miss Sampson. Please give me your address and a telephone number, area code first."

I watched him key in the data, all of it displaying on the screen. He misspelled the city name, "Phenix," moved his cursor into the word, correctly typed "Phoenix," and then the telephone number. I started to say something, but Caraveo nudged my arm and shook his head, then bobbed his head forward to the monitor.

"And how will you be paying for this today, Miss Sampson? Visa. And card number, please?"

As the man typed the credit card number, four groups of asterisks appeared on the screen. When he asked for the expiration date of the card, more asterisks.

"Thank you for ordering from us, Miss Sampson. You should expect delivery within five business days." About to click a switch on the headset wire, he paused and laughed. "Yes. Well, I hear *that,* Miss Sampson. Thanks."

He clicked the switch and ten seconds later he started talking again. He never once looked to see who'd been watching. Caraveo took me back up onto the catwalk and across to the server cage. He squared his face a few inches from a square white panel and said his name aloud. A bluish line moved across his right eye and a few seconds later the door lock clicked open.

"Retina scans," he said as we went inside the cage, the door relocking automatically. "You ask me, it's the only real security in this place. Got any questions about how it works down below?"

I hesitated, unsure how much I could tell him.

"No problem," he said. "I know about the scam, but I don't have a clue how it's happening. I've been over the software here a dozen times. I've written in different code blocks to trap things. Figuring, if there's an information leak, it can only happen two ways. Either the operators are memorizing a whole lot of data, not impossible. We've had several guys in here with photographic memories. But pretty unlikely, given how we screen and rotate the guys. So. Option two. The weakest link is between the servers and the Internet uplink."

"Where do you send the data?"

"Secure satellite." He saw me smile. "Yeah, well, as secure as it's gonna get these days. It's only an uplink. No downloadable trojan horse programs. Not that I don't sweep the hard drives daily."

"So. How are they doing it?"

"Well, Laura," he said, emphasizing my name, "I guess that's why they're paying big bucks to the experts. I can't find it. And I'm good. How good are you?"

19

Two hours later, running through all of Caraveo's software, I couldn't find any programming bugs or trojan horses. Nothing. No hacker security attacks. No viruses, no Internet programs we couldn't identify. Nothing.

"Clean," I said grudgingly.

"That's a relief. I could give a shit if my company has screwed up. But I love my code, I write clean code, and I just couldn't see any problems with it. So?"

"When do you change work shifts?"

"Another two hours."

At the cage wall, through twelve-gauge steel diamond webbing, I watched the operators below.

"They don't seem to pay us much attention."

"Don't believe that for a second," Caraveo said, holding up a laminated plan of the workstations. "See the guy at station thirteen? No, no, no, don't look at him, look somewhere else, but keep him in your peripheral vision. You'll see him cut his eyes up at you every few minutes."

Okay. So they watched me. I've felt watched before, I've been stalked before, but here I had the positive security of being separated from the inmates by locked doors and solid steel.

"Just him?" I asked.

"I don't want to freak you out. *But every man down there*," Caraveo said slowly and emphatically, "is *watching you*." He saw me cock my head slightly to the side, eyebrows raised, a half smile on the left side of my face. "You ever been watched by so many men before?"

"Never."

Caraveo twisted one of his rings, a snake that wrapped itself around the second joint. When he saw me looking at the rings, he smiled.

"You're wondering, how the hell does that guy work a keyboard with rings on every finger. Right?"

"Especially a laptop," I said. "Crowded keys."

"Not really." Flexing his fingers, studying two of the rings as though he'd not paid them any attention for a long time. "Writing programmer code, I can fly way above one hundred words a minute. Mostly, they're from another time. Pony tail, rollerblades, living in New York City. I'd see another cool ring, I'd just buy it."

He twisted off a golden thumb ring, showed me the inscription inside.

"From my girlfriend," he said. "My partner. It's Hebrew. Something from the Song of Solomon." He put the ring back on. "I lived right in the heart of west Greenwich Village once. Ten years ago. Just two doors down from the Erotic Bakery."

"Erotic? A bakery?"

"Lots of cookies." He shrugged. "You know. Woman's breasts, with pink icing. Penis with blue icing. That kind of thing. Anyway, I've never been looked at by more people since. Men or women. Course they were all men."

"Why are they watching me?"

"Inside, you *al*ways watch the keepers."

"Oh. So, just because somebody watches me more than somebody else, that doesn't mean anything about the credit card business?"

"Nope. What do you want to do now?"

I'd already thought about that.

"What do you do if your server goes down?"

"You mean, if the inmates can't enter orders from the callers?"

"Uh huh."

"If the down time only lasts a few minutes, the callers get a recorded message that there's a heavy backlog, please be patient, stay on the line, we'll be right with you, that sort of crap you've heard a hundred times."

"For how long?"

"Six, seven minutes. That's the longest I've been down with a short term problem. Anything longer than that, I have to shut down the servers to find the problem. All calls get rerouted to a backup call center. Somewhere in Kansas, I think. Or Nebraska, or . . . somewhere."

"And if you have to take the server down, what happens to the inmates?"

"They wait. If I get it back up, they're online again. If not, they go back to their cells."

"Take your servers down."

"Whoa. I can't do that," he protested.

"I think I know where the problem is."

He waited for an explanation, but I kept silent. He fiddled at his keyboard, uncertain, and then executed a short program. Instantly, all the inmates looked up at the cage. Caraveo picked up a headset, held the microphone stalk to his mouth.

"There's a problem," he said, his voice booming over a loudspeaker. "I have to shut things down. This person is here to help me fix the problem. Server will be down for the rest of your shift. Correctional Officers will arrive to escort you back to your cells."

He unplugged his headset, dropped it on his desk, fiddled with his mouse before he looked at me.

"I hope to hell you know what you're doing."

We waited for half an hour until all the inmates were cleared out of the work center. Finally, certain that we were alone, Caraveo let us out of the cage.

"Can you get below the floor plates?" I asked.

"Helluva lot of work."

"I may not need to do that, but I need to know if it's possible."

I picked a cubicle at random, sat in front of the workstation. Caraveo gave me a four-inch screwdriver with a special head.

"Not Phillips," he said, "and not slotted. You'd think it was so specifically different that it would last a lifetime. In here, somebody will make a tool just like it within a few months, so we refit all these things every forty-five days."

He pointed to a dozen screws. I removed them and the plastic case separated in two parts. The CRT was awkward to work around, but I finally isolated the motherboard, borrowed a jeweler's loupe and stuck it in my eye, looking for

improvised soldering, anything that would indicate that
somebody'd altered the motherboard.

Nothing.

"Never been that thorough," Caraveo said. "What next?"

"All the other workstations."

"We'll be here all night!"

"But only tonight. This place creeps me out. If there's a
hardware clooge, I want to find it now. How can you stand it,
working behind bars every day?"

"What are you looking for?"

"I don't know."

"Can I help?"

"If *I* don't know," I said impatiently, "how will you?"

Five hours later, I'd looked at all the motherboards. Caraveo followed me, reassembling the workstations, tidying up
after me. At one point I asked for a copy of the map of the cubicle area that numbered each workstation.

Finally, I had seven red crosses over seven cubicles. The
last workstation lay disassembled in front of me.

"What does that mean?" Caraveo asked.

"I don't know. But there's something, I don't know what,
somebody's altered the motherboards."

"That's impossible."

"People said that to Galileo."

"Am I going to have to close down the call center perma-
nently?"

"No," I protested. "That's a dead giveaway. How do you
assign who works at what workstation?"

"Randomly. By shift."

"And what happens if a workstation fails?"

"I've got six spares."

"Get one," I said. "Put it right in this cubicle, then make
sure that nobody is assigned to this machine for a few days."

I yanked on the power cord, snapping off the connections
to the motherboard. Two more yanks and the ethernet and
phone cables were free.

"You can't take that!"

"How do *you* bring hardware in and out of here?"

He shrugged, nodded. I yelled for Brittles while Caraveo brought another workstation out of his cage. Quickly setting it up, he studied the motherboard I'd pried loose, shaking his head. I handed him my loupe and he saw it immediately. A small break here, there, unexplained components, an extra chip.

"What is it?" he asked.

"Don't know. I'm not a hardware guru."

"How'd you spot that?" he said with awe. "Man, I thought I could do anything with these boxes."

"You're young," I said. "Give it time. You'll learn. But while you're waiting, we'll need to know the names of anybody who's had access to these workstations over the past year. You must have, what do you call them, trustees? Helpers? Inmates, whatever?"

"A few," he said, eyes narrowing to slits and then popping wide open. "There was a guy. Seven, no, eight months ago. I'll get his name."

"Brittles!" I shouted. "Come here."

Caraveo made a short call, turned to us, his jaw hanging open. The person at the other end had hung up, but Caraveo stood motionless, in shock, until the phone started beeping a message for him to hang up.

"What's the inmate's name?" Brittles asked.

"Marriott. William Marriott."

"Let's go talk to him," Brittles said to me.

"You can't do that."

"I'll get the permissions. Thanks for your help here."

"No. You don't understand. Marriott was shanked yester-day. He's dead."

Finally outside the prison, outside that grim, cold place, I sat at a picnic table on the grounds, crying again. Brittles hung nearby, turning the motherboard over and over in his hands, reluctant to bother me. He laid the motherboard on the table, started to ask me something.

"No," I said. "I'm done with all this. I'm done with the deal. Get me my daughter, let the two of us alone."

"Okay, okay," he said. "No hassles. But, as a starter, I need to know what's wrong with this computer thing. We need to tell Don."

I wiped my eyes with the three soggy tissues in my pocket. Took out my cell, punched in Don's number. He answered immediately.

"Wi-fi," I said. "Motherboards on some computers have been altered so that everything typed is being sent over a wireless network."

"Outside the prison," Don said. It wasn't a question. "But where?"

"I'm out of this now, Don."

"Don't you have a Mac Powerbook? Doesn't it have software that detects these wireless nodes?"

"Yes, Don," I said sarcastically. "And you have the same equipment and the same software. *You* look for the outside source."

"Is Nathan there?"

I handed the phone to Brittles, but he said nothing, listening to Don for only half a minute and then making another call, walking away from the picnic table so that I wouldn't hear the conversation.

"Here's the deal," he said, shutting down the cell. "You don't have to do anything. But you'll have to wait until we pull your daughter out of the camp."

"Let's go there *now*."

"Can't do that. She'll only be released to the custody of that friend of yours who pretended to be the stepmother. I just checked."

"I don't have to do anything," I emphasized. "I wait, I get my daughter."

"That's the deal."

"So will you take that motherboard back to Don? Just leave me alone?"

"Okay. Want to get something to eat?"

"Later. I'm going to get a few things from my house."

"Only if you let me drive you there. I'll feel safer. You'll feel safer."

"Drive me there," I said reluctantly. "But once I'm home, you leave."

Brittles called Zeke Pardee, told him to pick up the motherboard at Friedlander's CIU office. I knew Brittles struggled with the decision. He wanted to carry the board directly to Don, he wanted to take me directly to my house.

20

But once we pulled into my carport, I didn't feel very safe. Without thinking, without *wanting* to think about it, I kept my legs going to the door. Barely inside, all my anxieties from the past year rose like ghosts, as though I'd never achieved any natural balance to life, never moved beyond the frantic rhythms of keeping busy, using hacking as a fourteen-hour-a-day distraction from my anxieties and addictions.

Wandering the house, kicking dispiritedly at some of my cartons, I felt things nagging at me, something I'd forgotten, some data I'd discarded too quickly. I went from room to room, standing in doorways, standing at the patio door for a moment until the biker's helmet blossomed in my imagination and I had to turn away.

Gradually I realized that most of Rich's things were gone. He'd sorted out what he didn't want and dumped them on the floor. Clothes, books, CDs, even his guitar, everything lay exactly where he'd dropped them.

I finally found a handwritten page on a kitchen counter.

Lines from one of his children's stories that he tossed off, dreamed of getting published, though he never contacted a publisher.

> *"How far are the stars?" Rich asked Laura one day.*
> *"I don't know," she said, "they seem pretty far away."*
> *He asked his dad, who said, "Ask your mom."*
> *He asked his mom, who said, "Ask your dad."*
> *Rich was out of ideas and feeling sad.*
> *Late that night Rich awoke.*
> *His room was glowing and he began to float.*
> *His room disappeared and he heard a voice say,*
> *"Welcome to our sleek space boat."*
> *"It's called a space ship," Rich said, "and why am I here?"*
> *"You're on our space ship to take a space trip,*
> *So come on, Rich, let's get it in gear."*

And below this, Rich had written in red ink

I'm outa here—toss my other stuff into some of your boxes—or just burn it all

Opening the fridge, I started to pull out a can of Mountain Dew, popped the top, and had it to my lips before I recognized the old pattern. I emptied the can into the sink, ran the water, drinking right from the faucet. My heart rate slowed, gradually, the pulses no longer resonating in my head, and I recognized that my life *was* improving, *was* growing more holistic, more cohesive in purpose and tranquillity, despite the stress of meeting my daughter and the bittersweet contradictions between finding Rich and uncertain what to do about Nathan.

Also wondering about Rich's reaction to the trashed sliding door, and the obvious bullet holes stitched around walls, cupboards, and ceiling. Maybe he thought I'd shot it up myself, yes, that must be it, expressing my anger at our relationship, at him. But that made no sense to me at all, how some-body could think that way. I looked for another note. Maybe he'd written some questions, something friendlier, some-thing . . . I didn't know what. I picked at the top layers in the garbage can, but found nothing.

Brittles walked across the backyard, studying the biker's footprints, running a hand over the wall next to the sliding door, finally disappearing around a corner.

One last tour of the house, collecting a few things, most of them just picked at random. The house seemed, at last, to be empty. Just a few days ago, I'd never have considered that, never have dwelled much on my cardboard boxes. I won-dered how many times in the past few months with Rich I'd lived with the assumption that life was good, life was not to be questioned. A false assumption, I knew now. How many other false assumptions did I have? Was Abbe Dominguez *really* my daughter? How does one know a blood relation, if you haven't seen that person since she was only two years old? How much time did people spend their lives with false hopes and assumptions, with that inevitable sense that life, down underneath, is not a joy but a hopeless, unfulfilled burden?

Enough of this, I thought, nodding to myself, nodding hard with the acceptance that this house really was empty for me, that, like Rich's note, I was moving on. Bye bye. Outa here.

"Come on," Brittles shouted from the front door. "Don's got something."

revelations

Tamár Gordon carefully stacked all the brown envelopes on top of each other. She squared the stack, turned it on its side like a deck of cards, and fanned the envelopes out onto her round stressed-oak table.

"Fifteen identities," she said.

"Praise the Lord," Micah said.

"Praise the INS," Tamár answered. "If it wasn't for my connections with immigration people in Phoenix, this would have taken years."

" 'I knew a man in Christ,' " Micah said, bowing his head, not noticing that both Tamár and Galliano exchanged cynical smiles. " 'Whether in the body, I cannot tell, or whether out of the body, I cannot tell.' " Micah looked up, beaming. "Second Corinthians twelve, most of verses two through four. The fourth of the sixth Raptures. And how many innocents are delivered up by these documents?"

"Seventeen," Tamár said. "Mostly Chinese, several from Burma, one from Tibet, and four from Colombia. Fourteen are for girls, three for boys."

"Political refugees," Galliano said, crossing his legs at the ankles, smoothing out the creases in his linen trousers. "It's a nice metaphor, Micah. Delivering these girls from political terror."

"The Raptures are not metaphoric," Micah said calmly. "Without Jesus, the flesh will not be saved on The Day."

"These girls would have had their flesh ravaged. They would have been raped, probably again and again. In the wrong hands, they'd be imprisoned without a trial. In the worst hands, they'd be tortured and killed."

"Anthony," Micah said in his business voice, "please, how you wish on your own time to discuss women, and the use of their bodies, is for you and not me. I know of these things, but I do not speak of them."

"Agreed," Tamár said. "Now. I have seventeen identity kits. How many girls are in the Rapture camp?"

"Eleven girls. Two boys."

"Excuse me," Galliano said. "I thought there were three boys."

"Rudolpho Corazon left yesterday."

"Yes, I know he left, but didn't he come back?"

"No. He left with his friend Emilio, but only Emilio returned."

"Excuse me," Galliano said, standing. "I must make a phone call."

"Stay," Micah said. "I must get back to the camp. Another girl is coming this afternoon. I must be there when she arrives."

"Don't explain the Raptures to her just yet," Tamár cautioned him.

"I never do at the first meeting. I let the other girls make inquiries. I let you do background checks to verify the girl is a legitimate candidate for Rapture. And so, my dear Tamár, good-bye."

He stood forward to place a hand on her hand in benediction. Galliano intercepted the hand as it moved to her. Micah tried to remove his hand, but Galliano held it firmly.

"I shall let myself out," Micah said. "Thank you again for these documents. 'And when Jesus had spoken these things, while they beheld, Jesus was taken up and a cloud received Him out of their sight.' Acts chapter one, nine through eleven."

"Have you ever heard my story about the Raptures?" Galliano asked.

"No." Micah smiled. "Please, Anthony. Tell me."

"A friend of mine. From South America. From a very privileged family, nothing too expensive for her. Spoiled, bad spoiled. Her parents preached the Raptures to her. Preached of Revelations, the Second Coming, the Judgment Day, when sinners would be left behind."

"Good parenting."

"They bought her a brand-new Range Rover. Power this, power that, every conceivable option, including a giant sunroof that she could power back. Being wild and careless, she loved to set the car on cruise control, kneel on the front seat at high speeds, and stick her head up through the sunroof while driving."

Micah tried to pull his hand away from Galliano, but couldn't.

"So. The second week she had the Range Rover, she's on a mountain road, following a slow truck with stake sides, filled up with something. Those mountain roads, those South American drivers, bad things happen. To shorten the story, an oncoming car smashed into the front of the truck. A gigantic collision, and several dozen people started flying upwards from the open back of the truck. My friend, she saw all those people going up, she went from being terrified that she was going over the cliff to being ecstatic that she was witnessing the Raptures."

"Ahhhh . . ." Micah said. "And it was a hallucination?"

"Oh, no. That's the moral of my story. She stood on her front seat, half her body out of the sunroof, thinking she was in her moment of redemption and would be raised unto Heaven. But the truck was loaded with inflatable dummies, going to a rich landlord's birthday party. Since the dummies were full of helium, when the truck crashed, all the ropes gave way and the dummies floated up, like balloons."

"And your friend?"

"She forgot to brake her car. She smashed into the back of the truck and was decapitated."

"I have hope for you yet, Anthony," Micah said reluctantly as Galliano released his hand. "Perhaps another day. Good-bye."

From a window, Tamár and Galliano watched his chauffeured car pull out of the garage and move on down the street. Galliano lit a thin cigarillo, moved his upper lip back and forth across the lower lip, rolling the cigarillo as he smoked. He wrapped his hand around one of her wrists and suddenly squeezed so tightly she gasped in pain. And in that moment, she realized with *real* fear that she no longer controlled him.

"That was . . . messy. The thing on Campbell Avenue."

"We've got to close it all down," Galliano said.

"The Prejean girl was in custody. We couldn't get her away from them legally. Left us no alternative."

"Still . . . it was messy."

"Necessity is often untidy. But they missed that other woman."

"Who is she?"

"We're looking at a computer security firm. Aquitek. I can't find it listed anywhere in Tucson, so we're checking Phoenix. Another necessity." Tamár smiled, patted Galliano on the cheek. "You're such a dignified gentleman, Antonio."

"Anthony."

"Dignified. Calm. Efficient. Brutal."

"The whole chain of custody will have to be eliminated."

"And Father Micah?" Tamár asked. "Does he have to be one of them?"

"Rapturized."

"He might see it that way when it happens. How *will* it happen?"

"I'm not sure, yet. There are two others I'll have to deal with first. How do you want to handle the girls at the camp?"

"We'll bring them here one at a time. I've already made

arrangements on the Circuit, they've all been assigned. So they will stay here overnight and then fly to whatever city they're assigned."

"That anthropologist that I saw on the news." Tamár crossed her legs, quickly uncrossed them. "Sorting the bones. Should we deal with him?"

"They'd just realize the bones were even more important, and bring in experts from all over the country. No. The anthropologist is nothing."

"And the bones?"

"Our only real problem," Galliano said. "I doubt seriously that they can easily be identified. Perhaps not at all, but that won't keep the crime scene forensic people away."

"Here is the list of the others," Tamár said nervously.

He crumpled the paper in his hand without even looking at it.

"Don't you even want to check the names on that list?"

"There's one final thing. The information circuit. We may not have any more use for it, but I've taken care of the man at the prison. I need to find this computer firm. They may have access to all the data transformed over from the prison. If they do have it, we need . . . how shall I put it?"

"Another . . . rapturization?"

"Are you frightened?" he said.

"How frightened should I be?"

"A lot more than usual."

"You're hurting me, Antonio. And you're really starting to scare me."

"Don't play with words like that," he said. "Frightened. Scared. You'll get used to saying those kinds of stupid things, you'll say them to the wrong person someday. You've moved young girls around this country without much thought about what will happen to them in another ten years. AIDS. Beatings. All kinds of abuse, once they're no longer beautiful enough for the Circuit and drop down through the next levels of selling their bodies."

He let go of her wrist when she nodded. She rubbed the white marks of his fingers, massaging her wrist, cocking her head as a new understanding came to her.

"You'll be leaving me soon."

It wasn't a question.

"Soon," he said.

"When?"

"When the chain of custody is all . . . rapturized."

"Anthony the gentle brute. You have such metaphors for murder."

"In this country, 'murder' is a police term. A legal term. Nothing more. Without being able to establish chain of custody, there are no problems."

"But you're not a policeman in this country."

"How far can I trust you?" he said.

"Trust me," she said. "But when your murder list grows every day, I can't help but be frightened that you'll add one more name at the bottom. Mine."

"Only if you're arrested," he said casually.

Staggered, she rubbed sweat from her forehead with the back of a hand.

"I'd never tell anybody about you, Antonio."

He dropped the cigarillo butt onto her Chinese carpet. She automatically stooped to pick it up, but he put a shoe on top of her hand and pressed down.

"In *my* country, when the *policía* arrest you, nobody makes a deal with judges or lawyers. If you even smell guilty, the *policía* let you free, send you outside with protection, and young boys assassinate you on busy street corners."

"Is that a threat?"

He ignored her, studying a small brown stain on his silk shirt.

"And your young boys? Are they also on the list?"

"In this country, they're too young to be afraid," Galliano said. "They kill without any real understanding that it's a terrible thing to take someone's life. If I told them that everybody had death coming, they simply wouldn't understand me. Back in Medellín, I'd be wary of them. They'd kill for me, but given the right incentives, they wouldn't hesitate killing me also."

He removed his jacket, stripped the shirt off, and threw it on the floor, shrugging back into the jacket.

"Your green tea," he said. "It leaves stains."

"I'll have it cleaned."

"Just burn it," he said, and left the room.

laura

21

Aquitek's offices occupied the top three floors of the newest building in Scottsdale. A prime and expensive location, situated between two hotels and only a few blocks from the center of Scottsdale. Faced with pale lavender sandstone in the atrium area, the building's exterior was pretty much fifteen stories of tinted, mirrored glass. Six stories up, the building's size jogged inward floor by floor, so that Don's floors were roughly two-thirds the size of the bottom of the building.

The lobby, seemingly open and accessible because of all the glass windows, in fact could only be entered by one door. An armed security man stood inside and studied Brittles's ID before unlocking the door to let us in, immediately locking it behind us. He took us to the central security desk, a horseshoe-shaped configuration about waist-high, with dozens of small security screens showing views of the entire building. He made a short phone call, nodded, pointed behind him.

The elevator bank had two lifts to most of the floors, and a special elevator to the top. Brittles keycarded an expensive device next to this elevator door, then bent over to peer into it for a retina scan. The doors slid back and we rode directly up, the doors opening into a small lobby with a single door, again protected by a keycard and retina scanner, which let us into a sally port area with yet a third security combination, a punch-code device and a palm scanner.

Don sat waiting just inside. Typically, he didn't even say hello, as though he'd just seen you an hour before. Yet another elevator door stood open and we went up two floors and followed Don into a conference room, where three men rose from their chairs. Two I didn't recognize, but I was surprised to see Justin Wong, who came to hug me, standing sideways during the hug and clapping me on the back, one of those nongenital-contact things, or maybe even his martial arts training to have one side free in case he needed to move suddenly. His right arm was slightly withered, hanging at an odd angle from his shoulder.

"You okay?" I said, pointing at the shoulder.

"Still frosty."

"Nathan, Laura," Don said. "This is Michael Briggs. FBI, Phoenix office. That's Louie Youker. He keeps all the noncomputer gadgets working around here, but he's also learning a lot about computer hardware. And Justin Wong is in charge of all my security."

Nobody shook hands. Don gathered us around the conference table, punched some buttons on an LCD panel. The window blinds glided shut and a projection screen lit up with an image, rapidly scrolling data, nothing I could recognize. I looked around the table.

Youker settled somewhat uncomfortably in his chair, obviously not a man used to spending much time at a desk. An unlit cigar clamped between his teeth. Barrel-chested, with a slight belly and an expensive haircut obviously dyed with a color so black it gleamed with a dark purplish sheen. Wearing a blue cotton short-sleeved Polo shirt and pressed khaki Dockers, two gold chains hung around his neck, a cross on one, an Italian pepper on the other. He said nothing, sat patiently, waiting to contribute if asked, but not actively involved in discussions where he had nothing to contribute. Youker looked like somebody who dealt with hardware effortlessly, without much thought although his knowledge was encyclopedic.

Briggs was old, really old. Hands and head dotted with liver spots, his neatly combed hair very sparse and in some places just individual strands. But he waited with courtly patience until I was seated, standing ramrod-straight, still several inches taller than six feet, with a very brushy mustache that made him look at least ten years younger.

"You young farts," he said, sitting down. "You probably never really wonder how things will be when you get near my age. Your technology will have changed as much as your friendships, with most of who and what you once knew dead and buried. You'll learn, like me, to just keep going. You can't look back, because you'll realize that what the newer group of young people call the future doesn't have any place in it for you except as a memory. Like the first personal computer with no hard drive. And that was barely twenty years ago. You've got to have that will to keep going, you've got to tell your primary care doctor that if he sees you've lost that will, lost that spirit, especially if you've lost all your humor, that doctor has instructions to put something in your veins right then and send you off for cremation."

"You're a long way from that," Don said.

"I am. Indeed, I am. But it's a goddam nuisance to think that when you get up each morning you take a moment to realize that, yeah, you're still here."

Don spent half an hour summarizing every detail of what we knew. It wasn't much, and he called up three PowerPoint screens in succession.

KNOWN

Bones of possibly more than twenty people found in Coolidge
Credit card scam run from Florence 800 # call center
Theresa Prejean and US Marshal assassinated in Tucson
Laura Winslow assassination attempt fails
William Marriott murdered, helped install call center
computers

"Five facts. Five independent bits of data. We *assume* they're connected, we just don't know *how* they're connected. We can also assume the following."

CONJECTURED

Bones tentatively identified as female
Prejean is connected to Winslow because of bikers
Call center data sent by wi-fi outside prison

"You'd better explain that wi-fi thing," Youker said.

"Institute of Electrical and Electronics Engineers started work on wireless networks back in the early 1980s," Don said. "Sneaker-net was a bore, taking a floppy disk from one computer, carrying it to another. So IEEE set a standard, 802.11b, officially adopted in 1999 when Apple Computer built it into some of its machines and called it AirPort 802.11b. Some marketing guy, maybe Steve Jobs himself, started calling it wi-fi, for wireless fidelity."

"This guy reminds me of Hugh Downs," Youker said to the rest of us. "Old-time TV announcer. If you asked him the time, he'd tell you how to build a clock."

"Okay," Don said. "So here are the major questions we have to answer."

UNKNOWN

Who are the victims, where did the bones come from?
Who are the bikers, where did they come from?
Why is Winslow targeted?
Is Brittles also targeted?
What's the common link between all of the above?

"Focus on that last item," Don said. "There are absolutely no reasonable ideas why all the listed events are connected. I don't want to even spend much time conjecturing."

He switched the screen back to the scrolling numbers.

"I'm crunching the entire call center database from the

last six months. Hundreds of calls, thousands if you count the ones that didn't result in orders. Once I get it all crunched, I can process and sort it a dozen ways from Tuesday, looking for any kind of pattern. Right now, I want to start at the prison. Data was being transferred outside the prison by a wireless network. We have no idea, yet, where the signals were going."

"We're getting around to me," Briggs said.

"We appreciate the courtesy of your being here," Don said. "We've worked together before, so you know the drill. Any problems with what I want to do?"

Taking time to consider the question, Briggs shot his cuffs, straightened his tie, aligned the American flag pin in his lapel. Up to this point, other than beyond the introductions, he'd listened carefully without saying a word, taking no notes, written or with a tape recorder, his concentration intensely focused on whoever spoke.

"Okay," he said finally. "I can't authorize any federal personnel or equipment for this electronic search. But as I understand this wireless thing, when you set up a wireless network, you broadcast a signal. You create an electronic node that's accessible to anybody nearby. Am I right?"

"Yup," Don said.

"Our computer security people back in DC tell me that with these broadcasts, no laws are being broken. Am I right? Anybody can legally tap into an open node?"

"Yes," I said.

"So anybody can use anybody else's Internet connection, if you're close enough to the active node?"

"Yes."

"How far away can you be?" Briggs asked.

"It was originally set up just for use in a house or an office building. Some colleges these days have set up wireless networks on the entire campus. I think a few cities are doing the same, mostly in the San Francisco area. Berkeley. Santa Cruz, farther down the coast."

"How far away can you be?" he patiently asked again.

"Probably no more than three hundred yards," I said.

"So your theory is that the database info from the prison call center is going somewhere outside the prison walls?"

"It's not a theory," Youker said. "My men have isolated a small portion of the motherboard in the sample computer Laura brought back from the work center. It's been altered to include wireless transmission."

Briggs laid circuit diagrams on the table, took a ballpoint pen in both hands, and traced out a circuit for us with both hands moving from the sides into the center to indicate a specific area of the diagram. He set the motherboard on the table, used the pen to point to some circuit board components.

"If the data is going out, it doesn't matter if it's from one computer or twenty. We need to find where it's being received. Justice says it's a go for you. We have no authority to interfere. Depending on what you find, we may have jurisdiction. I reserve that option. To step in if we so decide a federal crime is being committed. Now I've got to leave. Anything else?"

"Thanks," Don said. "We'll let you know anything new."

Briggs left. Once the elevator doors closed on him, Don took out a thick folder and spread it open on the table.

"Just as well he doesn't know everything. I've been digging into financial records of the Rapture Warriors Camp. Can't find any traces of a corporation with that name in Arizona records. Has to be some other state. Given the structure of cash flow for the camp, the corporation may even be established offshore."

"What now?" Brittles asked.

"These financial records, including the bank accounts we know about, show that a Tucson woman, Tamár Gordon, was the rainmaker. Anything needed at the camp, Tamár paid for by check. Somebody named Anthony Galliano also has power to write checks. I'm trying to find out now who he is. All finances legal enough to survive both state and federal audits. Micah Posada drew a salary, paid by Tamár. Posada paid all expenses at the camp, including staff salaries and equipment purchases. At the bank, all deposits from the camp were by check. Other cash deposits, some from people who sponsored kids there, but no ability to trace the source of a lot of cash."

"What now?" Brittles asked again. "I don't see how you make any sense of this."

"That's the trick," Don said. "Some of it will *never* make sense. All we can do is try to eliminate the false hopes, which we can only do by checking out everything. Frustrating, if you get impatient, if you try to play a hunch without the data to support hunches. At some point, we'll know we're on the right track. But right now, just out of the gate, it's foolish to make any predictions or play hunches."

"I said I couldn't find any traces of a corporation," Youker said. "But I'm sure I know what to look for. The problem is time. There are so many offshore banks in different parts of the world."

"Or maybe," I said, "it's a corporation in name only. I've been looking in the wrong place. I'll bet the ranch that it's referenced in Arizona DBA files."

Brittles said he had to go to the bathroom, and Wong followed. Youker stood up, impatient to leave the room, and Don waved him away.

22

Don asked me again to summarize anything I'd seen at the prison or in the town of Florence, but nothing yet seemed relevant. A blown-up grid map of Florence's streets and roads hung on one wall, a red marker pen ready to make crosses marking locations of wi-fi nodes.

"Gotta take a break," Don said. "Come on."

Wheeling into his office, he started to brew up another pot of his Arabian mocha triple-roast coffee. I stood outside the glassed wall of his office, watching him carefully measure and grind beans, adjust the temperature of his espresso maker, a headset running down to three different cell phones. He'd click from one to another, using a small switch in the mike cord, the cells rigged to take voice commands. Seeing me, he waved me into the office.

"Close the door," he said. "Take a break with an old friend."

"I'm too scared to relax."

"Keep me posted every ten minutes," he said into his stalk mike. "Whether you find anything or not."

He turned off the cell connection, removed the headset.

"Coffee?"

"Got any Mountain Dew?"

"In that small fridge."

I took out a one-liter plastic bottle, cracked the screwtop, drank deeply.

"Yikes," Don said, settling into the leather backing of his wheelchair, which popped and crackled. "Gotta get this upholstered. Okay. We're in a holding pattern."

He studied a single sheet of paper, crumpled it, smoothed it out, and tore off some tiny strips, wadding each strip into a jagged pellet, setting them on the edge of his desk, aimed at his wastebasket to flick each pellet six feet away.

"Got any ideas?" he said.

"Titanium Powerbook. Node sniffers that will show any open wi-fi nodes."

"Already got that covered, Laura. Trust me. I've got three different people on scene with computers, already checking for nodes. One of them thinks there's a pattern to the south. But nothing specific yet. Florence is a bigger area than it looks once you start dealing with just a three-hundred-yard radius."

He flicked the last pellet, missing the wastebasket by several feet. Rolled his chair back and forth a few inches, hands on the rubber rims, thinking.

"Just so it's clear," I said, "I'm not participating. I've done my part of the deal. There are too many dead people connected here. I just want my daughter, and nothing else."

"What's up with you and Nathan?"

"Nothing."

"What happened to that nice guy I met at your place a few days ago?"

"Rich?" I said, bursting into tears again, good Christ, crying *again*.

"He seemed kind of a control freak."

"Stay out of my personal life, Don."

"I said that wrong. He seems pretty much focused on the long ago. Dead bones, ancient artifacts. Nathan is focused on long ago, but he deals with that by working hard to live in the here and now."

"Don, fuck your psychobabble."

"You know me. I say whatever's on my mind."

He handed me one of the cells he'd been using.

"Okay. Take this cell. Keep it on. Here's an extra charged battery. Here's two. I figure it'll be an hour, maybe two before I get complete reports from my crews in Florence. So, right now, why don't you and Nathan go somewhere? Soon as I hear something, I'll give you specific directions to the nodes."

"Okay with me," Brittles said from the doorway.

Don let us find the elevator by ourselves. When we got off two floors below, one of the coded doors was open, Wong waiting for us.

"Let me show you what I've got," he said to Brittles. "Just so you know in case you need equipment of any kind."

Going through yet another sally port, complete with even more elaborate coding devices, Wong opened the inside door to a small corridor ending in a steel-plated wall with a huge vault door standing open.

"Fort Knox vault door," Wong said, spinning the five-spoke wheel just below the combination dial. "Executive Model 8240. Weighs six tons, with twenty-four locking bolts. Modular interior, set with shelves and racks. Electronic snooper stuff on the left, armament on the right, ammo in the center drawers. Anything you want to start a small war, I've got it here."

Brittles looked over a rack of assault weapons.

"AK-47. M-16. AR-15. Take your choice, if you want one. Two dozen different handguns ranging from .22-caliber to .45."

"I used this piece when I was in the Shadow Wolves," Brittles said, taking down an elaborate weapon with a long barrel and a short, squat shoulder stock.

"You were in Shadow Wolves? Cool, man. When this exercise is over, you gotta tell me about that. I hear it's an elite unit, all Indians. Part of US Customs, or the Border Patrol, whatever. I've been in all kinds of elite units. I was a LURP, in Nam. Used older sniper rifles, but the principles are the same. You in Nam, man?"

"Yeah."

Brittles held the weapon carefully.

"M600 Special Light Anti-Matériel Rifle," Wong said, as though he were quoting from a gun manual. "Put one of these in the hands of a super marksman, you've got a .50-caliber single-shot system capable of delivering exceptionally accurate fire on targets in excess of fifteen hundred yards. I've personally sighted this one in for twelve hundred yards. I can light a kitchen match at that distance."

"Night vision optics?"

"Raptor NightVision. Barrel length from the factory is twenty-eight inches. I added another three inches, rebalanced the weapon to give me another five hundred yards for an extreme shot."

"Whatever happened to Kyle Callaghan?" I asked.

"He's in South America. I always thought . . . you two . . ."

"Nathan." I tugged at his sleeve. "Let's go."

"Right." He handed the rifle back to Wong. "We ever need to shoot somebody at two thousand yards, we'll give you a call."

"No problem. Good to see you again, Laura. Sorry I mentioned Kyle."

"Who's Kyle?" Brittles asked.

"Just somebody we once knew," I said. "C'mon, let's go."

"What was *that* all about?" Brittles asked when we got onto the street.

"I worked with Wong earlier this year. Wong was part of a kidnap rescue team, headed by a guy from New Zealand. Kyle Callaghan. A sweet man, with a very sweet daughter. During the final rescue assault, Wong took two bullets in his arm and shoulder. I'd not heard from him until today."

"So. What now?" Brittles asked.

"I'm a wreck, Nathan. Part of me doesn't want to do anything. Part of me wants to do *every*thing if it helps get my daughter back."

"So I want you to hang with me," he said finally. "Where I go, you go. That's the only way I'm going to know that you're safe. Come on. It's getting dark. I've still got those extra bedrooms. You just go in there, I won't bother you at all."

23

"That's Hopi pottery," I said, pointing to an old brownish pot on a bookshelf, with faded lightning bolts and frogs painted on the sides. "Do you know who made it?"

"I was over on First Mesa once," he said. "Went to meet a guy who might have been taking some of my father's sheep. Or maybe not. But the guy wasn't there, or he didn't want to talk to me. His kid came out. I had this wool cap. You know, the kind that pulls down over your head, over your ears if you want. The kid eyed the cap, so I gave it to him. He looked around that old stone house, wanting to give me a young eagle feather. But he couldn't find it, so he gave me this beautiful Hopi pot. Some months later, when I was seeing a woman who worked as a curator at the museum in Flagstaff, she told me it was a rare fifteenth century pot."

I picked up his TV remote, punched some buttons, but only got on-screen messages for different video inputs. Several channels had flickering pictures, the sound very buzzy and the video streaked by interference.

"How do I get the news?" I said. "How do I switch to your antenna?"

"You can't."

"Nobody has a TV that doesn't get the news."

"I'm not hooked up to an antenna," he said. "Or cable. Or dish. I just watch movies. When I'm here, I don't want to be bothered with news or any other junk on those five hundred cable channels."

"No live TV," I said to myself in wonder, since I was the only other person I knew at that time who didn't get live TV.

"The spare bedrooms are along the hallway. Pick either one, settle in. I'm going out to strip down the engine on my '31 Henderson."

Later, as I sat at the window and watched the sunset, Brittles emerged from inside the workshop. Standing in the doorway, backlit by a dull yellow glow from some lamps. He leaned sideways, flicked a switch, and the lights went out. I watched his shadow move across the caliche drive, headed toward the house. He went directly into the kitchen, and I watched in silence as he took off his wristwatch and the silver bracelet on his left arm.

Removing his work clothes, folding them carefully as though they were dress clothes, he laid them out neatly on top of a wicker laundry basket. He seemed unfazed by his nakedness in front of me, but didn't even look in my direction.

Filling the sink basin with cold water, he stuck his face underwater and used his hands to thoroughly wet his hair. Finding the bar of soap, he raised his head, splashed water on his arms and chest, and lathered himself from his chest to the top of his head. He rinsed his head in the sink, let the water out, turned on the cold water faucet, and carefully removed all the soap from his body before toweling himself dry. He wrapped the towel around his waist and went to his bedroom for clean clothes.

Returning, he stood in shadow, staring out the living room window, his face hidden from me. But I found enormous assurance in the way he stood erect, working out some inner problem. Watching him, not even seeing his face, I understood the complexity of my conflicted attraction to him. He turned, his face dimly lit by the reflected light from the bedside lamp. A slow smile blossomed on his face, but he said nothing. There was nothing he *needed* to say to me. I went to him and he folded me in his arms, turning both of us back to the window.

"Sorry about no news channel," he said.

"Sometimes I wish my life was like video on demand. Hit Pause if something ugly happens. Hit Rewind if I think I can edit the tape."

"Hey, let's try this. If your life was movie theme music, what would it be?"

"That's a stupid Baba Wawa question," I snorted.

"I've got a lot of that kind of music in my head."

"So? What is *your* theme?"

"*Lawrence of Arabia*. No. *Once Upon a Time in the West*. Listen to this." He threw his head back like a wolf. "Wah *wah* wah. If you know the movie, you know the sound track. And this."

He whistled another part of the theme music.

"So let me ask you one," he said. "What music would you choose for this very specific moment?"

"I can't handle this, Nathan. You're coming on to me,

and . . . and . . . I feel so like a wimp, for being so scared."

"I've got your back, Laura," he said. "That's all you need to know."

My cell rang. I held it between our ears.

"I just wheeled into the data center," Don shouted. I could hear at least three different voices in the background and several sets of hands dancing on keyboards. "We've located some wi-fi nodes in Florence. Nathan, I think you'd better go up there, since you've got federal authority as a U.S. Marshal. My man will meet you at the L&B Mexican Restaurant."

revelations

"Abbe. Are you one of us?" the Chinese girl said.

"Us?" Spider said, thinking she was completely alone. Also thinking that she wasn't so quick anymore in responding to the name Abbe.

"The Rapture girls."

"Uh . . ." Spider edged away, not wanting any religion. "Jesus and all?"

"No, silly." She giggled, one hand over her mouth. "One of the girls. You know, the Rapture girls."

Spider thought carefully for several minutes, the Chinese girl content to look beyond the low-planked fencing, across the road to a field ripe with thick bolls of Pima cotton.

"I *think* so," Spider said finally. "But I'm, like, so new here. Nobody's really said anything to me except to tell me where to sleep, where the bathrooms are, what the rules are, plus all that Jesus Raptures stuff I can't quite relate to."

"Ahhh," the Chinese girl said. "I am Jennifer Mao."

"Abbe Dominguez."

"Welcome," Jennifer said, embracing Spider.

"I guess," Spider said, wondering where the conversation was going. "So, like, how do I find out about, what did you call them? The Rapture girls? If it's some prayer meeting group, or bible study, I'm not much interested."

"Bible study." Jennifer giggled again. "In a way. We are told about the Circuit book, but until we leave here we don't see it."

"Oh, yeah," Spider said, "the Circuit book. I've heard about it."

"And where are you from?"

"All over."

"Where did you get that beautiful hair color?"

Spider brushed her hand across the top of her head, surprised for a moment to find it so short, cropped almost against her scalp on the sides and the back of her neck. Brittles had run her through the hair salon so fast that Spider hardly knew what happened after her shoulder-length dark brown hair lay on the floor, expertly scissored off.

"I changed it. Before I came here. I wanted to be a different person, inside here. I thought, like, you know, I look different, maybe I can *be* different."

"Shut *up,*" Jennifer said, lightly punching Spider's shoulder. "That's too awesome that you'd think that. Did you know people on the Circuit, did you know that blondes have special status in some of the houses?"

"So where's your dorm?" Spider asked.

"Dormitory! Shut *up,* girl. Rapture girls have their own private rooms. This would be the sweetest tricks you ever turned." "One man a night. You just make him feel special. Sometimes, you'll turn him on so much, you'll get the same man for several days, a week, even a month's travel somewhere exotic. Paris, I've been to Paris twice. Geneva, Rio, Amsterdam, Saint Barthes, especially Saint Barthes around the end of the year, when the filthy rich sail their yachts into the harbors and party twenty-four seven. And sometimes, if it's negotiated right, one of these men will buy you from Tamár or one of the other Circuit managers."

"Buy me?"

"Money's nothing to them. Used to be a twenty-thousand-dollar buyout. I figure it's gone up five or ten thousand in the past year. Then you belong to him."

"I don't understand," Spider said. "I've got a criminal record. Lots of these girls must have records. So I guess that lets me out."

"No way. They give you a whole new identity. Credit cards, driver's license, Social Security number. Of course, you've got to take a new name. And usually you don't have any say what name you get."

"Who arranges that?"

Jennifer cut her eyes sharply, realizing she'd already said too much. She fiddled with the sleeves of her tee shirt, rolling them up and underneath her bra straps.

"You'll find out," she said finally. "If you're chosen, you'll get it all."

"How do I get chosen?"

"Just be a good girl." She smiled. "Good things come to good girls."

"Jennifer, yo."

Two adolescent Hispanic boys came across the yard.

"Oops," Jennifer whispered to Spider. "Don't tell them anything I've said."

"Okay."

"See you later, Abbe."

"Jennifer," one of the boys said. "You're wanted."

Jennifer left, no giggles this time, almost backing away to avoid the boys before turning to run into the main complex.

"I'm El Ratón," the taller boy said. "What's the haps, girl?"

El Ratón's hair was buzz cut all around except at the bottom of his neck, where a half ponytail dangled. *Mullet cut,* Spider thought. *Michael Craven told me that's a mullet cut. Not quite a ponytail, not quite trailer-trash-biker-prison cut.*

"Nothing much," Spider said, readjusting her awareness of being careful, the boys standing one in front of her and the other in back. She turned sideways so she could see them both, but they also moved, perhaps boxing her in, perhaps just being adolescent boys. "*Quien sabe.*"

"*Bueno,*" said the shorter boy. "*Yo habla Español?*"

"I *habla* with my friends," she said.

"We want to be your *amigos,*" El Raton said.

"Hey, you a regular *lenguilargo,*" the other boy said.

"No," Spider said quietly. "I'm so *not* a tongue-wagger. Especially with kids like you. See you later."

She started to walk boldly away, but the two got in front of her. She moved sideways, but they circled with her.

"Okay," she said with contempt. "You can do the chicken dance. What now? Just tell me what you want. My money? I turned it all in. My jewelry, my wristwatch? I turned that in, too."

"Chicken dance. Oh, *amiga,* check this out."

El Ratón began clucking wildly, fists on his hips, elbows extended and flapping as he picked up one leg and stomped in an exaggerated gesture.

"He's some little mouse," Spider said to the shorter boy. "I can see why he calls himself El Ratón. And who are you?"

He slowly pulled a color xerox from his back jeans pocket, unfolding it in front of Spider's eyes. She held her breath for one scary moment, but knew enough of role playing to keep in character. The xerox was a copy of the photograph of her and Jonathan, the same photograph that Laura had shown her at Perryville. She reached for the paper, took it from the boy's hands, looked it over dismissively.

"Around the eyes. Maybe. But I never have long hair."

"There are people who cut off hair."

"Never, ever wear hoop earrings. Not those big ones, those are black girl earrings. J Lo earrings."

"You've got the holes here, *amiga.*"

He touched both of her earlobes.

"Studs. Took them all out before I came here. Diamond

studs. One and a half carats, both sides. In the left ear, I also had a ruby and a fire opal."

"Where'd you get such fine things?" El Ratón asked. "Cluck, cluck, the chicken wants to know. Luis wants to know, don't you, Luis?"

But Luis was carefully studying Spider's face, cutting his eyes from her face to the photograph. He finally folded the paper and stuck it back in his pocket.

"So. Can I go now?"

"Sure," Luis said.

"As soon as you apologize for dissing me, I'm on my way."

"Dissing you?" El Ratón said with a wide grin. "You don't like chickens?"

"Not you, mouse. Luis, why'd you front me like that? Why are you checking me out? Pretending I'm somebody else."

"We check out all the new people," Luis said.

"So you made a mistake."

"Maybe," he said.

A bell rang over the sound system, a heavy clang like a cook beating a dinner triangle. Luis took hold of both of Spider's hands, turned them over, rubbed her palms and fingertips.

"You gonna pick some cotton now, girl. Better wear gloves. Don't ruin those pretty white hands. You are a white woman, aren't you?"

"My father was from Medellín," she said, a calculated guess.

"Hey, Luis—"

"Shut up, dude," Luis said to El Ratón.

"That's where you boys are from, right?" Spider said.

"Maybe."

"Somewhere down there. Some country where they let young punks be *sicarios*. They do all the things that grown men avoid, because the young punks rarely get prison time for things like drugs and murder of *bazuqueros*."

Luis looked at her with eyelids half shut, nodding slowly.

"Maybe I'm wrong about you. You're a beautiful thing, *amiga*. You ever been a working girl?"

Ahhhh, Spider thought. That's *what the Rapture girls do.*

"I never had any use for a pimp," she said. "Especially a snot-nosed young punk like you."

"I'm no pimp," Luis said. "How old are you?"

Spider had a brief moment of panic. Her fake ID showed her a few years younger, but she couldn't remember if she was twenty or still a teenager.

"Old enough to turn two or three thousand a night," she finally said.

The bell clanged again and people started gathering around some wide-body staked trucks, piling empty sacks in the back.

"All *right,*" Luis said. "Now we gotta pick dat cotton."

"Tote dat bale," El Ratón said. "And all the nigger jive field hand stuff."

laura

24

I located the first node in a small complex of single-story stucco homes, arranged in a cul-de-sac on a dead-end street. All of the houses gleamed with new white paint, the intense glare so painful I put on my sunglasses. Tired, so tired, I wanted to let the sun heat my face, lay my head back, and sleep. Brittles nudged me as my head bobbled, offered to pour me more coffee from the thermos.

"Nobody there," he said. "Nothing inside at all. House has been totally emptied. Everything. Right down to the kitchen cupboards."

"No computers?"

"Nothing."

"Okay. See that thing on the roof that looks like a big coffee can?"

"Yeah."

"Well, it probably *is* a coffee can. I've heard that some people have experimented with extending wireless range with homemade antennas like that. So we're going to have to follow the coffee cans until we find the end of the line."

I studied the red X marks on my street map of Florence, gave Brittles directions as we drove slowly out of town. We followed the coffee can wi-fi antennas along State Road 287, moving steadily west to the junction of 87 in Coolidge.

Every few hundred yards the signal would fade, my Mac lap-top losing Internet connection. When this happened, we'd backtrack to the point where connection picked up again, un-til I found another coffee-can antenna high on a power pole.

Eventually, we covered the entire road from Florence to Casa Grande National Monument, where connectivity died out completely. Going back through Coolidge, we turned South on 87, the antennas hard to spot in the town, but luck-ily nobody in the small town used a wi-fi connection node in their homes so we drove steadily into Randolph, a smaller town less prosperous than Coolidge. South of Randolph I lost connectivity again.

Directing Brittles back into Coolidge, I steered him from one street to another, the signal getting stronger the farther we got off the main streets. Somewhere between LaPalma and Eleven Mile Corner Road, I knew we were close.

Tracking coffee cans on an empty highway was easy, but once inside Coolidge I asked Brittles to pull over to a curb-side parking slot and got out a detailed street map. "Follow those power lines," I said, scrabbling through the glove box to find a purple marker pen. "I'll mark off every street as we check it."

We crisscrossed a grid pattern of the main streets south of Casa Grande Monument, ending up on an old street, asphalt cracking and humped from years of no maintenance, the white and yellow traffic lines faded from decades of sunlight. Telephone and power poles tilted with the cracked sidewalk, so that power lines sagged between some poles and were stretched taut between others.

"Look," he said, pointing above an old Laundromat next to a tiny bodega.

From there, the rest was easy. What we found, I still don't like to remember.

25

Brittles turned onto an unpaved, unnamed street, more a dirt road with old transient laborer shacks on either side, finally dead-ending at a trash heap at the edge of the desert, with nothing ahead of us but weeds, bunchgrass, creosote bushes, and a few agaves. Turning the car around, I saw three single-story wood houses.

"One of them," I said.

Smashed windows in the first house, half the roof missing from the second. But newspapers covered the single front window of the third. Brittles moved the car a few feet so we looked at a corner, saw one side of the house with two more windows covered with newspapers.

Brittles drove a block away and parked in front of a house that had far better care taken with house and lawn than anything else in the neighborhood. Bougainvillea flowing from the roof in front, the left and right sides of the house separated from neighboring lots by huge rows of red hibiscus. The lawn area was groomed and raked like a Japanese Zen garden, rocks and cacti placed in random locations.

As we walked up to the front door, I could hear an old air conditioner clanking from the house next door, the compressor and the fan obviously not taken care of for a long time. I heard a stereo playing somewhere. We rang the doorbell. An elderly black woman opened the door, her face set in both suspicion and resolve. A can of diet Coke in her left hand, an aluminum baseball bat trailing from her right hand, the bat resting on her polished oak floor. Music swelled from inside her house. The Ink Spots, I thought, or maybe some sixties smooth doo-wop group with that Detroit Motown sound.

She waited, silent. Brittles immediately showed his ID card.

"If you could just spare us a few minutes," he said.

She studied his ID carefully, asked for his driver's license, then leaned the bat against the doorframe. Brittles asked about the house at the end of the block.

She snorted with disgust.

"Everybody else on this block is just trash. Redneck and nigger trash, all of them. I'd move on out of here if I could sell my house. What chance you think I'd have of selling?"

"Not much," I said, looking at the debris in the street.

"You got that right, honey. Down at the end there, at that dead end, that's where people just dump their trash. We got no regular garbage pickup here for free. Nobody's gonna pay for trash, they just run it down the block and pitch it out."

"Do you know the man who lives in that end house?" Brittles asked.

"Honey, knowing him's bout the bottomest thing on my mind. Was a depitty sheriff once, I think. I don't refreshify my memory so good anymore. But he's redneck trash. A Mexican trash friend comes around now and again, I think."

"Thank you," Brittles said.

"You're a right good looking couple," she said. I blushed. "And you folks got money, too. I can see it in your clothes. I can see it in your haircut, young man. See it in your car. Wish I had a car. I'd drive back to Alabama. If I knew how to drive."

"Thanks," Brittles said, trying to lead me away.

"You good looking young people with money, you ever stop to think what it'd be like you *wasn't* so good looking? You didn't have that car, that money? You ever think what it's like to be a loser, like me, surrounded by redneck and nigger trash that are even worse losers than I am?"

We started to the car, but she followed us, held the door for me, looked around inside the car.

"My Elmer, he had a Buick. Bought it second hand from a jeweler, down in El Paso when Elmer was working the railroad. We had money then, some money, enough money to rent a two bedroom bungalow. I grew chile peppers, vegetables, some flowers, we saved money from that so Elmer could buy that Buick. But being black in Texas, folks always looked down on us like we was just plain ugly losers that oughta get out of the neighborhood. We weren't ugly losers inside, but they beat that pride out of us, too."

Back at the end of the street, he turned off the engine. The hood and engine block tinked and pinged as they cooled.

"Think anybody's in there?" I asked.

He slid off his grip holster, pulled out the Glock, and racked the slide, leaving the hammer at full cock. Studying the house. We waited half an hour. Nothing moved in the house. Even with the car windows all down, the afternoon sun warmed the car like a fifty-gallon oil drum used for a barbeque. Sweat soaked clear through my blouse to my bra, which started to itch and nettle me when I moved, so I reached inside my blouse and took off the bra.

"How did you do that?" Brittles asked.

"Tell you later," I said. "Why don't you go inside?"

"You stay here."

"I'm getting out of this oven."

Metal creaked as I opened the door, the outside metal so hot it partly blistered my finger and I kicked the door shut while sucking on the finger. Brittles raised his Glock in the Weaver stance, turning slightly sideways, his left palm underneath and supporting the right hand on the grip. Walking slowly, he circled the entire house, disappearing around the back so long that I went to the front door, climbing up some concrete construction blocks used as steps onto a small porch. The glass in the door covered by newspapers, I couldn't see anything inside. I tried the door handle. Locked. I knocked and heard nothing.

"Get back in the car," Brittles said, coming around to the front of the house.

"Why?"

His Glock stuck in his belt, he wiped sweat off his fore-head.

"Just go back there, okay?"

"Is this the place?"

"Oh, yeah," he said shortly, wearily.

"Is the back door open?"

He waved me toward the car, went around to the rear of the house. I followed a few steps behind and he didn't notice me until we got to the rear door. The nearest occupied house was at least two hundred feet away, the back door shielded by three giant mesquite trees that grew along a dry creek bed. A half-rusted hibachi barbeque sat on concrete blocks, two aluminum folding chairs on either side of the hibachi. The green and white webbing on both chairs was frayed and worn so badly that nobody could possibly sit down without falling through. Twenty feet away an ancient Ford pickup bed sat on wooden sawhorses, with nothing left of the rest of the pickup. Wheel rims of all sizes lay around the yard, some with tattered retreads mounted, others bare and dented. Brittles walked over a small rise to the creek bed, where some-body had shoved the frame of the pickup, the engine still mounted, but the cab missing entirely. Hooked to the frame, a long rope went off behind one of the mesquite trees and I got close enough to see the bodies of two rottweilers, their gutted stomachs teaming with flies.

A slight breeze ruffled the mesquite branches, but standing in their shadow I could feel hot air drying the sweat on my shirt. I opened the shirt to below my breasts, grabbed the two sides, and flapped them, trying to get air inside the blouse to dry the sweat, the air roasting me, roasting my head, the inside of my head, as I stared at the rottweilers, and there was no smell, I tell you, they'd been dead awhile, but I was upwind of the bodies, the breeze blowing from me to them, so my only horror was the thick mass of flies and a slow awakening of fear at what might be inside the house.

The breeze picked up, like a late afternoon Santa Ana, like those winds that blow across the Sahara for days and days and drive people mad. *I am* not *mad,* I thought, but I just had to see what was in the house, nothing else made sense to me, in reality, nothing made sense at all except that the breeze dried all my sweat.

Unless I dried off from fear.

The back screen door hung from the bottom hinge. Nothing recent, the closing spring keeping the top of the door dangling. Somebody had smashed the glass window on the top of the rear door, and it stood open. I walked to it, but Brittles stopped me again.

"You don't want to go inside."

But it was hot, you see, I was *so* hot, so scared, so mad and out of my mind about where all of this was going and only wanting things to *stop* so I could get Spider out of prison, so I pushed Brittles's arm aside and went inside the door into a room so small and so dark, windows covered with layers and layers of newspapers. I couldn't see a thing.

"Is there a light?" I said.

"Power's off."

He ripped some of the newspapers from the window and I took a step forward and nearly collapsed with horror as I slipped in a pool of half-dried blood.

Through a doorway I could see a filthy kitchen. There was only one other room in the house except for a small toilet and shower stall partially visible behind another door. A faded, stained sofa was pushed back into a corner, opposite an ancient black and white TV set with rabbit ears wrapped with aluminum foil. The lath and plaster wall between this room and kitchen had been punched with holes, and two men stood side by side, flat against the wall, crucified against the framing studs, bodies sagging, their wrists and ankles across some of the punched-out holes and bound with barbed wire wrapped around the wall studs. Industrial-

strength staples pierced both palms, the hands flat against
the studs. The man on the left was heavy but muscular, his
skin bronzed by the sun and his Indian blood, his face covered with dried blood from a dozen staples in his forehead.
The other man's face was undamaged, but he'd been gutted
like the rottweilers, his blood pooled on the floor where I'd
slipped.

"Jesus God!" I said.

If I'd just not felt that madness, not seen the rottweilers or
felt the breeze, I wouldn't have crossed over that doorsill,
crossed from light into horrible darkness.

That's the defining story of my life.

Knowing what will happen when I cross a border.

Knowing I *have* to cross over, against my will, against all
my past crossings where, once the step was taken from one
second into another, things changed.

Irrevocably.

"Let me see if there's a computer here," I said dumbly.
"Let me just find the computer. Then we leave."

"It's in the other room. I'll get it later. You go back outside."

But I'd never seen anybody crucified. It was like looking
at the rottweilers, except there were no flies in here yet, although now that Brittles had smashed open the rear door
some flies were already buzzing outside.

"Cover the door," I screamed, but he looked at me as
though I were crazy.

I grabbed some of the newspapers he'd ripped off the window, the masking tape still with a bit of stick to it. I first shut
the back door and then covered the broken window with the
newspapers, a single fly buzzing in the room, but *I can stand
just one fly, I can stand anything now,* I thought.

"Who are they?" I said.

"Don't know them well."

"But you know who they are?"

"This one's a deputy sheriff."

He started to unfasten the barbed wire around the man's right wrist, staring so intently at the damaged face and recoiling as he saw the staples through the palm. I thought he'd have noticed that before, but I realized he was streets ahead of me, not focusing on the immediacy of the torture but trying to figure out *why* they'd been so cruelly treated. He turned to the other man.

"This one, I've forgotten his name. A maintenance worker at Casa Grande Monument. I met him two days ago. Met both of them. At the housing development where they found the bones."

I felt dizzy and didn't realize I'd started to faint until Brittles grabbed me under the arms, holding me up against the door, propping me there.

"Go outside," he said.

"Can't move."

"Then lean against the door. Close your eyes. I'm going to get the computer and that other electronic stuff."

But he called out two minutes later.

"You're going to have to come in here and tell me what's worth taking."

"Shouldn't we call the police . . . somebody? Shouldn't we call?"

"I'm the police," he said.

"But we should leave things here, we should *leave everything here and just go away*!"

"We leave this computer, we may never find out what's on it once the Tucson Police Department, or the FBI, or whoever comes in here and takes all the evidence into custody. We've got to take this computer now."

"Okay," I said, stepping around the blood, going into the other room.

A black Dell computer stood on a cheap deal table next to a refrigerator, the monitor stacked beside a printer, keyboard, and mouse blackened with grime, as though an auto mechanic had used it for months. A two-burner portable kerosene stove sat on the floor, the grill covered with grease.

"What have we got here?" Talking to myself, trying to be logical and technical, just shut off the rest of my head. "That's the computer box. Unplug it."

He took a clasp knife from his pocket, opened it, and slashed all the cables.

"Okay. Cutting them is okay. We don't need the cables."

"What else? This?"

"No. That's just a monitor. And that's just a printer. Look for CDs?"

"Music?"

"Same size. But not music. Data."

He raked stacks of paper off the deal table, opened the single drawer, crammed with junk. He turned it upside down to empty everything on the floor. There was a small, unfinished pine bookcase, just three shelves stacked with pornographic videotapes. He swept the top shelf on the floor, left me to pick through the tapes while he cleaned out the second shelf, then the bottom one. Just tapes. He picked up the bookcase, turned it around, and seven CD jewel cases were taped to the back.

"These?" he said.

I nodded and he crammed them into his pockets. Shouldering the Dell computer, he backed out of the kitchen, motioning me with his palm to step where he stepped. When he opened the back door a swarm of flies rushed into the room, filling my hair and the inside of my blouse, driving me truly mad for a moment, and I ran, I ran to the car, stripping off my blouse, brushing off flies, not wanting to swat them, not wanting their bodies stuck to my skin. When Brittles got to the car, I sat shivering in the heat, leaning against the front bumper.

Down the dirt road, an old black man stood on his porch, holding his screen door open with one hand, a twelve-string guitar in the other. Staring at me.

"Get in the car, Laura. Put on your blouse."

"Yes," I said.

Yes, anything.

The black man stood absolutely still as we went past him, except his head swiveled to follow us until he couldn't turn his neck around any farther. He didn't have the will or the energy to bother turning his body until we disappeared.

26

We drove, we drove, we drove. Brittles pulled over at the Tom Mix Memorial, trying to comfort me. Done with crying, I sat motionless, slumped against the door, staring at the half-inch thick steel outline of a cowboy on a bucking bronc, the steel pocked with bullet marks, one of them a hole through and through and probably from somebody who got tired just dinging the metal and went home to load his assault rifle with a full metal jacket slug, hand-loaded with extra powder.

We drove past Catalina into Oro Valley, the outlines of Pusch Ridge dark against the sun. Brittles started working his cell phone, but I couldn't hear anything with my window down, the air whistling by and the steadily increased roar from traffic. Or maybe I just didn't want to hear anything. Brittles turned off Salina at the Tucson Mall, went across to Stone, and pulled into the parking lot of the Five and Diner.

"I'm not hungry," I said.

"Well, I am."

Ahead of us, a family of five pushed open the front door. The mother held a crying baby girl nestled in her right arm, her left hand gently urging the other three children toward the order counter. They all clumped together at the cash register, waiting to be seated. Our waitress motioned them into the left side of the diner, patting each of the children on the head as they passed her, the mother ordering all the meals in Spanish without looking at a menu, finally quieting the shrieking baby by opening her yellow cotton blouse so the baby could suckle.

Brittles steered to the right, way in the back to a red leather booth underneath all kinds of pictures of Marilyn Monroe. A young waitress plopped two menus on our table, got two large plastic glasses full of ice water.

"What you want, hon?" she said to Brittles.

"What's good here?" he said.

"Well, you asking what I like myself?"

"Sure."

"Well, *okay*. All soup is homemade and fresh, absolutely delicious. Especially the clam chowder and the potato-leek. We got a turkey club sandwich with fries, spices or no spices please, a kickass chicken sandwich, onion rings. To drink, dynamite malteds, chocolate or vanilla, or either vanilla diet Coke or cherry Coke. All drinks are fountain-mixed and hand-stirred with lots of syrup."

I opened the thick menu, all burger-and-fries kinds of things, one of which Brittles ordered. I couldn't stand the thought of eating meat and ordered macaroni and cheese.

"You'll like that, hon. We make it ourselves. What to drink?"

"Two large diet Cokes," Brittles said. "No straws."

"Comin' back atcha."

He stared out the window, his mind completely elsewhere, not even noticing the waitress leave the diet Cokes. His cell phone rang. He listened without talking, folded the cell shut.

"You okay?" he said.

"No!" I shouted, and people looked around. I leaned forward, arms on the table, facing him, whispering. "No. I am so *not* fucking okay."

"Yeah."

"That's a stupid thing to say to a person."

"What? What's stupid?"

" 'Are you okay?' "

"It's just a thing," he said.

"A thing."

"You know. In bad times, that's what people say to each other. You okay?"

"It's stupid."

He drank half the diet Coke, rattled the ice, finished off the Coke, and waved the glass at the waitress, who brought him another.

"Okay," he said. "I'm sorry. I should have asked how you were doing."

"Not good. I just want out of this, Nathan. I want to get my daughter pardoned, I want to take her away from all of this."

"We're not done yet."

"*I'm* done," I hissed. "I found out how the credit card stuff got out of the prison, I found where it all went. That's our deal."

"Half the deal."

"The other half is your half. Not mine. I've done my half."

"It's all a piece." He tried to hold my hands and I jerked them away from him and put them on my lap, under the tabletop. "You found out how."

"And where."

"You found out how and where."

"So you do whatever's left."

"Why?" he said. "That's the missing part. Why?"

"I'm not helping you with that part."

"No," he said carefully. "But your daughter will."

"Uh uh. She's outa that place. She's outa there. We're both done."

"Laura, let's get this clear. For now, she's *in* that place. She *stays* in that place until we figure out why that place, that camp, why is it involved."

"Oh, Jesus," I said.

"Laura. You're just not getting the picture at all. I'm thinking of your daughter's safety."

"Don't shit me, Nathan."

I couldn't understand his logic, you see, I couldn't see how staying in that camp made Spider safer than her being released in my custody. But I could also tell that whatever *I* wanted to do, Nathan would reject. He had a plan. I could see it working from one side of his head to another, knew he was figuring how to work it, how to put it into words and so into action.

"I've got no choice in this, do I?"

"Don't do that."

"I'm not doing anything. You won't let me do anything, you won't listen to what I want. What I need."

"I meant, don't trade on our relationship."

"Excuse me?"

"Don't let whatever we have come between me and my job."

" 'Whatever we have,' " I mimicked. "There's another stupid phrase. Something from a Sunday night movie of the week, from people who think they can use clichés and play a lot of fake feel-good piano music in the background."

"Let me tell you what we need to do."

"California Dreaming" came on the sound system. I listened to the entire song without even looking at Nathan. The next song prattled on about having fun in the seasons of the sun, and during the next song, Nathan's cheeseburger and fries arrived, he poured ketchup on the fries, and started eating. At some point I stopped paying attention to him, to the music, the colors and chrome of the fifties interior, the pictures of Marilyn and Elvis and James Dean.

I didn't want to think. I got up to look at the jukebox.

All the songs were fifties and sixties rock and roll. Mostly sixties. The music I grew up with and still love, CDs, the three-inch mini-size, no vinyl 45's like a genuine jukebox. But the style was amazingly accurate. An old-style Wurlitzer, all woody-looking with the colored light tubes going up from the base over the curved top and the air bubbles bubbling up inside them. No doubt available from Wurlitzer by mail order, or from the Neiman Marcus catalog.

I saw the waitress headed to our table with my macaroni and cheese. Delicious. I ate the whole bowl, spreading fresh layers of ground pepper after eating through the previous layer. On the wall, I fiddled with the sixties-style control heads for the main juke, the kind that were typical at every diner during my youth. All chrome and plastic, a rounded top and bulbous front with a large window displaying pages you flipped using the metal dingus things protruding out the slot in the bottom. Songs were listed on small labels that slip into the pages, about twelve labels per page, each label listing one song, the artist, and the button combination to punch to hear it.

At the bottom of the control head, two horizontal rows of square plastic buttons having white faces with one red letter or number on each. One song for a quarter, five songs for a dollar. Feeding it quarters, I punched the two button codes each for five choices.

Elvis. Beach Boys. Connie Francis.

I barely paid attention, and the five songs ended quickly. I found some more quarters in my purse, stuck them all into the coin slot, and punched combinations of buttons until all my money was used up. The sound system started up with the little old lady from Pasadena.

Brittles had finished his food, sat quietly waiting for me to say something. At one point he half stretched a hand across the table to touch me, but pulled it back. I worked on deciding how I could play all of this and finally realized there was no other choice except to follow whatever he wanted me to do. *That's the only way I can get Spider out,* I kept repeating to myself. *The only way to get her released.*

"It's the only way," I said out loud. "Let's hear it."

"All of it?"

He pushed his plate aside. Wiped his mouth with several paper napkins. Wiped his fingers. I nodded.

"Those two men," he said. "The house belongs to Jesus Totexto. Don looked up his police record. A dozen arrests, most of them misdemeanors, a few felonies. At one time he seems to have been a bad-debt collector, another time a repo man. Got in trouble just last year. Chased a guy who owed money into a McDonald's, pushed the guy behind the counter, and stuck his hand into the deep fat fryer.

"He was also a maintenance worker at Casa Grande. I figure he was at the housing development when you and I were there. He saw you, he told somebody. Who, I don't have a clue. I also figure that he buried all those bones there. He knew exactly which spots had been excavated and wouldn't be touched for years. Better than just dumping things out in the desert, where some new housing developer would run a backhoe through, laying sewer lines, dig things up."

"The desert's a big place," I said. "Kinda dumb not to just drive over toward Yuma and pick a spot no developer is ever going to touch."

"I never said Totexto was smart. But smart enough to know the exact plans of which areas on the grounds weren't scheduled to be looked at for years."

"Which one was Totexto?"

He hesitated, not wanting to describe the mutilations.

"The bigger guy," he said finally, hurrying to talk so I wouldn't dwell on the blood. "The other guy was called Early Thumb. A Pinal County deputy sheriff, although he'd been dismissed from the force some months back. He worked as a security officer at the boot camp, and for some reason he just kept wearing his deputy uniform. He was the next level up the food chain."

"You think he set up the computers?"

"No. Somebody else did that. Probably Thumb collected the data, transferred it to a CD, delivered it to somebody. Except Totexto might have been smart enough to make copies for himself."

"There's a lot of holes in what you're telling me."

"This wasn't random violence," Brittles said. "Somebody knew exactly what information they wanted, figured out who was most likely to tell what. None of this happened quickly. Whoever did it was very cool, very calculating. He started with this one, slicing him up, letting him talk, and letting the other guy shrivel with fear. Probably whoever did this promised the second guy that he'd not be tortured or killed if he could get the first guy to talk.

"Please," I said. "Just . . . leave it."

But he couldn't.

"Torture requires patience," Brittles said. "You can't hurry it, you always got to make your head control what your hands are doing. You play games with the clock, judging how many minutes to torture and maim, how many minutes to stop it and let the victim hope it's all over. You have the patience to judge the victim's hope, rising up a curve, and just when it peaks you cut him again. I like old movies. You like movies. We've watched hundreds of hours of movie violence. But the only true violence you see on film is what happens to machines or animals."

"*Apocalypse Now,*" I said.

"The water buffalo. Body almost completely chopped in two with one mighty swing of the . . . the, I don't even know what the person used."

"Enough. *Enough,*" I said, hands over my ears.

"It's getting dark, it's getting late. Don is going to call when he's got more data. For now, let's go back to my place."

Too fatigued to think of anything else, I followed him mutely out the door. A small lime-green Volkswagen was parking beside our car. A bumper sticker on the back said WHAT WOULD JESUS DRIVE?

"What the hell does that mean?" I said rudely to the young couple in the car.

"Jesus wouldn't drive an SUV," the girl said with a huge smile.

"Jesus," I said to myself.

27

I poured myself some pinot noir, looking at all of Brittles's books. The only light in his study came from a west-facing window, and the falling sunlight lit up the room like a movie set. Rows and rows of books were highlighted against the walls, arranged by subject matter, standing exactly vertical, held together by all shapes and sizes of Mexican ironwood carvings serving as bookends. On another wall, an elaborate rack made of mesquite ribs held five wooden flutes, one of them distinctly different in design and texture from the others.

"That's my shakahashi," Brittles said from the doorway, toweling off after his shower. "Japanese. A bitch to learn."

"Show me."

He dropped the towel, walked nude into the room with no self-consciousness about his body. He raised the flute with both hands from its place in the rack, motioned me with his head to follow into the living room, where he sat cross legged on a three-foot-square soft velvet cushion. Expecting him to raise the flute horizontally, I was surprised that he held it vertical, his lips at the top so that he blew across the opening there, producing a mournful, delicate, elegiac sound that wavered in tone and intensity. He held the one note, then moved his fingers on the holes to play a sequence of notes in a minor key until suddenly he made a squeak.

"Sorry."

"More. You aren't even done by half."

Hesitating, he put it to his lips, not playing for a moment. I thought he was thinking that we had no time for this, or that he wanted to get me in bed again, but as he slowly moved his lips on the flute, caressing his cheeks with the mouthpiece, I saw he was just trying to decide what to play.

The piece lasted four minutes, although I swear he played no more than half a dozen different notes and repeated sections again and again.

"Now your turn," he said.

"I can't play that thing."

"No. Your turn to do something."

"Do something?"

"Sing. Dance. Recite a poem."

"What do you think about hiphop?" I said finally.

"Just do it."

I sorted through different raps I'd written, not trusting to reveal myself yet with my latest rap about my life.

"Okay. Here goes."

They call me Shorty but a tower over Bushwick Bill
The girl round the way with the same guy still
Chill with my girlfriends one night a weekend
Love J. Lo though I'm not Puerto Rican
I've been mistaken, smoked weed with Jamaicans and
    Haitians
While on vacation in the greatest city in the nation
That's N.Y.C., I'm a b-girl with a capital B
And a rappin MC
So if you happin to see me
Just give me props if you've gots love for hiphop
And it don't stop so cop the heat, hip the hop.

"Something more personal," he said. "About you. With this."

He knelt in front of me with his flute, blew a single note, sustaining the note by breathing somehow through his nose while he played. *Who is this man?* I thought, picking through all my raps to find the perfect one for him.

Not tonight dad
I have a headache

Put the chessboard away
If you're busy I know where it's stored away
But my favorite book is by my bedside
Could you read? That's what I need.
There's a story bout Adam and a story bout Eve
A story bout Noah, and a story bout Jonah
And when it's all over, you can tuck me in
My one prince charming with disarming grin
While all these other men like to smile and front
But when my bedtime comes they know what they want
And some are so cute that I can't resist
But I'll always think of you as the handsomest
Who taught me that there's nothing I couldn't do
Now I count sheep chastised about for them what I
    wouldn't do.

Setting aside the shakahashi flute, he sat on my lap facing me, kissing my neck, slowly removing my blouse, moving down . . . but if you've done it with a lover, you know what happens, there's nothing more I need to tell you.

And yet . . . and yet . . . after he fell asleep, I went into the living room and watched the night sky. Brooding about why I was there and not with Rich. I mean, casual sex is one thing, and the first time with Brittles I'd mostly put out of my mind. But tonight our relationship had moved light years beyond casual.

I spent hours comparing the two men. Rich's interest in Indians pretty much had to do with old bones and artifacts. Brittles *lived* as an Indian. An unfair comparison. On the few occasions when I talked with Rich about my attempts to find my daughter, he seemed to think it was more comforting to push me toward believing that it would be best if I never found her. Brittles liked her. He liked the two of us together. Not quite so unfair a comparison.

One thing seemed irrevocable. My Tucson house was never my home.

Brittle's house *felt* like the home I'd been searching for.

Not the actual house, but the *kind* of home I wanted.

The kind of home I'd make for my daughter.

With all these conflicting thoughts in my head, I didn't fall asleep until the wine finally made me drowsy. I laid my head sideways against the chair back, pulled up my legs onto the chair, and the last thing I remember before I fell asleep was the wonder of that flute and the magic.

revelations

Spider picked cotton for half an hour. Back and thigh muscles aching from continually stooping over the waist-high plants, removing the fluffy boles and stuffing them into her sack. Father Micah was in charge, picking himself. Some of the staff stood by, carrying water, some food, making bathroom runs every twenty minutes back to the main complex. Her sack filled, Spider brought it to one of the trucks. El Ratón stood on the wooden bed, about four feet high, hands on hips, watching her struggle to heave the bag up. Reaching down a hand, he took a bag and in one fluid motion threw it to the back of the truck. A red and gray motorcycle burred in the distance, slewing around a turn and braking quickly beside the truck.

"That's enough, *amiga*," Luis said, taking off his helmet and holding up a cell phone shut. "I got a call. You checked out just fine. Leavenworth, *amiga*. What you doing in a bad place like that? Caught stealing credit card numbers, maybe? Sending lists through the mail, some federal fraud stuff? That you, *amiga*?"

For the first time since she came to the camp, Spider was afraid. But the rest of the day passed without anything happening, except that Luis gave her a ride on his motorcycle back to the main complex, dropping her off at her dorm.

"So what now?" she said.

"Tomorrow. We gonna clean some brush tomorrow. Chop

some weeds, pick up some trash. Tomorrow, we gonna tell you more. Give you a test."

"You'll tell me about joining the Rapture girls?"

"*Quien sabe?* Just wear old clothes, bring gloves, wear a hat. Tomorrow you'll be out in the sun all day."

He revved the throttle, popped the clutch, and roared away.

But at three in the afternoon on the next day, Spider still waited, all the other girls in her dormitory off picking cotton. She thought of exploring the main complex, of trying to find the private rooms that Jennifer had told her about. Bad move, she thought. Wait it out. Wait for the test. Wait for Luis.

To her surprise, Father Micah came to get her at three-thirty.

"Some of that discipline duty," he said with a broad smile.

"Picking up trash?"

"That's part of it."

"Why not early in the morning?"

"You mean, why not in a cooler part of the day? Three o'clock, that's when it's hottest. That's when discipline really means something."

He let her sit with him in the front seat of the truck. Several boys and girls sat in the back, Luis and El Ratón standing just back of the truck cab, their hands beating out rhythms on the metal roof. Another truck driven by a staff woman carried another dozen boys and girls. Father Micah drove south, leading the small convoy through Coolidge, stopping at a wide expanse of desert. He passed out heavy-duty plastic trash bags and some tools. Everybody seemed to know what to do without asking. Some picked up hoes, others took short-handled weed whackers, two others followed behind the laborers stuffing the trash bags.

Unlike the day before in the cotton fields, Luis and El Ratón now worked with everybody else. After two hours, one of the trucks was filled with trash bags, dead branches, some cacti leaves and stalks, and separate bags for paper and plastic litter. Luis and El Ratón jumped into the back, fixing the

wooden tailgate and chaining it solid. Father Micah started
up the truck, motioning Spider to sit with him. Reluctantly,
she climbed into the cab.

"Where we going?" she said.

"End of the line. The place where we dump all the trash."

"How's that done?"

"Paper and plastic gets recycled. Brush and dirt gets processed."

"Processed?"

But he'd shifted into third gear, the transmission so noisy
that talking was impossible. She slouched against the door,
trying to look casual, wondering if she should just open the
door, jump out, and run.

After ten miles or so, Father Micah turned onto a dirt road,
slowing for fifty feet until he stopped in front of a twelve-
foot-tall chain-link fence, topped with razor wire and surrounding a large warehouse building. Luis jumped down,
took keys from Father Micah, and opened the gate, closing
and relocking it after the truck went through. Luis jogged behind the truck to the warehouse, using more keys to unlock
the main door, punching a button so an electric motor wound
the door up. Father Micah turned the truck around and
backed inside. The door went back down, Father Micah shut
off the truck engine, and he and Spider got out of the cab.

"Our moneymaker," Father Micah said, gesturing at a
huge machine in the middle of the concrete-slab floor.

"What is it?" she asked.

"The CBI Magnum Force 4000. Fifty feet long, weighs
thirty-seven tons, cost half a million. Paid for by Pinal
County, leased to Rapture Warriors Camp as part of a contract to continually clear all brush in Pinal County."

Luis and El Ratón unstaked the tailgate. Luis started
throwing down the trash bags, the few containing paper and
plastic going into a pile that Father Micah carried to huge
mounds of similar trash bags in one corner of the warehouse.
El Ratón started piling all the other bags at one end of the

huge machine, next to a ten-foot-wide bumper rail.

"What is this thing?" she asked.

"Woodchipper," El Ratón said. "Chops things up."

"Not just a woodchipper," Father Micah said. "Grinds up everything into mulch, which we sell to landscaping companies in Tucson. Luis, get her going."

Luis walked to a far wall and threw two huge red-handled switches. The machine began whirring and groaning. El Ratón slid back a metal guard across the entrance chute, hefted the first trash bag, took out a curved box cutter, slit the bag, and emptied all the brush into the hopper. The machine started grinding. El Ratón and Father Micah emptied trash bags, while Luis beckoned Spider to the other end of the machine, where mulch started to spit out.

"So let's talk," Luis said.

"Cool."

"So we've got a proposition for you."

"We?"

"Some people. Connected to the Circuit. You know what that is?"

"Back East, some girls talked about a circuit of very exclusive houses. Only the best working girls, the best conditions, the biggest payoff. I never knew anybody that went on that circuit, though. But I heard girls made lots of money."

"How'd you like to meet the woman who manages all the Circuit houses in the Southwest?"

"Sure," Spider said with a forced smile. "What do I have to do?"

"Well. There's this little test."

"Take me to the woman. I can pass any test."

"Here. The test is here. Come on."

He led her back to the front of the machine, where El Ratón and Father Micah were tossing the last of the brush into the hopper. Luis and El Ratón exchanged looks, and El Ratón brushed dirt off his gloves, standing close beside Father Micah.

"Most of the younger girls, they come from overseas. They don't have to pass the test, because it's all been arranged. Their new identities, where they'll be assigned, everything. But girls like you, who kinda come along by chance, you have to make your bones to get inside."

"Make my bones," Spider said. "Uh, if that means what I think it means, like, whoa, dude. Not me."

"Well, *amiga,* you've got no choice. Come over here."

He took her hand, the two of them coming up alongside Father Micah.

"What's the test?" Spider said, totally frightened, wondering if she could get to the electric door and raise it enough to slip outside and get away.

"We're gonna throw him in there. You help lift him, you pass the test."

"Test?" Father Micah said, removing his gloves, wiping sweat from his protecting eyeglasses. "What test?"

"You don't help lift," Luis said, "you fail."

Frozen stiff, Spider tried to move away. Luis and El Ratón each clapped Father Micah on his shoulders, placing their gloved hands on his upper arms. Luis looked back at Spider for ten seconds, enough time to see that she'd made half a step backward, horror written all over her face.

"Here's your Rapture, Father," Luis said.

"What are you doing?" Father Micah shouted. "Put me down. Turn off the machine and put me down."

Pulling a bulky gun from one of his baggy pockets, Luis held the gun to Father Micah's neck. Blue sparks sizzled and Father Micah's body slumped unconscious.

"Stun gun," Luis said with a grin. "Lord, Thy will to be done." He turned toward me, flicking the stun gun at me once it recharged, a small, jagged, glaring white vee of lightning that arced six inches from my forearm.

"Don't *do* that," I said.

"It's a test. You're at the border, *chica,* you got to decide if you crossing over, if you coming to our side of the line."

"What test?"

"What test," Luis mimicked.

"I'm not firing that thing at Father Micah. If that's the test, I pass."

"He's just another bag of trash. A *heavy* bag of trash. Two people can't lift him into the chipper. You'll have to help us."

"Whoa, wait, wait," I said, my hands up in front of me, pushing the idea away. "Not me. No way . . . what . . . why are you even saying that?"

Luis crackled the stun gun again, turned to El Ratón.

"I think she just said no."

"Yes," I said. "I mean, no, I'm doing that."

"You just failed your test."

They grabbed and lifted him.

"Up and over," Luis said to El Ratón, and they started to swing Father Micah between them. "One. Two. *Three!*"

They tossed him head first into the hopper. The machine, running smoothly with the last of brush already processed, groaned again as Father Micah's body passed through the cutting disks and grinding wheels.

Luis went to check something on the side of the machine. El Ratón turned to Spider, grinned at her, and reached out a hand toward her. She kicked him solidly in the crotch, knocking him against the lip of the hopper and knocking him out. Without even thinking about it, she grabbed his ankles and flipped him into the machine. She ran to the electric door, punched a red button, screaming at the door to move quicker. When it was up a foot she reached to hit a green button, and as the door shuddered to a stop, she threw herself on the floor and rolled underneath before the door banged shut.

Starting for the gate, she saw a green SUV heading down the dirt road. She ran to the back side of the lot, stopped at the fence, quickly pulled off her shoes and removed her jeans. She climbed halfway up the chain links, her toes finding places to grasp, and when she neared the top she tossed her jeans on the razor wire and in one motion threw herself onto her jeans, some of the razor barbs digging into her stomach and bare legs, and in great pain, thankful none of the barbs held her there, she climbed down the other side of the fence and started running.

An engine revved behind her. Taking a chance at looking back, she saw the SUV slewing around the corner of the fence. She tripped over a teddy-bear cholla and fell heavily, her legs and arms laced with needles. The SUV stopped beside her. Anthony Galliano got out, removed his sunglasses, and dangled one of the side pieces from his mouth.

"That's gotta hurt," he said. "But I think after what I'm going to do to you, you're going to hurt a lot more before you tell us what we need to know."

laura

28

"I've got three different data sets to show you," Don said on the cell. "I don't see you hooked into the satellite downlink yet."

"Working it," I said.

One of the few things I'd brought from my Tucson house was a SATCOM phone device. Don gave me specific coordinates and frequencies, but I still couldn't connect my Powerbook to the downlink. I kept hearing snorts in my earpiece, Don impatient and frustrated that I wasn't doing things fast enough.

"I think I've got it," I said, clicking through the last set of windows.

"Yeah. Okay. I just got pinged, we're connected."

"Is this a secure link?"

"Everything Aquitek does is secure. Okay. Here's the first data set."

"Hold on. I'm going to transfer this call to a speakerphone, so Nathan can talk if he's got questions."

Brittles huddled on another chair just behind me, one hand resting against my neck, his breath on my ear. A short list of names popped onto the screen, the list divided into two groups. Seven names in the bottom group, three on top.

"Father Micah, okay, we know him," I said. "Who exactly

is Tamár Gordon? Who is Anthony Galliano?"

"Galliano, I don't know yet. I've got an idea, but I'm wait-ing for input. Gordon, I ran her through Coplink, out of Tuc-son. Took one hell of a lot of persuading, they don't like private companies using the data. But they knew me well enough, and I called in a few favors from Justice in Washing-ton. Tamár Gordon, which seems to be her real name, is a member of the Circuit."

"What's that?" I said.

"Brothels," Brittles said, his coffee breath strong.

"Not just any old brothels," Don said. "The Circuit has been around in some form for half a century. Thirteen of the biggest houses were just closed down, the madams—or man-agers, as they're known—arrested and charged. But probably new houses have already been set up to replace the ones that closed. They use only high-class women, they have no pimps, they arrange exclusive client dates, and every few months, sometimes just a few weeks, the girls are moved to another location to keep fresh bodies in front of the clients. Rates usually from a thousand a night all the way to ten thou-sand once two girls are involved."

"I don't get it," I said. "So there are expensive whores. So what?"

"Keep those names in your head. Okay. Here's the second data set. It's huge, so I'm just going to give you one screen's worth."

A list of items, names, addresses, phone numbers, and credit cards.

"From the call center?" I asked.

"Every order or information inquiry from the last six months."

"How much data is there?"

"A ton. From all fifty states. The Caribbean, Europe, Japan."

"What does it tell us?" Brittles asked.

"Nothing," I said. "It's just raw data. So how are you sort-ing it, Don?"

"Ten different ways. My hunch, though, is that the sort I'm doing just for names in the Tucson area will tell us something."

"How long before you're finished crunching all the data?"

"Ten, fifteen minutes. When it's done, you'll know. Okay. Look at this."

A third data set came onto the screen. I scrolled down, saw it was about three pages long. A list of names, ages, sex, addresses, and phone numbers. I saw Abbe's name in the list.

"From the camp," I said. "Is this everybody?"

"Just the residents. I've got a separate listing for the staff, but I've found something really interesting here. Wait one."

He manipulated the data, and my screen now showed just female names.

"Thirty-seven girls there," Don said. "But let me call up one more thing . . . okay, check this out."

The list on my screen now showed just eleven names.

"Print that out," Don said. I hit the printer icon. "Now, here's our real Christmas and birthday present all in one."

Another list appeared, male and female names arranged in two columns.

"Left side, girls and boys in the camp. Right side, the sponsor who signed them in and paid the fees. Notice anything?"

"Twenty-seven," Brittles said, running his finger down the screen. "And twelve. Twenty-seven and twelve. Wait a minute, wait just a minute!"

"Tamár Gordon sponsored twenty-seven girls over the past year. Galliano sponsored twelve boys."

"How did you get this data?" Brittles said.

"The camp computer had an Internet connection. For their website. I got in through a back door, a flaw in the Microsoft web server. I've got all kinds of data on both residents and sponsors, but these lists just jumped right out at me. Like seeing a typo in a book you're reading, pop, you lose interest in everything else and focus attention on the typo. Now. Are you ready to hear more about Tamár Gordon?"

"Come on, Don. Just tell us, no need to boast about it."

"Ah, Laura, you know I love nothing better than success with data. Okay. Gordon is the true money behind the camp. We've tracked her bank accounts, the accounts of the camp. Enough shifting of her money into camp accounts to leave no doubt that she's in charge. And . . . she owns a big house in Tucson."

"Give it to me," Brittles said. "We'll go there."

"No, no, no," Don said. "I've got a much more creative idea."

"How about Galliano?" I asked.

"Tough nut to crack. This is totally conjecture. No records in any U.S. law enforcement database on Anthony Galliano. But in New York City there were three arrests for assault in the past year for an Antonio-Chelín Galeano. Colombian."

"So?"

"That biker in your backyard," Don said. "With the gun. He was Hispanic, no? He was young, no? Well, I traced the name Chelín Galeano to Medellín. He's dead, murdered a year ago. One of their thirteen-year-old hit men. A *sicario,* they're called. Murder squads for the drug cartels. These young boys are never sent to prison because of a government law, so they go to rehabilitation camps, spend a few months there, get back out on the streets. I talked with a captain on the Medellín drug squad. He says that somebody else took Galeano's name a few years ago. An older man, probably in his forties. Their passport control showed that Galeano flew to the States fifteen months ago. Nobody knows where he is. My guess—"

"Is that he's got really good identity papers," I said.

"That's right. Anthony Galliano. Somehow connected to Tamár Gordon. I'd suspect that he's chief of her security. Handles all her dirty laundry."

"I want to pull my daughter out of that camp," I said to Brittles.

"Hold on," Don said. "The director of the camp, a preacher named Father Micah, lives on the premises, but never came home last night. I've got the Florence Police Department looking into a possible disappearance. I don't want to pull your daughter out, I don't want to do *any*thing that might spook Gordon and Galliano."

"No way," I shouted. "I'm going up there myself."

"Laura," Brittles said. "If this man is really that Colombian, then he's supervising young kids recruited from the murder squads in Medellín. Look at that list of the boys he sponsored. Some of the Colombian kids may be in the camp. One of them may be the biker that shot up your house. If you show up, both you and your daughter could be in serious trouble."

The speakerphone remained silent as Brittles's words took hold of my heart.

"I can't just sit around and *wait* for something to happen to her."

"Well," Don said, "I've got this really creative idea."

"Go," Brittles said, squeezing my shoulder.

"Let's rattle Tamár Gordon's cage. If I'm right, she's got Galliano taking care of business. Somehow, those girls that Gordon sponsored are related to her work on the Circuit. They're probably recruits. The names all look foreign. Lots of Asians, which are in hot demand by Circuit clients. So Gordon somehow has got all she wants from this camp, and she's got Galliano killing everybody that knows. The two men you found dead and tortured, they undoubtedly had some part in things, like that young girl. Theresa Prejean. And unless I'm really wrong, Father Micah isn't going to turn up again."

"That leaves me with one real question," I said. "What the hell does the credit card scam have to do with any of this?"

"Whoa," Brittles said. "I've got it. Don. Have your machines finished that list of people in Tucson who are in the call center database?"

"Just done."

"Sort out all the men. Then, how much trouble would it be to run the list of women's names against the actual people? I mean, can you verify that all the women are still alive?"

Don must have been struck with the same horror and understanding that silenced me. Brittles saw my comprehension, waited for Don to talk.

"Identity theft," he said finally. "A whole new wrinkle on an old scam."

"Used to be," Brittles said, "people who wanted fake identities just went to newspaper clippings or cemeteries, looking for names of children who'd died really young. That name would be turned into an almost hundred-proof guaranteed new identity. So if there are women on your list from the call center who are single, probably with no real family ties, maybe even new to Tucson, but women who've mysteriously disappeared in the last year—their identities could be given to the young girls from the camp. They go out on the circuit with names guaranteed to have no arrest records for prostitution. Absolutely clean names. Kept clean by the Circuit. Am I right or am I right?"

"Stay there until you hear back from me," Don said.

"How long?" Brittles asked.

But Don had already hung up. He never wasted time talking when he had a hot lead on data. I disconnected the satellite downlink feed, hung up the phone.

"He never told us his creative idea," I said.

29

He called back in fifty minutes.

"I picked one name at random, a woman from Tucson who has moved out of town. Apparently an orphan, no known relatives, no forwarding address. I picked another name at random. Same pattern. I've got somebody here tracking down more names, but I don't want to wait. I checked those two names against a standard informational database. One woman is now living in Kansas City, the other in New Orleans. Only problem is their age, which is at least twenty years younger than that of the two Tucson women who disappeared."

"Call Tamár Gordon," Brittles said.

"I'm about to do that. I've got her cell number and I'm going to make her an interesting proposition that she'll find hard to refuse. Okay, I've patched you into another cell here, you'll be able to hear my call, but I'm going to cut out your ability to talk. Just listen and make whatever notes you want. Laura, what's the swankiest place in Tucson where we could rent a very expensive, very private set of rooms?"

"Arizona Inn," I said. "That's the only one I think of."

"Good. Now. When my voice comes on, I'll be running it through a filter. Won't sound like me at all. Ready?"

"Ready."

Clicks and pops on the line, suddenly a dial tone.

"Yes?" a woman's voice said.

"Tamár Gordon." Don's voice was deeper, with an Eastern European accent. "My name is Stefan Grozny."

"I don't know that name. How did you get this number?"

"I work in Bangkok, Miss Gordon. You must have a way of quickly verifying my name and what I do there. Do that. I'll call you back in exactly ten minutes."

He disconnected, his real voice coming back.

"I had an Interpol contact set me up with that name," he said. "A procurer of Asian girls for European brothels. Unknown in the States, but well known overseas. He was just arrested last week, held without bail or communication from anybody."

He hung up and nine minutes later dialed Gordon's number again.

"You checked," Don said.

"Stefan Grozny has three scars on his torso. Where are they? What shape?"

"I have two scarred bullet holes in my left lower abdomen," Don said. "And a long knife scar running down my right leg, from a time I was careless at the beach."

"Let's say that you really are Grozny," Gordon said. "Why are you calling me?"

"You know what I can provide?"

"Yes. Young women."

"Girls. Only Thai girls. No Vietnamese, no Laotian, no Chinese."

"Yes?" Gordon said.

"I know how your Circuit works."

"How did you find that out?" She took a deep breath and sighed.

"Your Circuit has been smuggling girls through Hong Kong for several months. Since young, pure Thai girls are very rare these days, I thought you'd be interested in a one-time supply."

"And how much product are we talking about?" she asked.

"Fifty girls. All with guaranteed identity papers, U.S. citizenship."

"And how much for this product?"

"Ten thousand a girl."

"Out of the question," Gordon said.

"If I know enough about you to call your private cell phone, I also know how your finances work. These girls would draw top money. But I'd make an even better suggestion. Sell them. Lots of rich men in your hemisphere like to buy young girls, keep them secure, keep them happy. I know of many such transactions where the product sale price is well above twenty thousand. You'd make one hundred percent."

"Where are you now, Mr. Stefan Grozny?"

"Mexico City. I have a potential client here, but his understanding of the value of this product isn't so high. He likes Hispanics to screw Hispanic girls. I'm booked into New York tomorrow. If you don't agree to meet me tomorrow morning, I'll just fly to New York."

"Cancel the ticket," Gordon said. "Where can I meet you?"

"I'll arrange a secure, private location. I'll call you in twelve hours."

"I'll need more time to get half a million dollars."

"Here's my proposition. I'll arrange a location that will house, say, half a dozen people. You contact other managers on the Circuit, you have them fly into Tucson, and I'll discuss the product with all of you."

"If you can guarantee this to be a continuing relationship, I'll bring in seven other women. But if it's a onetime thing, just me."

"If you're satisfied with the product, and if I'm satisfied with your money, I'll absolutely bring another batch with me."

"I'll need a day to think about this," she said.

"Miss Gordon," Don said. "I'll give you fifteen minutes to decide. If you have to consult somebody about your decision, I'll give you five minutes. Then I'll hotline your cell and land-line phones."

"Hotline?" she said.

"I'll shut them down. You won't be able to call anybody for ten minutes. At the end of your grace period, I will call you back."

He hung up.

"Hotline?" I grinned. "That's what the phone companies tell their deadbeat customers. I didn't know you could do that."

"I can't," he said. "But it rattled her anyway. Okay, kids. Why don't the two of you get into Tucson and see what's available at the Arizona Inn?"

30

Brittles drove slowly down Elm Street, past the entrance to the inn. Half a dozen older couples stood in front of the inn, a few with champagne flutes. All expensively dressed in that typically rich Tucsonan style that looks just about two inches off true elegance to somebody from New York or San Francisco or Paris.

We circled the entire block, eyes cutting back and forth at all the cars, people walking, backpacked University of Arizona students on bicycles. Brittles turned even farther from the inn, down a parallel street, pointing at a large home as we glided past.

"They say Joe Bananas used to live around here."

"Who?"

"Mob boss. From back East. Came out here to be respectable. I don't know if he lives there or not. Good story, anyhow."

"Why don't we park somewhere?"

A few turns later, we came up on the western side of the inn property to a large gated compound, the old, greened gates standing open. He stopped, backed up, and drove through the gates. We parked at the far end, where a young man waited for us, watching. He wore dark blue shorts, a white shirt, and a loose-woven hat with a blue band around the brim with the words ARIZONA INN.

"Can I help you?" he asked.

"Is that the Greenway House?"

Brittles pointed at a stucco wall surrounding a compound, two steps up to the front of an open doorway, planters of agave and roses everywhere.

"No. That's the Breasted House. But it's currently occupied by a private party. I apologize, but they've asked not to be disturbed this morning."

Brittles turned to an expanse of perfectly green grass, one side interlaid with heavy stepping stones. Behind a wall exploding with purple and red bougainvillea, I saw a two-story colonnade, rounded arches just under a flat red-tiled roof. A second part of the property stood like an equal-sized leg of an "L." Blue window casings on both buildings, a huge palm tree in the courtyard just at the base of the "L," with lawn chairs and planters surrounding a private swimming pool.

"And the Greenway House? Is that unoccupied?"

"Yes, sir. I believe it's vacant for the next five days. After that, it's booked solid through the summer."

"Excellent," Brittles said. "Who can talk about renting it?"

"We don't 'rent' rooms," the man said. "But to reserve the Greenway House, please go inside the main building and ask for Janet."

"Janet," Brittles said to me. "Well, my sweet. Let's go ask for Janet."

"Out*standing,*" the young man said, keying a portable radio. "And who shall I say is coming?"

"I am," Brittles said with a grin to me, taking my arm.

"Sir, I meant," the young man said with absolutely no loss of dignity or even a smile at the joke, "if you'd give me your name, sir."

"Mister and Miss," I said.

"Outstanding. If you'll follow me to the main building, please? And welcome to the inn."

"Polite guy," I said as we passed a large patio dining area.

Inside, a middle-aged couple sat across from each other, both slumped against their seat cushions. The man said something, gesturing with his hands, but the woman just stirred the straw in her cherry Coke, listlessly ate another french fry. The man continued talking, but I could see tears on the woman's face. She turned sideways to avoid him, saw me looking at her, grabbed a napkin, and swiped it across her eyes. The man looked at me also and shot me the finger. He threw money on the table and they both went outside to the parking lot.

"Sir?" the front desk clerk said with a Scottish burr. "Can I help you?"

"Janet," Brittles said.

"Go to my left, to the first open door. Inside, knock on the door on the left side of the room."

We knocked. A young woman opened the door.

"Are you Janet?" Brittles asked politely.

"I am," an older woman said from her desk on the right, a cheerful smile on her face, a wireless headset secure on her bobbed hair. "Are you Mister and, was it Miss or Missus? About the Greenway House?"

"Marc Becker," Brittles said. "And my wife. Tara Prindle."

"How can I help you?"

Unlike the young man in the hat, Janet was a stronger combination of business and affability.

"We should like to, uh, how do you put it? Rent the Greenway House?"

"We don't rent, Mr. Becker. But it's available next week for five days. You could check in late Sunday afternoon, stay until Friday."

"Outstanding," Brittles said. "Per*fect*. May we see it, please?"

"Certainly. Let me get the assistant manager."

"You'll do."

"Well. That's not right, that I show you the property."

"But we like you. Don't we, honey buns?"

"Yes," I said with a huge grin as Brittles brushed his hand across my buttocks as he slid it around my shoulders for a hug.

"All right." Janet nodded at one of the other women and removed her headset. "Would you like a brief tour of the inn's public facilities? The library? The restaurants, the gardens, the main swimming pool?"

"Later," I said.

"We'll eat on the patio, darling." Brittles squeezed my shoulder.

"I should go over the daily rates," Janet said, not forgetting business for a minute as she led us past the gift shop and an open formal dining area.

"Whatever," Brittles said, waving her off. "We're only interested in the privacy, and the number of bedrooms. We'll be having six or seven people flying in for the week. Some of them may stay just a day or two, but I'll want the house for the entire week. Will twenty thousand do?"

"I'd drive you to the moon and back for a week at that money." Janet grinned as we stood in the house's courtyard. "Okay. It's two stories. Six thousand square feet. Gated entrance, off-street parking, for privacy. Five bedrooms, each with private bath. Two of them are suites, one with a Jacuzzi. Heated pool. This separate residence has two more guest rooms, with a joint living area, fireplace, and patio. Would that be enough bedrooms?"

"Let's go inside," I said.

Heavy two-by-twelve stained oak rafters on the ceiling of the spacious living room, with all-white fabric chairs and sofa set informally around a huge glass-top coffee table on wrought-iron curled legs. Iron railings surrounded a balcony above the open dining room, where ten chairs surrounded a beautiful oak table, inlaid with an edging of rosewood. The pool stood just outside a sliding glass door.

"There's a kitchen," Janet said. "A breakfast room. Should your guests want to eat here, rather than in the public rooms."

"Definitely not in the public rooms," I said. "Much too public, right, darling?"

"Will you provide staff for twenty-four-hour service?" Brittles asked.

"That can be arranged."

"And our own chef. A good chef. An *ex*cellent chef."

"That, too, can be arranged."

"Out*stand*ing," Brittles said. "We'll rent it."

"Reserve it," Janet said. "And how will you be paying, Mister Becker?"

"I like you, girl," Brittles said with a slight bow. "I like people who have something excellent to offer for money. Do we have to go back inside?"

"I can take down the information right here," Janet said, taking a pad and lavender pen from her bag and writing down what she needed quickly. "Welcome to the Arizona Inn. And if you care to eat out on the patio, the inn will be your host."

Half an hour later, Brittles forked up the last bit of poblano chile and chicken quesadilla. I'd picked at a salad vicoisse, but wasn't really hungry. Patio service stopped at three in the afternoon, but three other tables were still occupied. A foursome played bridge, shuffling and dealing nonstop with little talk.

Inside the banquet room, a wedding party sang Mexican corridas. A young woman, wearing a brocaded silk evening gown and four-inch lavender shoes, came along the walkway pushing a gold-gilded harp toward the banquet room.

Inside, a guitarist struck up a flamenco arpeggio. Through the half-open door, I saw the bride and groom strike dance positions, facing each other. The bride's wedding gown reached from the floor to her neck, but when she turned to take position, I saw her bare back, the dress open at the shoulders and tapering to finally close at the base of her spine. Her shoulder blades, her muscles, her vertebrae, all stood in naked fleshy contrast to the imperial whiteness of her gown.

At the first minor chord from the guitarist, the couple started tapping their shoes against the tile floor, their bodies motionless, like Irish dancers, just the feet moving. The bride bent her shoulders and the groom swiveled his hips, hands in front of him holding an imaginary bullfighter's cape.

Young, I thought. Twenties. No more. All their future ahead.

Three fortyish women sat near us, all of them on their fourth drink, and another foursome, one couple obviously French, talked and laughed quietly. I'd been listening to the three women, one of them complaining constantly about how she'd been cut out of a large real estate deal by her boss. A mousy blonde kept trying, unsuccessfully, to be both a friend and a therapist, but the complainer hardly stopped whining. The third woman, a dark-haired Latina, spoke little around her margarita glass, but she was the one facing me and finally stood up, unsteady, shoving her metal chair back so hard it crashed on its back. She finished the margarita and came up to me.

"You want to join us?" she said bitterly.

"Excuse me?" I said.

"You've been listening so hard, I thought you'd be able to hear better if you just came and sat at the table."

"Audrey," the blonde called. "Get back here."

"This bitch is fascinated by us. I thought this bitch might join us, so we can all talk at once."

"Audrey!"

Brittles half rose from his chair.

"Oh. That's so sweet. You're going to protect her and all."

"Leave us alone," Brittles said.

"I'll leave hell alone," she shouted. "Until this cunt apologizes."

"Please," I said. "I didn't hear a word you said."

Two waiters appeared on either side of the woman, one of them holding a large aluminum serving platter in front of him, defensively I thought at first, but he very carefully got between me and the woman, talking quietly to her, offering her another margarita if she'd please go back to her table, there was a wedding party she was disturbing, please, ma'am, the inn asks if you'd please sit at your table.

"Oh," the woman said, lurching against the serving tray. "Who's getting married? Let me see, I have to see if I know her."

"They're from Nogales," the waiter said. "I doubt you'd know them."

"Nogales," she said in surprise. "Greasers can afford to get married at the goddam Arizona Inn? Huh. Listen. Girls. Lemme tell you who's getting married."

A waiter held her chair ready, and she slumped into it as another waiter brought a fresh margarita. The bridge four-some barely looked up at the whole exchange, concentrating on the blue-haired lady in a SISTERS IN CRIME tee-shirt who brought home a small slam.

"I'm sorry," a woman said behind me, "for the . . . slight confusion."

"Not a problem," I said.

"And would you be Mister Becker and Miss Prindle?"

"Yes," Brittles answered.

"Janet said I might still find you here. I'm Judy Vaughn. Head of housekeeping. She said you wanted, um, special arrangements? For next week at the Greenway House?"

She held a pad, ready to write.

"Yes," Brittles said. "All seven rooms will be occupied. I'll want housekeeping to provide a person for each room. Two more staff on call. Can I also arrange the kitchen and wait staff with you?"

"I'll take down what you need and pass it on."

"Outstanding. Here's exactly what I want. And if you'd ask Janet to arrange it, we're both very tired. I think we'd like to stay in one of your other rooms tonight. I want to see your evening menu. Talk to the chef."

We started to get up, but the Frenchman began a story, in French, about the true French meaning of savoir faire. Nathan listened closely and smiled. When the storyteller fin-ished, to polite laughs and clapping hands, Nathan took me to the front desk to get our key.

"I didn't know you spoke French," I said.

"Don't speak it well, but I can understand it. A Frenchman brings home a friend for lunch. Arriving at his apartment, he hears a slight noise in the bedroom, opens the door, and sees his wife in an incredible position with another man. '*Excusez moi*' the husband says, and closes the door. In his kitchen, while making some espresso, his friend congratulates the man on his excellent behavior. 'That is the true Paris feeling of savoir faire,' he tells the man. '*Non, non,*' the husband says, and goes back to the bedroom, opens the door again, and says '*Continuez, s'il vous plait.*' "

"So what do we do now?" I said.

"Compliments of the inn, I'm going for a swim."

We sat around the main pool, the sun low enough so that half the pool lay in shadows and the sun worshipers kept moving their chairs around to catch the last rays. An elderly couple finished their martinis, ordered two more, clinking the new glasses together in a silent toast.

A woman swam slow, steady laps, pausing at the far end of the pool to reach up to stroke the legs of a young bronzed man sitting on the curved edge. Neither of them paid us any attention. When the woman varied her path to swim closer to me, I saw she was at least in her sixties, her face surgically altered more than once, forehead smooth from Botox.

After one more round of martinis, glasses again raised in a toast, the old couple left. Finishing her last lap, the swimmer slowly rose from the pool by pulling herself up the man's body, eventually straddling his pelvis and facing him. Brittles moved his chair on the tiles, and they both looked startled by the slight screech, as though they thought they were entirely, absolutely alone.

"I think it's time to go find our room," Brittles said.

revelations

Tamár welcomed the wait help and instructed them to set seven chairs at the table. In front of each chair, Tamár placed a leather-bound notepad, a gold Cross pen, and Steuben crystal ashtrays and flower holders, each holding a single white rose. At an old teak serving table, the wait staff carefully set up silver coffee jugs and a silver teapot. Dominique, the youngest of the wait staff, presented a silver tray with four different-patterned Limoges teacups for Tamár to inspect.

Each bedroom was furnished with thirties furniture. An oak trestle side table, a carved mesquite wall hanging, an ornate spindled headboard on the beds. Each room had cellophane-wrapped food baskets and freshly cut and arranged flowers in Hopi pottery vases. The bathrooms were also completely stocked with toiletries. Brand-new thick velour robes hung in the closets. The bedside tables held bottled water, small boxes of French chocolates, a silver ice bucket, and full-sized bottles of bourbon, scotch, and gin.

Satisfied, Tamár dismissed all the staff, sat nervously in the huge living room.

By midday, she'd left dozens of cell phone voice messages. None of the seven Circuit women had arrived. None of them answered her phone.

The front door opened. Irritated, ready to show anger, she rose, sat back down, and carefully composed herself. Expecting to see a friend, she gasped at the two people coming inside.

laura

31

"Sorry. Expecting somebody? Gee. They won't be here. All of them were arrested at the Tucson airport when they got off the plane. So it's just us three chickens."

"Do I know you?" Tamár said.

"Personally? No. But you've heard of both of us. My name is Nathan Brittles. This is Laura Winslow."

Stunned, she stood up, staggered slightly, had to put one hand on her chair. I could see her mind spinning, spinning, spinning like mad, it was all over her face, trying to work out what we wanted, trying to figure how to get rid of us.

"Time for a little chat," Brittles said.

To gain more time, Tamár went out to the pool, slumped into one of the aluminum-framed chairs. She lay her head back, carefully folded her hands on her lap, staring at the brilliant blue water. Composing herself, I thought. Preparing a story, trying to stay calm and look innocent. Brittles picked up an ashtray and flung it into the pool. She shivered at the splash, her hands clenching tighter, breasts rising and falling as she fought to keep her emotions under control. Just when she settled herself again, a tiny smile on her lips, Brittles kicked the chair, knocking it a few feet sideways. Her head slumped to her chest and she took an amazingly deep breath and let it out slowly. She rested one hand on the glass table, pressing the palm down, lifting it again, studying the faint aura left behind. She abruptly rubbed the table clean, completely erasing the palm print. She sat forward, hands folded again in her lap.

"Okay," she said. "Tell me what's in it for me."

"Hard time," he answered. "In Perryville."

"I'll tell you what I know. But I'll never testify. Put me in court, I'll swear you two bullied me, threatened me."

"So talk," Brittles said, promising her nothing. "Who else?"

"You know the others already," Tamár said after a while. "Father Micah, from the camp. Anthony Galliano, my security chief. We've used a few people from around here, but none of them really knew what the other was doing."

"The identity theft?" I asked.

"Just that. We needed identities for the girls who'd go out on the Circuit."

"Why didn't you just forge them?" I said.

"We thought about that. At first."

"Why did you kill those women? Just to get their identities?"

"I didn't kill anybody. That was Anthony's work."

Tamár wanted to talk, probably believing that in talking she'd not get charged with murder. But I hardly trusted anything she said. Lies, persuasions, diversions, inaccuracies, nothing could be believed just because she'd said it. Tamár ran a lucrative, secretive, and hidden business. Tamár herself could be no different than that. What might appear to me to be a willing flexibility to give us the truth was in all probability her manipulation of what she thought we wanted to hear.

When Brittles asked her about Theresa Prejean, Tamár's face softened. Just for an instant, tears welling in her eyes. I thought she was going to tell us everything then, but the moment passed so quickly I wondered if I'd really even thought her vulnerable.

Halfway through another of her stories, Brittles stood and kicked her chair violently. It teetered on one side and Tamár stood up quickly to avoid falling over. Brittles lifted her body and threw her into the pool. She surfaced, treading water, moving to the center of the pool, turning in the water to track Brittles's movement as he walked around the edges of the pool every time she tried to move to a wall and climb out.

"You're not living on the edge anymore," Brittles said to her. "*I* control the edges here. *I* control what happens. You're totally out of it now. You're so out of controlling things that you'll be bored for years, wanting to get back the edge, get back control. Right now you're figuring how you'll save yourself from the death house up at Florence. You think that because you never killed any of those women, because you never saw them killed, that you'll walk past the death house. You'll cheat the state out of executing you. Well, lady, I've seen a lot of people in the same situation you're in right at this moment. You're trying to be calm, trying to be in control, still trying to figure how to get the edge on me. But you're going to stay in that pool until you finally realize what's happening to you. Your scheme wasn't supposed to end this way. But you're the one who might drown. When I see that look of total desperation take over, then maybe I'll let you out."

He flung one of the chairs into the pool, the backwash ripples washing over her face and filling her mouth with water. She sputtered, choking.

Defeated.

She nodded. Waited submissively for his approval.

Brittles waved her to the edge of the pool, gave her a hand up onto the tiles.

"I know what it's like," he said gently. "You tell one lie, it's nothing. A white lie. You tell another. Finally you start linking all your lies together. Odd bits of truth in between, until you convince yourself that it doesn't matter."

Dripping wet, shivering, nipples huge under her blouse because she was so cold. He found several towels, handed them to her. Gently. She didn't even bother to rub herself dry, just draped the towels across her body.

"Galeano," Brittles said.

"I'm cold."

"You want another towel?"

"No. Antonio. He's cold. Lifeless. A robot with charm. Continually bored as he makes nice with expensive society women. Sits in the dark a lot. Just his cell phone blinking, no other lights. He makes calls all over South America."

"So do you control him?" Brittles asked. "Or does he control you?"

Shuddering, Tamár drew one of the towels tight across her shoulders.

"Both," she said finally. "He had his moments. I had mine. It was all about money. And I was his passport to some of the wealthiest people in Tucson."

32

After the Tucson police took Tamár away, we toured the house again, looking for anything. But other than the small address book in her purse, Tamár had brought nothing to the meeting.

Brittles flung himself onto one of the beds, beckoning me to join him.

"This is crazy," I said. "What are you doing? I don't want to spend a night here. I want to get my daughter."

We lay on the king-sized. All the curtains closed, the lights off, but sunlight filtering through the side window. Brittles nudged my left breast, but I sat on the edge of the bed, shaking my head no.

"The dining room opens at six," he said. "We've still got half an hour."

"No." I started getting dressed. "I want to get my daughter."

"Until we hear from Don, we can't do anything. Let's have a good meal."

"I can't eat."

The phone rang, a tinkling sound, and a red light blipped on and off with each separate ring. I pounced across the bed, picked up the phone.

"Get to Florence," Don said, his voice shaking.

"What's happened?"

"The sponsors of all the camp residents have been notified. All the kids are being told the camp is closing and they have to leave. So far, everybody's contacted their sponsor except those boys and girls sponsored by you know who."

"And my daughter?" I shouted. "What about her?"

"The Florence police have the camp sealed off. They're running a second check for . . . for your daughter."

I slammed down the phone.

"What's wrong?" Brittles said.

"My daughter's disappeared."

I rapidly finished dressing, got my computer bag, tugged his arm to hurry, but he fiddled with his boots.

"You're going to stay here," he said finally.

I snatched up his car keys.

"You can stay if you want."

The door half open, he braced a forearm against it, shut it while keeping me inside the room.

"Think about it," he said. "Don't let your heart or gut do the thinking. Use your head. Remember, there's a chance—a small chance, but a chance—that this woman isn't really your daughter."

"Let me *out* of here!" I shouted.

"I'll go right to the camp. Talk to some of the other residents, see if they remember anything that happened. I don't want you to be seen at that camp. The kid who tried to kill you may be there. I can handle him. You can't."

"Watch me. You have no idea what I can do."

"I'll tie you up if I have to," he said, gripping me from behind in a bear hug.

"Goddam you!"

"Get it into your head. I'm driving up there by myself. I want you to stay here, stay by this phone that nobody knows about. I'll call you at twenty-minute intervals, and I'll have Don call you also. You two have done enough with your computers. Leave the rest of this to people who know how to deal with the problem."

"I can deal with any problem," I said.

"You're not leaving with me," he said.

Okay, I thought, *go ahead. I'll just rent a car, I'll pay the driver to go even faster than you do.* I slumped my body back against him, relaxing. He let go, tentatively, waiting for a trick, finally opening the door and standing out on the patio.

"I'll call every twenty minutes," he said. "If you're not here, I'll get the Tucson Police Department quick. All right?"

"Every twenty minutes," I said.

He kissed me, my lips clenched so rigid that he broke contact immediately. Going backward a few steps, he paused, then turned to run out to the car. Not even bothering to close the door, I went to the phone, called the front desk, and asked them to arrange for a car and driver for me as quickly as possible.

A minute after I hung up, somebody rapped on the open door.

"Oh," I said to the tall man in the linen suit, "you must have been waiting out on the street for a pickup."

"Oh, yes," he said, standing back while I came onto the patio. He closed the door behind me. "Yes. I've been waiting on the street for some time, Miss Winslow."

"Who?" I said, not remembering the names that Brittles and I had used to check in, but certain that the inn didn't know I was Laura Winslow.

"Nineteen minutes," the man said, looking at his wristwatch. "Your friend Mister Brittles will be calling in nineteen minutes. We'd better be leaving."

Behind me before I could move, he wrapped one arm around my body, pinning my side against the adobe wall, and using his other hand to press a handkerchief over my nose and mouth.

Ether, my brain shouted, but I couldn't make a noise, didn't even have time to think of a reaction, the ether and whatever else was on the handkerchief working so fast. I slumped in his arms, barely conscious. When he let go of my arms, I slapped him hard across the face, twice, until the fumes I'd already inhaled made me even groggier and I tried to slap him again, but he just caught my limp hand and held it for a moment. He stooped over, threw me over his shoulder, looked up and down the sidewalks in case anybody was watching, and went to an open gate on a side street. A tan Mercedes stood at the curb, the trunk already opened. In one fluid gesture he tossed me into the trunk and slammed the lid.

laura

33

My head fuzzy, eyes filmed over, I tried to see where I was.

"Hello?" I shouted.

My arms duct-taped behind me, ankles duct-taped together.

"Miss Winslow."

He turned on a flashlight, rose slowly from a plain wooden chair, his body uncoiling fluidly until he stretched, muscles flexing, and I could tell his body was immaculately balanced, a dynamo, ready to take on anything. His sudden, radiant smile seemed that of a politician, but genuine and reflected in his deep green eyes. *Vote for me*, the smile said. *Not because I'll get the job done, but because I'm a good person.* He smiled so energetically I thought his face muscles must hurt. And whether smiling or not, his face shifted with the emotional quality of whatever he said, his face like a small swimming hole that ripples and bobbles with the slightest vibration or summer wind.

The flashlight flickered away from me until I heard a loud thunk and the overhead lights came on. The inside of the warehouse all was in shadows, the bulk of a huge machine rising in the center of the floor. I could see a huge pile of trash bags and bales of cotton stacked here and there in dark corners so you couldn't really make out what was actually there. On two walls, high above, long, horizontally narrow windows without glass opened to the air for heat evaporation.

"My name is Galeano," he said, kneeling in front of me. "I'm sorry to see recognition of my name, as groggy as you must still feel. You and your lover have caused a lot of trouble. Tamár Gordon has been arrested. The camp is closed down. All of my boys are in police custody. Even Luis, who you met at your house. Luis rarely misses when he goes to kill somebody. Back in Medellín, he's killed twenty, thirty, I don't know how many people. And he's only fourteen years old."

I looked up at Galeano's face, his cheeks where I'd slapped them still flaming red against his even brown tan, his lips flattened to a horizontal pencil line, his eyes full of shock. He couldn't look at me and I felt very afraid.

In that moment I gave up hope of living. I lay flat on the oaken flooring, arms across my chest, like an animal who's rolled over into the submissive position. *Go ahead, here's my throat, rip it open.* I felt nailed to the floor by my helplessness, all hope crippled, damaged to the point of being completely relinquished. For an instant, I thought of coiling like a snake and striking when Galeano wouldn't expect it, but he saw my body tighten reflexively and just smiled at me.

"Not a chance," he said. "Don't even bother trying. You're going to need all your energy, where you're going."

"Where?" I said quietly, hope not yet extinguished.

"I'll tell you exactly where. Well. Not exactly. Let's say, approximately in the middle of the Sonora desert. East of Yuma. Near the border. I figure to drop you out there 'long about noon. 'Long about, say, hundred degrees plus. No water. You'll make it a few miles, I figure. You'll live just long enough to know what's going to happen. Your life is gonna be like the horizon, it's gonna shrink right down to a few yards around you, and then you just won't be able to look forward even just one more step, you'll realize what's happening and that it just won't go on much longer."

He slit the duct tape on my ankles with a box cutter, tossed it aside, helped me to my feet.

"But before we go," he said, "say good-bye."

He half carried me to the end of the huge machine. I blinked, my eyes smarting, suddenly filled with tears. Trussed up in duct tape, with a strip across her mouth, Spider sat on top of a huge metal lip of the machine. I shook my head hard, I knelt to the floor and banged my head on the concrete, trying to get focused and more conscious of what I was doing. He hauled me to my feet, forced me to look at Spider.

"I don't know yet how you two know each other. But I know you're connected, somehow. I'm going to have to find out from this young woman just what she knows. Back in Medellín, I was known as the best cleaner to call. You know, the guy who comes with the bottles of acid and the bags and gets rid of people. You, you're going for a long run into oblivion. Thirty-nine people have already died in the area of the desert where I'm going to drop you. And that includes the cooler months, includes the ones who froze and the ones who got dehydrated."

"Spider!" I shouted.

"Spider," he said. "A nickname? Tell me more."

I clamped my mouth shut.

"Or not," he said. "I don't care. Once I've dropped you in the desert, I'll come back for this little spider, this tarantula, this black widow that will want to sting me. But I've already arranged an identity kit for her, passport, tickets on a private jet, where she'll be stabilized with tranquilizers."

"Where are you taking her?"

"South." He grinned. "To my own place, in the mountains. I'll keep her there until she tells me whatever I want to hear. Then I'll do something with her. I just don't know what yet."

He pulled a roll of duct tape from his pocket, cut off a strip, and whipped it around my mouth. Punching the button for the electric door, he waited for it to clunk to a stop at the top.

"All right," he said. " 'Bye, my spider. I'll be back."

He dumped me back in the trunk, held the ether rag to my face again.

34

I groaned, tried to stretch, but stabs of pain all over. *Stop stretching. Don't move!* A taste of vomit in my mouth, behind that sour taste something chemical, something hospital. I'd been drugged, now I remembered.

Ran a finger over my teeth, trying to clear those tastes, trying to spit, but my mouth too dry. Reached for water, but of course none to drink. I thought of tomatoes and blueberries, of succulent and damp fruits, of raw eggs, of honey molasses, but calling up good-tasting things didn't get rid of the bad taste. Running my hands across the ground, I found a smooth stone, a pebble, and put it in my mouth to suck on. The pebble was flecked with an amber-colored substance, the yellow polished by decades of being rolled along by winds and rain.

I tried to figure the worst-case scenario.

Best-case, I corrected myself. *Best-case scenario.*

Negative. Dehydrated so much that sweat scarcely formed. Positive. Sweat didn't flow continually into my eyes, so they didn't burn anymore. Negative. Bleeding from at least a dozen scrapes. Positive. The smell of the blood so intense that I could focus on it to the point of ignoring some of the pain.

Heat. Negative. Well over one hundred and ten degrees.

Heat. Positive. At some point, temperature doesn't really

matter. The organism dehydrates, blood pressure drops. At some point, you don't think about it.

Negative.

I was going to die.

Positive.

I wasn't dead yet.

Always surprising what the human body can do if the mind is shut off from thinking about things too much.

Think, you die.

Stand up, one foot in front of the other, total body focus, you live.

What to do.

Getting to my feet. My bare feet, I quickly realized when I stepped onto the hot desert floor. Panic of sudden realization where I was, didn't know where I was except it was in the middle of the desert. Slowly swiveling completely in a circle, I saw nothing alive, no birds, no snakes or critters or insects. They were out there, but with the sun directly overhead, nothing wanted to move.

I *had* to move. I had to find water. I had to find somebody.

Nothing I could use to bind my feet, the first hundred yards excruciating on my soles as I limped across the desert. No shifting sands here. Just corniche. Lots of small, sharp rocks, tufted dry grass. Here and there, discarded plastic supermarket bags from undocumented workers crossing up from Mexico. I gathered a few, tried to tie them around my feet, but they quickly tore on the stones and grass.

Stopping at the first saguaro, I used a stone to bash a hole between two saguaro ribs, looking for water. I pulled out clumps of the pulp, trying to suck moisture from them.

A dark plastic bag. I pulled it over my head, tied the loops under my chin, some relief from the sun although after five minutes my scalp felt like it was in a dishwasher. Hot, moist. I couldn't afford the water lost through the sweat and ripped off the bag.

What to do, what to do.

I was in serious trouble.

Gripping large clumps of saguaro pulp in both hands, I guessed which direction was north, hard to guess with the sun directly overhead, but I *had* to pick a direction so I did.

And I jogged off into the desert.

When starting out, without realizing it, I'd taken in the sense of shadows from saguaros and mesquite and creosote bush. I mean the lack of shadows, the sun so precisely overhead that its vertical rays hit directly down on the anvil of the desert. Now, seeing a saguaro shadow about two feet long, I knew that time had passed. Both my feet bled, but not badly. I'd done so much long-distance running that my feet had built blisters on blisters, the soles callused enough for occasional pricking, but on the whole, and I had to focus on the whole, the total foot was okay.

But that saguaro shadow was ominous. I estimated it was at least an hour since I'd started running. At least a quart of sweat, of moisture evaporation that I couldn't replace. Weighing the odds, I picked up my pace to something like a twelve-minute mile. The extra speed meant I had to watch my step. A trip, a fall, anything like that could be painful at minimum, potentially dangerous to the point of fatal if I broke bones. I shifted my path several times, the ground increasingly rocky, and I sensed I was on an incline, running uphill, and I didn't like that extra effort, but I had little choice. A covey of quail scattered in front of me, their song like Indian flutes, but the beauty of those flutes scarcely registered. My head was buzzing, inside, almost a rattle, like the sun was drying out my brain and leaving it to twitch about like the tail of a huge timber rattler. I went up and over a small escarpment, down the other side with a thud onto solid rock, impatient with my progress slowing down as I fought against tripping and stumbling, my eyes so intent on the two and a half feet of my next stride that I misjudged the next rocky outcrop and fell on my rear, sliding down the rocks for several yards until I stopped, my panties shredding, bright lines of blood on my rump. I clawed at the rocky desert, got to hands and knees, not bothering to look at the scrapes, willing myself erect and running again to the top of the small outcrop, where I stopped with a deep sob.

As far as I could see, nothing but desert, as flat and hot as the bottom of an iron. In the winter, I'd been in the desert at night, with temperatures down around freezing, the slightest breeze chafing any bare skin, piercing your sinuses and eardrums. But that was the other side of the calendar.

Until falling, I'd not been thinking about anything but the immediacy of being in the desert, of needing to get *out* of the desert. But now my head was full of the future, of eternity in the desert. In extreme sports, you do *not* think of the miles left, the time to completion, the summary of mental and physical exhaustion which will be stretched out beyond comprehension. In extreme sports, this is unthinkable. You just put one foot in front of the other, swim another stroke, pedal the bike one more revolution.

This totally freaked me.

I stopped again. I wanted to just lie down, cry myself into wellness, into healing, into begging for somebody to find me.

Two years ago, I'd have done just that.

Given up.

Not this woman, I thought. *Not this time.*

I carefully gauged the shadows, figured I'd been running at least two hours, figured my mind wasn't rational anymore so it could be three or four hours, the shadows having that midafternoon, indeterminate length about them.

Raising both hands, I cupped the palms around my eyes, shading out the sun, looking at the horizon. At first, I thought the tower was just another saguaro, maybe half a mile off. I squeezed my eyes shut, opened them to slits, looked again carefully. It really was a tower. Maybe two, three miles away. I saw no other towers, so it couldn't be a power line, maybe a telecommunications satellite tower. That was bad news, since anything like that would be so tall that I was underestimating the distance to it. It's a survival tower, I said to myself. One of those emergency signals to those on the desert illegally because of the hundreds of illegal travelers who died every summer.

Water! Here! the tower signifies.

My entire map of existence shrank to those few miles. Even the horizon was blurred, indistinct. I kept that tower etched in my head, even when I couldn't see it, which was most of the time, both feet bleeding heavily now, and my pulse so faint I could barely pick it up except at the base of my neck.

I headed toward the tower. Trying to run, really just a loping pace, slowing now and then to a fast walk, gradually slowing even more to shorter steps, my mind hallucinating, my strength really going now, felt like my blood was boiling directly out of my skin, reducing my circulation, reducing blood pressure to the point where I knew I was light-headed and getting dangerously near that point of low blood pressure where the body just collapses into a coma. And out here, a coma meant death.

Double vision. I shook my head violently, huge globules of sweat flung left and right, but no luck. Every bush had a double image, both of them sharp, overlaid, like two serrated leaves, one laid almost on top of the other.

A black lightning bolt hit the ground, no, hit the prairie dog, the strike a blur, talons ripping into the prairie dog, ripping a long string of entrails as the hawk swooped upward, suddenly skittering a full ninety-degree turn as I waved my arms at it, furious. I'd watched the prairie dog, licking his paws, satisfied, no longer hungry, *alive* and then dead. The hawk wheeling in a disdainful arc. I was no threat. It flapped its wings slowly, rising on a thermal, disappearing into the sun.

Intent on the ground, I didn't see the three-wire fence until I smashed directly into one of the metal poles. Bounced off the pole, ran parallel to the fence without a thought in my mind, ramming another pole, and this time I got knocked to the ground. Sat on my butt, blood running from open gashes in both legs and arms, and suddenly I was blind. I swiped a forearm across my eyes. It came away wet. Red. Blood. Wincing, I felt a small gash in my forehead, but my blood pressure was so low that none of the wounds bled much. I was in real trouble.

35

The ambulance hit a dip in the old pavement, traveling so fast that when it rose up to the top of the next rise, all four wheels flew a few inches off the road. When the ambulance slammed back to earth, my hip banged the side panel and I came to.

A young EMT let go of the overhead grip, steadied himself as the ambulance rocked side to side. He checked a tubing that ran to my left side, and I moved my head enough to see an IV inserted.

"Where am I?" I croaked.

"Hey. Back to life, are we?"

"Where am I?" I asked again, my head very fuzzy and beginning to ache.

"In an ambulance." He switched the saline solution bag hanging on the rack above me. "Yeah, I know. In an ambulance. Bad joke. You're on your third IV bag so far." He looked out the rear windows. "We just went through Sells.

Another forty or so minutes, you'll be in St. Mary's Hospital in Tucson."

"Where . . . find me?"

He unwrapped what looked like a green lollipop, stuck it in a bottle of water, and put it between my lips.

"You're almost bone-dry, girl. I can't let you swallow any water, but squeeze this between your lips. Get things a little wet, so you sound less like a frog when you say something."

The moisture felt wonderful. I clamped on the spongy green square, sucking and squeezing everything out of it. He smiled approvingly, but I saw that the smile didn't extend up to his eyes and I knew I wasn't doing very well. He pulled on another pair of latex gloves, unrolled some gauze bandages, dipped them into a solution, and started to work on my right arm.

"*Je*sus," I screamed.

"Yeah. It's gonna sting. I got your left arm done while you were still out cold. Sorry about this, but I've gotta clean all these wounds. Oh. They found you kinda west and north of Organ Pipe, almost halfway between there and Cabeza Prieta. People that regularly check the emergency water towers found you at one of them."

The moisture eased my cracked lips and seemed to clear my head. I moved. Not a great idea at all.

"I'm gonna strap you down if you try that again."

Raising my head, I saw jagged scabs on my right arm, bandages all over the left one.

"More on your legs. What the hell did you do out there? Run through a bob-wire fence?"

I nodded yes, clamping my lips on the now-dry sponge, clenching my jaw against the pain of the cleansing antiseptic.

"Your forehead, too," the EMT said. "All in all, you're one lucky girl."

"Where . . . we going?"

"Tucson. I've already radioed ahead. St. Mary's emergency room is all set to take you in."

"No hospital," I said, struggling to sit up, unable to muster enough strength to do more than raise my head. "Got . . . other things . . . got to do other things . . ."

"I'd like to knock you out with a shot, but you're so weak, I want to keep you talking to me. So talk to me, girl. What's your name?"

"Name is . . . name," I mumbled.

I tried to raise the patterned disposable sheet covering me.

"Well, I had to cut them all off. I'm afraid you're kinda naked under there."

I spit out the green spongy lollipop. He dipped it in water, put it back between my lips.

"So, like, were you trying one of those endurance runs? Out in the desert? Except you got lost or something?"

The ambulance launched off another dip in the road. I remembered that road.

"Eighty-six?" I croaked.

"Oh, yeah. You were eighty-sixed outa that desert, all right. Oh. You mean, are we on 86 the death road between Sells and Tucson?"

I nodded.

"People drive pretty fierce along this road. Lots of shrines. I've responded to a lot of accidents. I'm based in Sells, in the Indian Health Services hospital. I'm Ojibwe, so when I finished IHS training, do you think they'd send me back to Michigan? Back up to the Upper Peninsula, back to L'Anse? Oh, no. They sent me out in the middle of the desert. Okay. We're done with that arm. Now. I'm gonna bunch this sheet here up around your waist. I've got to work on your legs. I'll try to keep your privates private, so to speak. But I've got to cleanse all the wounds."

However far up he bunched the sheet, I never knew. I passed out again and woke up in a bed in the emergency room, two nurses and a doctor hunkered over me.

"Awake," one of the nurses said.

"Name?" the doctor said. He looked Indian or Pakistani, his bedside manner limited either by his English or his concern.

"Name . . . Laura. Winslow."

"Laura Winslow." The nurse made a notation on a clipboard. "You still need me here, Doctor?"

"Do you hear me?" the doctor said.

"Kinda," I said, "but I understand her better."

They both laughed.

"Good, good. Humor. You got some humor. Good thing. Cool beans."

The nurse changed out the empty saline bag hanging above me for a full one.

"Five bags in twelve hours," the doctor said. "I think almost a record here."

"Twelve . . . hours? I've got get up."

"Not you, Miss Laura Winslow. Your tank was really low."

A blood pressure cuff squeezed my right arm and they both waited for the readings.

"Improving," the doctor said. "The EMT man, when he first found you, he had trouble finding a pulse on most of your body. Your blood pressure was seventy-five over thirty-eight. You were this far from going into a coma."

He held out a thumb and index finger, paralleled them about two inches apart.

"How . . . long . . ." I couldn't even seem to get out a whole question.

"We'll keep you here for at least another twelve hours. Until your systolic pressure goes over one hundred and your heart rate stabilizes. Right now your heart is beating steady but really low, barely above fifty beats per minute."

"Runner," I said. "I run. A. Lot."

"So you normally have a low resting heart rate?" I nodded. "How low?"

"Fifty. Nine."

"Well, Miss Laura Winslow. That is good news, then. You just relax. These are good people in here, but now we have to go see about a stabbing victim."

I lay there for hours, dozing on and off, until the shift changed and the tone of conversation grew louder, more people in the room, and more patients. I lay in the bed for at least two more hours until a nurse came to start moving my bed.

"We're moving you to the ICU," she said.

An aide came to help with the IV stand, and the two of them wheeled me out into the corridor, where people were stacked up in beds.

"Busy gangbanger night," the aide said to the nurse. "So how's your boy?"

"Didn't I tell you?"

"No. Last I heard, you were taking him to a nose and throat specialist."

They ignored me completely.

"Yeah, right," the nurse said, as they maneuvered my bed into an elevator. "Well. You know he's been snuffling for weeks, and he kept telling me he couldn't breathe through his left nostril."

"I heard that part. So? What did the nose doc say?"

"He looks up Sammy's nose. Now, Sammy, you know, he's barely three years old, he can't really describe what's going on, but he starts screaming like crazy when the doc puts a swab up into that nostril. So I'm there, his nurse practitioner is there, the two of us are holding poor Sammy down while the doctor takes out an extraction tool and goes to work up Sammy's nose."

We came out of the elevator, the aide asking somebody at the nurses' station where to move me, and we started down another corridor.

"So?" the aide said.

"I mean, like, this doc is twisting and pulling and finally

he gets the extraction tool where he wants it, he tells us get a firm hold, and he pulls out the green moss."

"Moss?"

"Looked like moss. Like moss that was *growing*. So what the hell is that? I ask the doctor. A pea, he says. A green pea. Kids like to stuff peas up their noses. I figure this one had been there quite a while. It was growing roots. Here we are."

They wheeled my bed into a room, docked the bed in an empty space, and hooked up all their gauges without saying another word.

A green pea, I thought. *What would that be like, having one grow up your nose*? I passed out again.

36

At two in the morning, the grogginess finally cleared enough for me to see that I was in a private room of the ICU. I got out of bed and peered down the hall at the nurses' station. Nobody sitting there. I yanked the IV needle out of my arm, IV fluid spurting from the dangling tube and blood oozing from my arm. I found a roll of gauze, used my teeth to rip off several feet, wrapped it around the needle hole, and tied it tight.

My clothes and belongings were all in a drawstring plastic bag. I checked quickly to make sure my cell phone was inside, then slung the bag over my arm with the gauze, covering it up in case I got stopped. But either the staff was helping other patients or on a break somewhere, so nobody confronted me. I edged up to each open door, looking around the corner to see if a nurse was inside. Most of the rooms were empty, the rest with sleeping people. At the very last room, a young girl with body piercing all over her face and ears was listening to an MP3 player. Without turning off the music or removing her earphones, she immediately recognized the bag across my arm, knew what I was doing.

"Go for it!" she whispered.

I could see inside her closet and I reached in to snatch a lightweight University of Arizona jacket and some blue sweatpants. She nodded okay.

"Yo," the girl said. "Some guy whale on you too?"

Left side of her face horribly yellow and blue with bruises, a ring of marks around her neck.

"You need money?" she asked.

"I'll make out," I said. "Soon as I get a taxi home."

"Jesus, girl, don't go home. You got to *stop* that beating, Jesus Christ, I mean, you looked like he threw a rope around you and dragged you through cactus. Besides, no taxi driver'll take you into his clean cab. Here. I got lots of money."

Reaching under her sheet, between her legs, she pulled out a small leather bag. Without counting, she grabbed some bills and thrust them at me.

"Oh, no," I said. "I can't take your money."

"*His* money," she said. "Drug money. If he hadn't'a whacked me with my favorite alarm clock, if the clock didn't get broken . . . but when he left for a drug sale I cleaned out his stash. Take it. Driver's license. Credit card. Take it all."

She crammed the bills into my hand.

"Give me your name," I said. "Your address. I'll pay you back."

"Girl, you got no more sense than a sack of hair. I been laying here, thinking of doing just what *you* are doing. Before he finds where I am, I'm moving east coast way. Change my name. Get a new address. Just keep the money. Use the ID. You get clear of *your* old man. Okay?"

I found the exit. In the parking lot, behind a huge mesquite tree, I ripped off the open-back hospital gown and didn't even bother with my blood-soaked clothing. And no blood seeping through the gauze, but I left it on. My arms and legs were covered with bandages, but once I put on the sweatpants and zipped up the jacket, I figured I looked presentable enough for the taxi I called for with my cell.

Hesitating when he looked at my face, I tucked a fifty-dollar bill into his hand.

"Just take me to the nearest car rental place," I said.

"Lady. Nothing's open this hour of the night."

"Airport."

"Oh, yeah. Right. They got that new facility open."

"Before we go there, I've got five hundred dollars if you'll connect with somebody who can sell me a piece."

"A piece of what?"

"A gun."

"Whoa, who you think I am, anyway?"

"Any kind of gun. Handgun, shotgun. I don't care."

He braked to a sudden stop in the parking lot. I thought he was going to ask me to get out of his cab, but he took a cell phone and made a call.

"You there?" I couldn't hear any answer. "Yo, just wake up, get that clean nine I've been storing under my bed. You cool with that, dude? Be there in fifteen."

He took me somewhere into South Tucson, a small street off Thirty-sixth where he blinked his lights and a young boy came to the car, handing the driver a paper bag.

"You get some more sleep now," the driver said. "I'll be taking you to school in just a few hours."

He handed me the sack. A very worn Glock 17. I ejected the clip, saw it was fully loaded. I racked the slide, not knowing if there was a shell in the chamber, but since the Glock had no safety I was taking no chances. In spite of the age of the weapon it had been cleaned and oiled just recently. I rammed home the clip, racked the slide again, and lowered the hammer.

"Five hundred's a rip-off price, lady," he said. "But I gots to support three kids, and five hundred is better than four days' work."

"Just take it. I've only got about ten bucks left, so get me to the airport."

He counted the five hundred, thrust it into his pocket.

"Airport's free," he said. "I might have expensive goods, but personally, I'm not a cheap guy. I won't charge you for the ride."

An hour later, I was driving through north of Tucson past Oro Valley, headed on 287 to the warehouse. I had no specific idea where it was, but I'd seen the road sign, knew it was just off 287, knew it had to be south of Coolidge.

I'd told the Avis clerk that I just got out of the hospital after my car had been blindsided by a drunk driver. "I feel much better than I look," I said to the woman clerk, who seemed caught between wariness at my condition and concern that my face, a woman's face, might be scarred for life. But all the ID checked fine, the credit card went through, and I drove off in a metallic blue Pontiac Grand Am.

Somewhere south of Catalina I pulled over and called Brittles.

"Jesus, Laura! Where are you? I'm going out of my head. I've already been back to the Arizona Inn, trying to find out what happened to you. And we never found out what happened to your daughter."

"I know where she is," I said, "and I'm in a hurry to get to her."

At any other time in my life I'd have wondered at the depth of love and concern in his voice.

"Where are you?" I said.

"At the camp. Don was here earlier, but when I went to get some food he'd left. Don't know where he went."

"Just listen to me. Don't talk," I said, pulling back on 287. "I'm just going through Catalina. On 287. Head south of Coolidge. Look for a large warehouse, on your left side. A

dirt road, maybe one hundred feet, to a chain-link fence
topped with razor wire."

"Is your daughter there?"

"I hope she's still there."

"Who else?"

"Galeano."

"Laura, Jesus Christ, Laura, just stop your car and wait
for me."

"Can't do that, Nathan."

"I'll call the Florence and Coolidge Police Departments.
The Pinal County Sheriff's Department."

"Call them from the road," I said. "And if I get there first,
you'll see a metallic blue Pontiac Grand Am. I'll be inside
the warehouse."

"Laura, wait, I've got another call."

But I hung up and turned the cell off. I didn't want him
ringing me every minute. False dawn light slowly came up in
the east as I passed Catalina, and I slowed down to forty,
thirty in those places where it was all desert. Twenty minutes
later, I saw a sign on the right.

PINAL COUNTY BRUSH CLEARANCE PROJECT

I drove past, recognized the warehouse. I made a U-turn,
went down the dirt road, and stopped at the gate. It was unlocked and open a few inches, which solved a huge problem.
Getting back in the Grand Am, I pulled back the Glock's
hammer and stuck the gun in the small of my back. I ripped
off all the bandages on my leg, rubbed several of the wounds
to start them bleeding. I wanted Galeano to think I'd just
come back from wherever somebody'd found me, that I was
out of my mind, that I wasn't clear-headed enough to be anything but a woman come to collect Spider.

Ready, I backed up ten feet and accelerated ahead to ram
the gate open, my hand on the horn button as I drove right up
to the closed doorway. I kept blowing the horn until the elec-

tric door started to rise. I left the motor running, got out, left the door open. Galeano's feet showed in the opening, and as the door went all the way up I first saw the Tek10 in his right hand and then the grin on his face.

"You're one helluva survivor, lady."

I half unzipped the jacket, pushing the sleeves up, taking care as if by accident to pull the jacket so that my left breast fell out. But none of this distracted him as he beckoned me toward him. Dried blood stiffened the left side of the jacket. I held my arms at my sides, vibrating my fingers. Aware that I was overcompensating for my fatigue, I had to keep some part of my body moving. I staggered, recovered my balance, wanting to be alert, calm, in control and ready to consider anything Galeano asked of me.

"Zip that jacket up, Winslow. I could care less about forty-year-old tits. Just turn around. Slow."

I tried to pull out the Glock, but the hammer snagged on the band of the sweatpants and he clamped his free hand around mine to take the Glock away from me. He clicked the release lever, the clip falling to the ground. Pointing the Glock to our left, he pulled the trigger and the slide locked open after firing. He flung the gun thirty feet away and led me inside, rolling the door down shut.

Spider stood behind Don's wheelchair. Don's hands and legs were bound to the chair with duct tape.

"Surprise," Galeano said. "I know, I said I was leaving right away. But I thought I could take care of my boys, at the camp. This old guy was the only person there. He runs his mouth a lot, told me way too much before he found out I wasn't just another friendly dad coming to pick up a stepchild.

"So I had to take this guy. Maybe he's caused as much trouble as you or your boyfriend. I don't much know, but I'm hoping the boyfriend shows up also. I want to clean up everything. That's what this big woodchipper is good for. Run the four of you through the machine. No leg sticking out. Yeah, I saw that movie, too."

A car noisily braked to a stop outside.

"And that'll be him."

Somebody hammered on the roll-up door.

"We'll have to get ready."

Galeano quickly wrapped a long string of duct tape around Don's neck and then around the barrel of an over-and-under shotgun. He ripped off another string of duct tape, wrapped it around Spider's neck, and used it as a leash, holding it in his left hand while he gently laid the muzzle of the Tek10 against Spider's neck.

"Push the wheelchair," he said to Spider. "Winslow, you walk in front. When you get to the door, open it."

The four of us moved slowly. I hesitated at the door, not wanting to open it.

"Now or later," Galeano said to me. "I don't much care, as long as 'later' isn't any more than two minutes."

I punched the red button and the door rose. Brittles stood outside with an AK-47, moving the barrel from me to Galeano, freezing, the AK-47 drooping a few inches before he snapped it back up.

"Put it down," Galeano said harshly. "Now!"

Hesitating just a few more seconds, Brittles bent over and laid the AK-47 on the ground, stepping back several paces.

"Take off your jacket," Galeano said.

Brittles hesitated even longer, but removed the jacket and threw it on top of the AK-47, turning around to show he had no weapon stuck in back.

"Now the shirt."

Brittles stripped off his shirt quickly, tossed it onto his jacket. He turned around again, faced Galeano, waiting.

"Drop your pants."

This time Brittles really hesitated and Galeano immediately shifted the Tek10 from Spider's head to point it at Brittles. Undoing his belt, Brittles let his pants fall to his shoes, revealing an ankle holster. He removed a .32 revolver and tossed it on the pile with everything else.

"Pull up your pants. But take the belt out. I want you holding your pants."

Brittles did this quickly, his face not moving at all, his eyes fixed on Galeano.

"Okay. Let's all go inside."

"No, Nathan," I shouted. "There's a woodchipper in there. That's where all the bones came from. He wants to put all four of us into the woodchipper."

Sirens sounded from both the north and south. Galeano stiffened.

"Ah, geez," Brittles said. "Now what you going to do?"

Three Tucson police cars pulled up from the south, swinging on the dirt road, cherry and blue lights revolving on the roof rack. Two cars came from the north, each with a single revolving red light on the roof. All cars fanned out around the entrance to the warehouse, policemen ducking behind open doors.

"Don't shoot!" Brittles shouted. "Everybody out there, don't shoot."

Galeano seemed as calm as ever, but his eyes narrowed, I saw muscles flex in his cheeks as he clenched his jaws. His head moved slightly forward and he put the Tek10's muzzle back against Spider's head.

"Don't kill my daughter," I shouted.

Brittles grimaced, slumped his head.

"Mother and daughter," Galeano said. "I should have guessed. That just makes things all the easier. You men out there. Lay down all your weapons. Move away from your cars."

"They won't do it," Brittles said. "They'll kill you first."

"No, they won't. And besides, I've been shot seven times and stabbed at least twice. I prepared myself to die a long time ago, that's why I'm still alive."

Brittles turned to the officers.

"Do what the man says," he shouted. Several of the officers put down their handguns and moved away from their cruisers. One man stayed, the muzzle of his shotgun laid on the edge of a door. "You. Drop the shotgun."

The officer rose up so his head was visible in the open window and without hesitation Galeano shifted the Tek10 and shot the officer in the shoulder.

"Now what?" Brittles asked.

"We're all going to move into that green SUV parked inside here. You'll drive. Winslow will get in the other front seat. You'll fold down the backseats, and I'll get in back with the cripple and the daughter."

Brittles quickly came in the building, seeing the SUV. He worked fast at lowering the rear seats.

"It'll be easier to do this with the wheelchair if I drive the SUV outside."

Since we were all standing by the door, and the SUV was in the back of the warehouse, Galeano nodded. Brittles started the engine, drove slowly and carefully out the door, and parked about ten feet past the concrete loading strip.

"Go to all those police cruisers. Rip out their microphones. Open the hoods, rip off the spark plug wires," Galeano ordered.

I couldn't understand why Brittles jumped so eagerly to doing whatever Galeano said. He worked furiously, flinging the mikes off into the desert scrub and ripping ignition wires out viciously with both hands.

"Done," he said finally.

"Okay, everybody. We're all going to get into the SUV."

As we moved just outside the door, Galeano stopped our little parade and looked off into the distance in all directions.

"No surprises," he said finally. "You should have warned these hicks not to play all their cards together. How far away, how long before more police come?"

Brittles shook his head.

"That probably means they're close. Okay, let's do this quickly. Brittles and Winslow, in the front seats. You, the daughter. Wheel the cripple up to the back and dump him in there somehow."

Galeano kept his fingers on both triggers until Don lay on the floor. Galeano gave a sharp tug on the shotgun, ripping the duct tape off Don's neck. Spider stood near the hatch. Brittles nudged my knee with his hand, starting silently counting.

One.

Two.

"*Spider!*" he shouted. "Get down, *get down!*"

Spider dropped to the concrete, Galeano triggering the Tek10. He started to lower the weapon, but his head exploded like a pumpkin hit with a sledgehammer. Three seconds later I heard a *crack* reverberate across the desert floor.

Brittles flung himself out the door, kicked the Tek10 away from Galeano's hand before kneeling to feel his pulse, but most of his face was gone and I knew he was dead.

"Seventeen hundred yards," Brittles said to me. "I've never seen a shot like that. I don't know how Justin Wong ever fit into your past, but he's the guy responsible for being way out there to keep your future going."

Numb, probably about to go into shock, I just stared blankly at him. He pointed off North.

"Up there," he said. "In that little notch, between two hills. Justin Wong is up there with that long range sniper rifle. We counted on some luck, getting Galeano out into the open. Justin said it would only take one bullet."

He shrugged out of his windbreaker, laid it over Galeano's pulped face.

"Just over there . . ."

Brittles pointed again to the notch, mouth slightly open, frown lines deep in his forehead, and I saw he was crying. He stood like that for a long time, until I stood behind him and wrapped my arms around his chest and pulled myself up tight against his body.

"What's wrong, Nathan?"

"Dead people," he said finally. "Too many, too many . . . I can't deal with dead people anymore."

Policemen and ambulance drivers spent ten minutes trying to get our attention, gently working at pulling our bodies apart.

revelations

"Final call for American Airlines Flight 9492 to Las Vegas. Now boarding at Gate Twenty-eight. Final call."

Brittles stood at least twenty feet away, hands crossed in front of him, head bowed so low his chin touched his chest.

"I don't want to lose you now," I said.

"You never really had me," Spider said, her eyes bright with tears. "Well. Not since I was two. And I hardly remember that."

"You'll call me?"

"I don't think so."

"Email. You've got my email address. Fax number."

"Don't wait for anything," she said

"You've got Nathan's number. I'll be living with him. You can call or email or do anything, any way you want. Just talk to me."

"Spider."

I waited, expecting her to rebel against my use of the name. Nothing.

"You're my daughter. I've been looking for you for twenty years."

"I forgot you twenty years ago."

"Isn't there any way?" I sobbed.

"For god's sakes, don't make this any more melodramatic than it is already."

"You don't know me," I pleaded. "At least give me some

time so you get to know me. So I get to know you."

The boarding agent came over to us. I tried to turn my back on her, turn my back on the other boarding agent who was waiting to shut the door to the ramp.

"Please, ma'am. You'll have to board now or we'll have to close the door."

A bright-faced young Asian girl, a broad smile with teeth as white and straight as dominos, a small bronze plaque pinned to her shirt with the name TEQUILA.

"Tequila." I laughed, a hard thing to do while I was sobbing. "Your dad and I, we had this thing for Cuervo Gold."

"Good-bye. Mom."

"After twenty years, is that all I'm going to get? A single word? Mom?"

"It's just too late, mom. Way way too late."

She turned abruptly and went through the ramp door and the agent quickly closed it behind her. I slumped into a bank of chairs, sobbing. I felt Brittles's hand on my shoulder. The boarding agents started to move to another counter for a flight to Los Angeles. Somebody thumped on the ramp door. The agents exchanged looks. One of them opened the door and Spider ran through to put a hand on my cheek.

"Well, maybe not," she said. "Maybe not too late. I'll think about it."

She ran back down the ramp. The door closed again.

I wanted to see the plane take off, wanted to see her face at a window, but Brittles took my hands, pulled me to my feet, turned me around, held my hand as we walked away. I turned back once as the tug started pushing the plane back from the loading ramp, but Brittles cradled my head in his hands, held my hand against his shirt for a long, long time until I heard the engines roar and the plane move away.

"Come on, sweet pea," Brittles said. "Let's go home."

laura's rap

I'm alone on my own,
On a road with no map to where I'm going
But my ambition's growing
Not knowing where I'll end up but welcoming adventure
And freed from dependence indenture
Rid of my affliction
Ritalin addiction
I center my mind on steps, not sure what I'm going to find
   next
As I climb this hill I'm resigned to let
Things unfold, unsure of some of the things I've been told
Or what the future might hold
I've decided to escape my fate
Can't sit around and wait
For something I don't know, with ten miles to go
On a cold desert road, with my mind in a mode
Dwelling on the fact that
The futures a dream you can never get back
 . . . Once you get there
So I'm taking small steps with my eyes on
The western horizon
Even when the sun's rising I'm trying
To envision a sunset that hasn't come yet
And a truth that I've been denying

On a path that I've been defying
As I pass another butterfly flying
I'm thinking about a place where my heart can rest
And my mind can be resigned to consider the time
While I'm taking my time instead of racing to find
A world that I'll never get ahead of
I'm keeping my head up
And looking to begin from all I've taken in
Too many mistakes to make amends
Too many enemies to be making friends easily
Too many times that I think I might have acted unreasonably
With the weather unseasonably cold and gray
I'm trying to stay warm and weather each storm that unfolds
    this way
Like a normal day from the comforts of home
With a life that's my own, organically grown
In the garden of variety, I try to be satisfied
And abide by the ratified guidelines
That decide my immediate timeline
I find mine unstable
And though I've put many things under the legs of the table
I'm unable to balance, lacking the talent of contentment
At length meant harboring resentment
To maintain my strength to escape the entrenchment
From a life, that I'm not sure I like
I'm tired of rolling the dice
And about to start selecting my slice through listening to my
    own advice

Written by Kwame Harrison, AKA Mad Squirrel

Acknowledgments

I owe great debts to many people for helping me with this book. One of the true joys of writing a series character comes from real insights from fans and new contacts in Arizona. Their comments made for real challenges and changes.

Two people provided so much help that I've used their names as characters. Ian S. Friedlander helped enormously with Arizona prison details. Ian is a Special Investigator in the Criminal Investigations Unit, Arizona Department of Corrections. Rich Thompson, a mineral physicist in Tucson, helped with details about archeology, paleontology, and bones. The fictional characters bearing these names are entirely my own.

Carol Ellick, of Statistical Research, Inc. in Tucson, provided essential guidance about NAGPRA, the Arizona Burial Agreement, and many other details of recovering ancient bones and artifacts. Carol also introduced me to other people in this field, including Dave Winchester, Park Ranger at Casa Grande National Monument.

Kwame Harrison wrote original rap lyrics, after delighting and convincing me that alternative hiphop/rap and rap music offered more than gangsta/thug material.

Thanks also to Theresa May, Nancy Priest, and Rosemary Pooler, for their insights and support.

Sarah Durand, my exceptional editor at Morrow/Avon, offered continual guidance and made key suggestions about both plot and character. More thanks to my agent, Jessica Lichtenstein.

And finally, my gratitude to the EMT crew of Green Valley, Arizona, and the ER and ICU staffs at St. Mary's Hospital in Tucson. Without them, I might not even be here.

Although most place names are real, this is a work of fiction. All mistakes are mine alone.

Catch the riveting new hardcover from
New York Times bestselling author Tony Hillerman
as Leaphorn and Chee join forces to solve a
puzzling new mystery, from the discovery of a
murdered man with no ID to covert activities
on a big game ranch.

TONY HILLERMAN
THE SINISTER PIG

ISBN: 0-06-019443-X
Price: $25.95/NCR

Available wherever books are sold
or call 1-800-331-3761 to order.

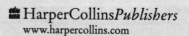
HarperCollins*Publishers*
www.harpercollins.com

SP 0603

Novels of Suspense by
New York Times Bestselling Author
J. A. JANCE

DESERT HEAT
0-380-76545-4/$7.50 US/$9.99 Can

TOMBSTONE COURAGE
0-380-76546-2/$7.99 US/$10.99 Can

SHOOT/DON'T SHOOT
0-380-76548-9/$7.99 US/$10.99 Can

DEAD TO RIGHTS
0-380-72432-4/$7.50 US/$9.99 Can

SKELETON CANYON
0-380-72433-2/$7.50 US/$9.99 Can

RATTLESNAKE CROSSING
0-380-79247-8/$6.99 US/$9.99 Can

OUTLAW MOUNTAIN
0-380-79248-6/$6.99 US/$9.99 Can

DEVIL'S CLAW
0-380-79249-4/$7.50 US/$9.99 Can

PARADISE LOST
0-380-80469-7/$7.99 US/$10.99 Can

PARTNER IN CRIME
0-380-80470-0/$7.99 US/$10.99 Can

Available wherever books are sold or please call 1-800-331-3761
to order.   JB 0503